The Catoctin Conversation

The Catoctin Conversation

By

JAY FRANKLIN

With an Introduction by
Sumner Welles

WILDSIDE PRESS

To My Wife

"Dux Femina Facti"

"As to the speeches which were made either before or during the war, it was hard for me, and for others who reported them to me, to recollect the exact words. I have therefore put into the mouth of each speaker the sentiments proper to the occasion, expressed as I thought he would be likely to express them, while at the same time, I endeavored, as nearly as I could, to give the general purport of what was actually said."

Thucydides.

ACKNOWLEDGMENT

I DO NOT CLAIM that *The Catoctin Conversation* ever took place. On the contrary, I contend that it is entirely imaginary.

Within that qualification, I have been at pains to give the utmost aspect of authenticity to the personalities, the policies and the points-of-view presented in this synthesis of Anglo-American statesmanship.

From February 13, 1941, until his death on April 12, 1945, I held a confidential and responsible relationship to Franklin Delano Roosevelt and his war policies. In this capacity, I had direct contact with numerous events and developments which afforded insight into the inner meaning and character of the war itself.

For their contribution—however involuntary—to this presentation of the ideas and issues which governed the Anglo-American allies in the struggle against the Axis, I wish to pay acknowledgment to the following individuals:

President Roosevelt;
Vice-President Wallace;
Secretary of State Hull;
Under-Secretary of State Sumner Welles;
Assistant Secretary of State Adolph Berle;
The Right Honorable Winston Churchill;
Lord Lothian, His Britannic Majesty's Ambassador to the United States;
Lord Halifax, his successor at Washington;
Sir Ronald Campbell, British Minister at Washington;
The Honorable David Bowes-Lyon, chief of the British Psychological Warfare Service at Washington;
The Honorable E. H. Coleman, Under-Secretary of State and Deputy Registrar-General, Dominion of Canada;

Adolph Hitler;

Hermann Goering;

Dr. Ernst Sedgwick Hanfstaengl;

Mr. Bernard M. Baruch;

Mr. Harry L. Hopkins;

Mr. Joseph E. Davies, American Ambassador to the U.S.S.R.

The Honorable Henry L. Stimson, Secretary of War;

General William J. Donovan, director of the Office of Strategic Services;

General George V. Strong, Deputy Chief of Staff, G-2, U. S. Army;

Major Albert Neumann, Counter-Intelligence Service, and numerous other members of the C.I.S., O.S.S., O.N.I., and M.I.D.

My thanks are also due to the Reverend Howard Sweeney, C.S.C., of Notre Dame University, South Bend, Indiana; and to Sir Willmott Lewis, Washington correspondent of *The Times (London)*, for their criticism and advice in the presentation of this material.

JAY FRANKLIN

Introduction

by

Sumner Welles

One morning in the summer of 1942, I received at my office in the Department of State a memorandum from President Roosevelt telling me that the President wished me to see John Carter and discuss with him a plan in which the President was deeply interested. The President later telephoned me to say that he wished to talk with me about some of the pros and cons of this plan after I had seen Carter.

John Carter, or as he is better known to the many readers of his column, Jay Franklin, came to see me that afternoon. He explained to me that Ernst Hanfstaengl, who had been living in England at the outbreak of the war and who had soon thereafter been interned by the British authorities, had recently been transferred to an internment camp in Canada. Carter had learned of this. He had interested the President in the possibility that the information which Hanfstaengl could give to members of the United States Government with regard to Hitler and the inner workings of the Nazi régime and, more particularly perhaps, with regard to the nature of the methods by which the Nazis were able to maintain and to consolidate their hold over the German people, might be of exceptional use to our Intelligence Services, and in the efforts which the American Government was then making to formulate plans for an effective campaign of psychological warfare.

Carter told me that the British Government was exceedingly reluctant to release Hanfstaengl to the United States even for a short time. The British Intelligence authorities were by no means persuaded that Hanfstaengl had actually severed his connections with the Nazis after his flight from Germany, and believed that there was some possibility that he had secretly been operating, like many Nazi agents, in the interest of the German Government at the same time that he was openly professing violently anti-Nazi sentiments. All attempts to obtain from the British Government the necessary permission for Hanfstaengl to come to Washington had, consequently, so far been unsuccessful. Carter brought me word from the President that he wished me to do what I could to expedite the arrangements for Hanfstaengl's transfer to the United States if I believed, as he did, that this might be of service to our Government. He suggested that in that case I enlist the personal intervention of Lord Halifax, the British Ambassador.

The project at once seemed to me to be worth trying out. I had, of course, heard of Hanfstaengl for many years, although I had never known him personally. I knew that his mother had been an American and that he had graduated some ten years before myself from Harvard, where he was generally remembered as "Putzi." I knew that he had maintained close connections with the United States during the intervening years and that his son had enlisted in the American Army. But what was much more sharply in my mind, and what made the plan seem peculiarly promising, was the fact that Hanfstaengl had been one of Hitler's most ardent supporters during the formative period of the Nazi Party. The Hanfstaengl art business had long been prominent in Munich. "Putzi" Hanfstaengl had been one of Hitler's early confidants at the Brown House headquarters in that city. It was often reported that his piano-playing had an especially soothing effect upon the Fuehrer in his more excited hours. After Hitler's rise to supreme power, Hanfstaengl had for some years continued to be one of his intimates and had been constantly associated with him. I had heard that Hanfstaengl had finally broken with Hitler and had fled from Germany, but I had not been informed of the circumstances nor of the reasons for the break, nor did I even know that Hanfstaengl had been interned by the British Government until Carter related this latest chapter in his history.

It seemed to me obvious that, even were the British Government correct in its suspicion that Hanfstaengl had not actually severed his connections with the Nazi régime, a series of interviews in the United States between Hanfstaengl and representatives of the American Intelligence Services might be productive of information of considerable value to our own Government. I immediately explained the circumstances to Lord Halifax and arranged for him to see John Carter. As a result of the Ambassador's personal insistence, notwithstanding the continued opposition of the British and Canadian military authorities, Carter went personally to Canada, and Hanfstaengl was finally brought to Washington where he lived secretly in nearby Virginia for many months under American military surveillance.

I remember that the President continued to follow closely the results of this experiment. While he later expressed to me some disappointment because of the lack of any very detailed or concrete information in what Hanfstaengl could be induced to communicate, he nevertheless felt that a good deal of useful enlightenment as to the mental processes of the Nazi leaders had been afforded our own authorities. He also expressed his own belief that Hanfstaengl was by then sincerely opposed to the Nazi Government, and that his rupture with Hitler and his flight from Germany had in reality come about because of his fear for his life.

During the next few months, John Carter from time to time gave me memoranda of the talks which Hanfstaengl had with him and with officers of the War Department's G-2. The accounts of these talks were all of them valuable to me, more perhaps because of what could be read between the lines than because of any new or startling insight into Hitler's Germany. The information afforded was more useful from the standpoint of psychological warfare than from the standpoint of military intelligence. I never spoke with Hanfstaengl myself. But the transcripts made available to me by Carter inclined me very definitely to the President's own conclusion that the project initiated by John Carter had proved itself to be well worth while.

It is because of my service as an intermediary in facilitating the arrangements made for bringing Hanfstaengl to the United States, and my knowledge of the talks which he had with some of our officials while he was here, that I have been especially interested in this book which John Carter has now written, entitled *The Catoctin Conversation*.

The conversation here reported is imaginary. But as a matter of fact, Hanfstaengl did ask to see the President and Mr. Churchill at the moment set for the scene here presented, and this account might well have been a true record had Mr. Churchill agreed to the interview requested. As it is the author has given an amazing aspect of authenticity to a dialogue which might so readily have taken place.

The Catoctin Conversation, in which Harry Hopkins and Bernard M. Baruch are also pictured as having taken part, now given to the public by John Carter, constitutes a convincing presentation of a conversation which would surely have been unique in modern history. For here you are given a report of an interview which is supposed to have taken place, at one of the most critical moments of the Second World War, between the President of the United States, the British Prime Minister, two of the President's closest advisers, a well-known columnist, and a German who had been one of Hitler's most intimate friends, and who was then a prisoner of the British Government. These strangely assorted individuals talk freely together as man to man, not only about conditions in Germany and the psychology and the ambitions of Hitler and his associates, but also about the manner of being of the British Empire, the future of Anglo-American relations, the basic essentials of post-war policy, economics and politics, and about the philosophy of government itself.

It would be hard to imagine such a highly civilized episode taking place under the auspices of any chief of state other than Franklin Roosevelt. One can in any event picture a very different scene had an American prisoner been brought for questioning before Hitler and his fellow-gangsters!

I must confess that the report of this conversation, as given us by John Carter, is to me all the more intriguing, because of the opinions which the major participants are made to express with regard to the probable nature of the post-war relations between the United States, Great Britain and the Soviet Union. It may not be'amiss for me here to affirm once more that in his talks with me President Roosevelt never wavered in the forthright expression of his conviction that, while the closest kind of cooperation between the British Commonwealth of Nations and the United States was indispensable to all of the English-speaking nations, the same kind of cooperation with the Soviet Union was equally indispensable to this country, and that the endeavor to secure Soviet-American understanding should never be prejudiced because of those conflicts of interest between Great Britain and the Soviet Union, which he so clearly foresaw must from time to time arise.

There can be no question of the outstanding importance of *The Catoctin Conversation* as an imaginative synthesis of Anglo-American statesmanship, at a turning point of the war, given us by a skilled and informed reporter in whom the President, I know, had great confidence. It will undoubtedly promote an innumerable number of controversies among those who undertake to write the history of our era. What makes it most valuable is the fact that the author was in a position to know what the actors on the stage which he has set really believed.

That is why the readers of this book will find in its pages a dramatic and illuminating revelation of the thinking and the personality of two of the three men who led the United Nations to victory, and who by their leadership so greatly helped to keep aloft the standard of freedom to whose service they had dedicated themselves.

1

Mars

1

THE EVENING was so cool that I hoped we would find a log-fire to welcome us at the lodge. Although it was mid-May and the city had been noticeably warm by day, here in the mountains and by evening it was cold enough for overcoats. As the car climbed along the shoulder of the Catoctins we could see, far to the West, the Blue Ridge like a wall against the afterglow. A single planet shone pale above the tumbling hills, as it had shone on Lee and Jackson, McClellan and Meade.

Three generations had passed since this peaceful land had smoked beneath the wheels of war, though it was still studded with the names that echo like drum-beats: Gettysburg and Antietam, Frederick and Harper's Ferry where they had hanged an old man who could not wait for freedom to march south of the Potomac. Only the Marine sentries at the entrance to the mountain drive and the occasional drone of a warplane on a practice-flight told of another war and armies bleeding far away in the still unwon battle for freedom.

We topped the last rise and stopped as another Marine sentry fully inspected our passes before waving us on to the house. It lay below us in a little funnel or fold of the mountain, flanked by cool green pines and shadowed by a large oak that had been young when General Braddock marched his red-coats westward to deal with the French at Fort Duquesne. White-washed rail fences held back the wild growth from the house, which had sprawled itself into the hillside as comfortably as a dog stretched out before a fire. There were irises in full bloom and the lilacs perfumed the night air beside the door, but otherwise the place was easy and half-wild—a mountain retreat and not a summer home. A thin snake of wood-smoke crawled out of the great stone chimney and there were lights in the small, square window-panes and the sound of voices back of the weathered oak door.

Putzi turned to me wordlessly and shrugged his great shoulders with that imperceptible gesture which carried him four thousand miles eastward to the old world where an army was poised at the ruins of Carthage. Colonel Starling strode across the parking space from behind the banked official cars and nodded to me. I introduced my companion and he told us to follow him. I glanced at my watch. We were on time.

The President is waiting for you, he said.

It had been mid-afternoon when the orders had arrived. I had notified Counter-Intelligence, signed the passes and proceeded to the Project, where I told Putzi to get ready. I had expected him to be nervous, excited, perhaps hysterical—since his liberty was at stake. He had appealed to Caesar and now he was to go to Caesar. Instead, he had been calm, fatalistic, only sorry that his clothes were shabby and not disposed to insist that his manuscript notes accompany him. I had not realized that he was so completely ready for the dictates of fate, especially when fate was represented by two powerful men on a mountain top.

The warmth of the crackling fire was pleasant after the cool outside, although the windows were still open to the

4

west and the scent of the lilacs mingled with the wood-smoke as the darkness gathered like pools in the folded hills and the planet sank towards the crest of the Blue Ridge.

The President was seated comfortably in an old, leather easy-chair, his legs freed of the heavy braces which weighted them by day. Mr. Churchill and his cigar roved around the broad, low-ceilinged room, now standing with legs spread in front of the hearth, now strolling to a window and tasting the night air, and at other times sprawled on a chair or the sofa. Hopkins and Baruch were still outside, presumably wandering through the woods, and it was not until much later that I realised that they would take part in the talk which carried us through to the morning and the fateful telephone call which brought to a close this Catoctin conversation.

2

How do you do, Mr. President, I said. And here is Putzi.

Grand to see you, Jack. Winston, this is Jack Carter, who's in charge of this combined operation. Hullo, Putzi. Good to see you after all these years.

Churchill nodded at me, pleasantly, and darted a swift, masked glance at Hanfstaengl.

Curiously enough, I almost met you in Munich, Mr. Prime Minister, I said, eleven years ago, and with Hanfstaengl. I was trying to get an interview with Hitler and so, I was told, were you. We both were unsuccessful.

I wish people would call me Hanfy and not Putzi, Hanfstaengl whispered.

Sh! I replied, the President is the only person on earth who calls me Jack.

After the normal greetings, Churchill looked at Roosevelt.

Sit down, Jack, the President said, and let Putzi find himself a chair so that we can talk this thing over.

Putzi, you wrote to both the Prime Minister and to me and asked us to accept your parole. You argued that you had come to this country by your own consent and wished to help us win the war against Germany. You said that your son was in the American Army, having volunteered nearly a year before Pearl Harbor. You also said that when the British authorities interned you in 1939 you had offered to help them and that they had refused. You asked for a personal interview so as to clear up any misunderstandings which either of us might have about your attitude. Now I want to make two things clear right from the start. You are a prisoner of the British Government which agreed to let us borrow your services for a time. What we would have done with you had you been in this country instead of a British prisoner is not a matter which I can consider. The final decision rests with the Prime Minister and not with me. The other thing is that the Prime Minister does not think that any useful purpose will be served by this meeting. He points out that both he and Mr. Eden refused to see Hess and has only consented to be present on the understanding that it must remain absolutely secret until the end of the war.

Does this mean, asked Hanfstaengl, that the only effect of this meeting is to insure that I shall remain in custody until the war is won? That is the only way you could be sure of keeping it a secret, *nicht wahr?*

It does. Unless, of course, the Prime Minister should change his mind after hearing what you have to say.

A little more than a year ago, Hanfstaengl replied, when

John Carter came to interview me in prison at Kingston, Ontario, he asked me whether I would be disposed to help the Allies win the war. I told him I was so disposed and gave him my reasons—which I repeated in my recent letter to you. Before I was flown down to Washington in an American Army plane from Canada, at your request I signed a paper stating that I was coming to this country of my own free will. The custody in which I am held is, I am told, not only to preserve secrecy but to protect me from possible Nazi agents. Do not forget that I fled from Germany in 1937 because my life was in danger from the S. S. and my life was in danger because Goering and Goebbels resented my warning to Hitler that he should not underestimate the America of Roosevelt or the England of Churchill. Surely there is an important difference between me and Rudolph Hess who parachuted into Scotland in time of war and as an important and trusted official of the Third Reich.

Our security chaps think that you, too, may have been a parachutist, as it were, said Churchill, in advance of the war and on the same mission, to neutralize England while Germany conquered Russia.

If I have to prove or disprove an assumed intention on my own part seven years ago, Mr. Prime Minister, as a condition of establishing my bona fides, then there is little use in this discussion. I shall be perfectly resigned to go back to prison-camp before I attempt anything so utterly impossible.

Hold your horses, Putzi, said Roosevelt. He has a good point there, Winston. After all, what we are considering is whether he can be helpful to us now and not what might have been in his mind in 1937.

I am willing and anxious to help, Mr. President, declared Hanfstaengl. That is, to help England and America.

I cannot pretend that I trust or admire the Soviets and the same I imagine, is true of others but I promise you that I shall answer your questions as truthfully as I can. John Carter, who has discussed these matters with me, can tell you if what I say tonight differs from what I have said to him often in the last year. But I have in the past shared some of the responsibilities of government and I know that the truth is not always welcome to the men who manage the affairs of state. Hitler did not welcome it, Goering resented it, Goebbels hated it. So tell me, please, if it is your wish that I should speak the truth or simply tell you things which are pleasant to hear in the light of what you and the Prime Minister have already decided.

We want the truth, of course, Putzi. Don't we, Winston? And the President cocked his cigarette mischievously at the Prime Minister.

Yes, we want the truth, Churchill said.

About Germany?

Naturally.

Why?

Because, Roosevelt said, if we know the truth, the truth may set us free.

Even if it sets others free, too.

I guess so, replied the President. Why not?

Will it set me free?

That depends, Churchill said.

3

We're going to set Europe free, at any rate, Putzi, Roosevelt observed. We're going to invade the Continent.

Natürlich! Will that be the Second Front?

I don't know whether Marshal Stalin will agree with us, but I'd certainly call it a second front.

He didn't consider the invasion of North Africa a substitute for what Moscow calls a second front, said Hanfstaengl.

Second front! grumbled Churchill. It's more like a fifth front. Egypt was a second front. Great Britain was a second front. The European Underground was a second front. And where was the Russian second front when we British and the gallant French stood in the West in 1939? What was the second front when England stood alone, for a whole year, against the Axis?

Yes, Winston. But just the same I think it can be said that the invasion of Europe is the Second Front in the bright lexicon of Moscow.

Europe is a large country, remarked Hanfstaengl. You are going to liberate Europe. But how much of Europe must you fight before you set it free? Will you fight the Catholic Church, for example?

Certainly not! Roosevelt snapped. We are the friends of the Church.

Does the Church know that?

Of course. When Pacelli was here just before the war, we—

I mean, Putzi continued, as the President's remark dangled incompleted, is the Church supporting the Nazis?

No.

Is the Church supporting the Fascisti?

No.

Has the Church excommunicated the Nazis?

No.

Has the Church excommunicated the Fascisti?

No. But neither has it excommunicated Winston or myself—not that we belong to it. But the Vatican hopes we win.

Is the Church in favor of Communism?

No.

And the Communists are allied with England and America?

Yes.

So your problem, said Hanfstaengl, is to liberate the Catholic Church from Fascism, which is peculiar to the Latin Catholic countries—Mussolini in Italy, Franco in Spain, Salazar in Portugal, and old Pétain at Vichy, not to mention General DeGaulle—with the help of the Communists who are anathema to the Vatican. It is a difficult moral problem.

The President nodded. You must remember, Putzi, he said, that the Church itself is in a difficult position. Not only is the Vatican opposed to Communism, as you pointed out, but Hitler has physical control of the lives of all Europe's Catholics. It is true that Fascism and Catholicism have much in common, but there is no such relationship between Nazism and the Church. The Vatican has repeatedly condemned many of the Nazi teachings and practices, but the Church does not dare expose Europe's Catholics to Nazi reprisals and so must be cautious.

Then, Mr. President, your problem is to attack Europe in such a way that it will be clear that you are not attacking Catholicism. You must draw one line between Nazism and Fascism and another line between Fascism and Catholicism. So you are going to invade Italy.

Who told you so? demanded Churchill.

But it is clear as daylight, Mr. Prime Minister, that Italy is the next stop on the Anglo-American train. You have conquered North Africa. The next move is to take the islands

—Sicily and Sardinia—and then land in Italy, which is also a sort of island because of the Alps. So you will land in Italy and rely upon the Italian people or King Victor Emmanuel or some disgruntled generals to make a revolt against Mussolini. Thus you can take Italy without fighting the Italians any more and can take Rome which is the city of the Pope. With Rome in your hands and the Italians as your allies, you can pry Latin Europe and Catholic Europe away from Hitler. That is the thing which you must do, provided that Hitler lets you do it. Have you thought that he might strike through Spain?

Naturally, Churchill said, but the Spaniards won't let him.

So! said Hanfstaengl. Franco will balance the forces so that Hitler will not try. Be assured that Hitler could be at Gibraltar within a month if he wished. If Franco pretends that Spain itself will attack Gibraltar and close the Mediterranean—

Putzi, Roosevelt interrupted. Let's get back on the rails. Spain will be all right, I think.

4

Then, Mr. President, it is that you plan to attack Germany on the Continent of Europe.

Exactly.

And you want to make it quite clear that it is Germany you are attacking, not the Catholic Church, not the Latin countries, not the Slavs, but Germany.

Yes.

Are you also attacking the German people?

Only so far as they serve Hitler and support the Nazis.

11

Do you intend to set the Germans free, too, or are they to be destroyed.

We shall set them free. There is no reason on earth why the Germans should not enjoy a peaceful, secure and prosperous life in Europe, just so long as they do not start a war of conquest and a reign of terror every twenty years.

Then you are trying to do what President Wilson did in 1918, to drive a wedge between the German Government and the German people.

Yes.

Does that mean that the Germans are not going to be allowed any government of their own?

Not unless they try to set up a government like the Nazi system.

Are you going to leave the Germans any choice in the matter or are you going to teach them to choose the right kind of government? I ask these questions, Mr. President, because, as you know, I helped put the Hitler Government in power and I helped create the Hitler movement. If I am to help you it must be by finding the means to dissolve the Hitler movement and destroy the Hitler Government.

Good! exclaimed Churchill. That's what we want.

In other words, you wish me to tell you what it is you are attacking so that you may know how to attack it.

Right!

You want to know what is the idea at Berlin which you must destroy and you want to know how to strike at it so that you will not also unnecessarily destroy anything but the Nazi Government and Hitlerism.

And Fascism, too! added Roosevelt. Fascism is as dangerous as Nazism, even if it is not as efficient. Fascism must go and the peoples under Fascist and Nazi rule must be set free to develop as they once developed—as Italians and as Germans with a citizenship in the world and a great contribution to make to civilization. Otherwise, there can be no lasting peace.

Quite, Churchill agreed. We don't want to destroy the Germans, not all of them. Europe needs Germany.

That makes the problem which you, Mr. President and Mr. Prime Minister, have set me much simpler than the original idea of invading Europe. I am asked to help you determine what it is that you are really attacking when you attack Hitlerism. Of course, you are both thoroughly informed by your intelligence services of the physical problems involved. You are asking me, as one of the architects of Hitlerism, to show you on the blue-prints how you can free Europe from German domination and Germans from Nazi domination?

Yes.

And I assume that I must leave Communism out of the picture, in the sense that neither of you want the Soviet solution. You do not wish or intend that Germany or Catholic Europe shall become Communist?

That's a fair way of putting it, Putzi, Roosevelt agreed. Russia is our ally and we have no quarrel with Communism in Russia but you yourself have pointed to the hostility of the Church towards communism. That means that we must not compel European Catholics to resist our invasion as they would certainly resist it if we planned to impose Communism on them. Do you agree, Winston?

Of course.

You are naturally not asking me, Mr. President, to discuss the military strength of Germany?

Not exactly. Although I seem to remember a great hub-bub in G-2 the day you arrived from Canada, because you pointed to Casablanca on the map and said that there was where the Allies must land. At the time it was a dark, deep military secret. That wasn't the remark of a military ignoramus, Putzi.

I must insist that I am not a military expert, Mr. President. I did my service in the Imperial German Army before the last war but, as you know, I was interned in this country during the war itself. And this war found me in England, where I was interned again. I am held as a prisoner of war and I have never fought in any war. In the case of Casablanca it was easy to see that it was the nearest place in North Africa where an American Army could land and be supplied and still have a direct effect on German strategy. You could also hope to win France to your side without landing in France or fighting Frenchmen, in this way, and also relieve Rommel's pressure on Egypt and Suez. To see that did not call for a military genius. It was so simple that I am amazed that the German General Staff did not see it themselves.

So am I, Roosevelt laughed, but they didn't.

The idea was too simple and obvious for the German military mind to grasp, Churchill explained. They had been listening to the Moscow broadcasts and thought that the landing must be in France in order to please Stalin, rather than to serve our strategy in Africa. And when they knew it was Africa, they were sure we were going after Dakar, because they had been reading the American newspapers.

Wunderbar! So I must assume that the Allies have able and experienced advisers who are competent to tell you all about the strength and weakness of the German Army, including the mentality of the German General Staff. I am confident that the Underground in Europe keeps you both well informed as to the disposition of German troops, the location of war-factories *und so weiter*. I am sure that you do not expect me, who left Germany seven years ago, to tell you about German industry, the Luftwaffe or raw materials. I am frank to confess to you that I am not a technical man. One of the things I most disliked about Hitler's Nazi group was that they were spiritually a set of chauffeurs. They knew about monkey-wrenches and carburetors and that rubbish but the only thing they knew about Beethoven was that he was absolutely Aryan. They could build Stukas but they couldn't play the piano. Am I correct in believing that you and Mr. Churchill—except for my little indiscretion about Casablanca—do not regard me as the indispensable expert on military strategy who must tell you how to defeat the Wehrmacht?

Roosevelt laughed and slapped his knee. You are one hundred per cent right about that, Putzi.

Then you want me to tell you, if I can, the real power of Hitler.

Yes.

That wretched man! said Churchill. His power is the power of evil.

But when you speak of Hitler, Mr. Prime Minister, you mean more than the single human individual named Adolf Hitler, do you not? You mean what I might call the mystical body of Hitler?

Mystical body, my foot!

What I mean, sir, is the whole group, the whole movement, the whole Nazi idea—the entire construction of men, methods, motives, ideas, ideals and purposes which has grown around Adolf Hitler and which he, as Reichsfuehrer, directs, controls and coordinates, and which, as I have seen it happen, determines what Hitler himself must do and say.

Do you mean his blinking intuition?

His intuition, Mr. Prime Minister, is often merely a

convenient expression for a decision which would otherwise offend one or another powerful group in the German Government. When strong forces are in balance, yet some action must be taken, the Fuehrer can summon his intuition—call it a hunch—to justify the action which he decides to take.

Quite.

Cousin Theodore used to call it thinking with his hips, said Roosevelt. Now, Putzi, let's get down to brass tacks.

5

I am sure, Hanfstaengl continued, that you do not need me to tell you of the political weaknesses of Hitlerism.

On the contrary, that is precisely what we do need.

Are you sure? I had believed that the weaknesses were clear to everybody and that it was your purpose to use them to destroy Hitlerism if only you could overcome its strength. Let me put it to you this way, Mr. Churchill. The weakness of Great Britain is her dependence on sea-borne supplies for her livelihood and, above all, for her food. The strength of England is her naval power, which holds the seas for her merchant shipping. Is that, on the whole, a fair statement?

How so?

Well, in two great wars, Germany has tried to defeat England by attacking her weakness—with submarines, surface raiders, aircraft, sabotage and terrorizing of neutrals. In neither war has Germany succeeded, because ships could be built faster than the sinkings and because British naval power was always able to apply counter-measures in time. Therefore, by attacking England's weakness and not her strength, Germany has lost two wars.

Abe Lincoln, Roosevelt remarked, made it a rule in a

law-case always to try to break down his opponent's strongest argument and not pick holes in his weak arguments. He said that the whole case turned on the strong argument, that the weak points were the tail that went with the hide.

Just the same, Churchill objected, I think we should know what Hanfstaengl considers Hitler's weaknesses. His view may not be the same as ours.

I hope so, Mr. Churchill, said Putzi. Because the weaknesses are so unmistakable. First of all, the regime hangs on the life of one man. If he were killed or assassinated or should die of apoplexy, there would be a struggle for power which would disintegrate the Nazi system, especially since one or another faction would seek Allied support for its coming to power. The Beer Hall bomb shows that somebody, at least, is aware of that weakness and I imagine that there will be other attempts to kill Hitler, directed by, shall we say Allied intelligence?

Churchill nodded.

Again, the Nazis are weak because they are hated by so many. There are all the German workers who are really Marxists in their hearts, whatever they may pretend in Berlin. There are the Catholics and the Protestant Churches, with their loathing of Nazi Paganism, youth-control and immorality. There are the millions of slave laborers, the war prisoners, the peoples of the occupied countries. There are also many German generals and officers who believe that Hitler has betrayed Germany into a disastrous war. This sum of hatred is truly immense and must be reckoned with, whenever it is possible to give it expression.

Quite.

Then there is the admitted corruption and irresponsibility of the Nazis themselves. Corruption in a police state is a terrible weakness because of the ease of blackmail and the mortal danger of betrayal. Irresponsibility is also a frightful weakness. You may remember the Blood Purge of 1934. There were many, many more killed than had been ordered. Grudges, personal revenge, hope for loot—what will you? It was a day when any Nazi who wished could take the chance to get rid of a personal enemy. No one was ever called to account for these crimes, not even by the Party whose discipline they transgressed. They set the final seal of irresponsibility on the whole regime.

Yet you went back to Germany in 1934, said Roosevelt.

Yes, that is so. I did. I got word of the Purge in church. It was a wedding at Newport. The bride was beautiful and the organ played *Lohengrin,* when into my hand was slipped the bloody telegram. At first I did not plan to go back. I might be killed, too. Who knows? But then men like Neurath, decent Germans, begged me to come back. They said it was my duty to try to restrain the Fuehrer as long as possible from the madness which threatened to destroy Germany and the world. I believed them and I went back to Berlin. I lasted less than three years before I, too, had to flee for safety to England.

Speaking of the Purge, Hanfstaengl, don't you think that Roehm and all that group of homosexuals in the Nazi Party constitute a weakness, Churchill asked.

Only esthetically speaking. I am not like your Sir James Barrie. I do not believe in fairies. One of the things which most disgusted me in the Hitler movement were all those people who fluttered around the Brown House. Yet it would be wrong to confuse my personal disgust with a view that this is a weakness in the regime. Both Rome and Greece were openly addicted to the same unlovely vice and they were truly powerful. Even today the Arabs are not precisely Methodists in these matters. It is all one. This is an age of

18

threes: the Third Reich, the Third Rome, the Third Republic, the Third International. Why not the Third Sex?

6

Hanfstaengl's list of weaknesses is not exhaustive, Franklin. I could add to it quite a bit, but it is enough to show that we are at least speaking the same language.

Winston, you know, I think that Putzi is quite right to say that it is the strength of Hitlerism which must concern us. Before we can strike at its weakness, we must destroy its strength. Putzi, what do you consider the true political strength of the Nazis?

Perhaps, Mr. President, I can best explain it to you as I saw it myself twenty years ago. It had the strength of a national resurrection, something beyond reason, something based on instinct, that made it like a tide or the sap rising in the trees after winter. I had been interned in America during the first war. My business was taken away and destroyed by your Alien Property Custodian. I married an American girl. My son was born here. In 1922 we all went to Munich. The first time I heard of Hitler was through your Military Attaché at Berlin, Colonel Truman Smith. Smith had come to Munich, heard Hitler speak, was impressed by him, put me in touch with him. So my membership in the Party was sponsored by the U. S. A.

Not really! I never knew that.

Germany had been beaten. The war was lost. The Allies were in control. There was inflation. There was disillusion. There was unemployment, hunger, despair. There were putsches and riots, Marxist uprisings, Allied reprisals, reparations. It was not pleasant for a German to contemplate

Germany. Then there came this man, Hitler—a guttersnipe, a nonentity, a voice. He believed in the German people. He believed in a glorious resurrection for Germany. He preached national unity, courage, self-discipline, patience, determination, organization. He called on youth to serve and sacrifice. He promised them a diet of hard knocks. And above all, he believed in himself. When we saw that even our great war-general Ludendorff was willing to take orders from this little corporal, we Germans believed in Hitler, too. It was, if I dare say so, Mr. President, not unlike your New Deal, only much, much more powerful.

I can see that, Putzi.

Hitler gave us courage, hope, pride. Germany could awake. The Treaty of Versailles, the Jews, the Marxists, all that scum and *quatsch,* would be swept away. Our girls could find husbands, our men could find work, our children would have secure, happy homes, and Germany would be born again—strong, young and purified.

You spoke of the Jews, Putzi.

Ja, Mr. President. The Jews. I mention them because they alone as a group in Germany were able to take prompt advantage of Germany's downfall. Everywhere you looked, a Jew popped up—in medicine, dentistry, literature, science, politics, industry, banking and all the nice profitable occupations. And you know that in Central and Eastern Europe, and in peasant countries the world over, the money-lender is hated and the Jew is hated. This is a fact which I do not defend, but it is also a fact that anti-Semitism was and is popular politics in Germany and perhaps in other countries, too. Myself, I did not share it but I went along with it as John Carter here might go along with the Solid South and the lynchings and the poll-tax for the sake of the New Deal. Anti-Semitism in the Nazi movement was at first only a weakness. It was not until after that Grynschpan business in Paris that it became something worse than a weakness.

You mean?

A strength, Mr. President. But before I continue I would like your opinion of what I have just said, and of course the opinion of the Prime Minister, too. After all, he is the presiding judge.

7

What Hanfstaengl says, Churchill observed is quite true, so far as it goes, which is only back to 1922. The strength of Hitlerism is built on the strength of Germany and the Germans have been a strong, warlike people since the dawn of history. Long before Julius Caesar, his uncle Marius had to fight back a terrible German invasion—the Cimbri and the Teutones. Tacitus tells us how the Roman Emperors used the Germans, as a sort of arsenal of military manpower. When Rome fell, it was the Germans who swarmed over the ancient world—the Goths and Lombards in Italy, the Visigoths in Spain, the Vandals in Africa, the Franks in Gaul, and the Angles and Saxons in poor old England. They ransacked the Mediterranean, they reached to Rome and Byzantium. They were the scourge and terror of the Middle Ages. Of course, after one group of Germans took England, another branch, the Norse pirates or Normans, took England all over again.

For a thousand years they ruled Europe and it was night, Churchill continued. Then, bit by bit, Europe recovered from the shock and became civilized. The Germans were pressed back into Germany and fell to fighting each other. It was no accident that old George the Third hired

Hessians to fight your American rebels, Franklin. It was in the blood. Germans were good soldiers and they cared not whom they fought so long as they were paid and on time.

When France, under Louis XIV, was the great enemy of freedom, we in England used the Germans to restrain him. Marlborough, as you know, fought in comradeship with Prince Eugene and his Germans. England and Prussia wore down France under Louis—all the Louis—and under Napoleon, too. Wellington and Bluecher won the Battle of Waterloo that sent Bonaparte to St. Helena.

About fifty years later, the Germans began to march again. Under Prussia and Bismarck, they became once more what they had been a thousand years before—a powerful, military people. They conquered Austria, they conquered France, they conquered Denmark. They paused to rest for another fifty years and then they attacked England. After Bismarck came Kaiser Wilhelm II, and after Wilhelm came Hitler, but it was the same Germany and the same Germans.

I tell you, Franklin, we in England not only live close to Germany but we know the Germans. They are a formidable people. They are strong in military power and they are strong in industry. They have science, they have coordination, they have discipline. Bismarck married the Prussian Army to German industry. It was Krupp, it was the I. G. Farbenindustrie. It was coal and iron, not blood and soil, as that mad mullah at Berlin declares. They built ships. They built a navy. They built aircraft. It was one for all and all for loot.

There is the real power of Germany. There is the true strength of Hitlerism.

Yes, Churchill continued, I know the other side, too. They are fine, handsome, cultured people. I know Munich and I love it, Hanfstaengl. It's a beautiful city, good beer, excellent food, fine people. Pity we had to bomb it. I knew it before Hitler and the R.A.F. The truth is that no German can control himself or his actions if a drummer passes down the street or a banner waves. They goose-step, they "Heil Hitler!," they follow the flag. They are the same people who sacked Rome, ravaged the Mediterranean, conquered England, and plunged the whole world into a thousand years of darkness.

Hitler is merely the self-appointed agent of German industry and the German General Staff. Hitlerism is merely what you would call stream-lined Prussianism. Granted that there was a great and wholesome national resurrection under Hitler, that means nothing. It does not explain how the Nazis turned their New Deal into a world-wide war of conquest and domination. For that you must go behind Hitler and his talk about the Dictate of Versailles, back of the Jews and Marxists, back to Bismarck, Nietzsche, Krupp, Frederick, Charlemagne and Barbarossa. Hitlerism is only the current expression of the German will to war, combined with the German will to be commanded, the German lust to kill and to obey that is recorded of the tribe since the earliest records of the human race.

What you say, Winston, Roosevelt remarked after a pause, is true as history but it does not explain the real strength of Hitler. Germany under Bismarck showed that the Germans could be strong, prosperous and peaceful. Bismarck had won a place in the diplomatic sun for the Germans, whom he had united under Prussian leadership. He had established the tariff union. He had humbled Austria and France, but opposed the annexation of Alsace-Lorraine. He had made Germany a great power. His policy was founded on friendship with England and friendship with Russia. That is what Germany was when Wilhelm dropped the pilot.

When I was a small boy I was taken to Germany and sent to German schools. When first I arrived, everything was calm, *gemütlich,* Bismarckian. While I was there, Wilhelm dropped Bismarck and the uniforms began to multiply. The railway workers, the postmen, the teachers, everybody in Germany began wearing uniforms. The country became militarized right under my eyes. It was not natural to the Germans, it was imposed upon them as an act of policy by a government which had already decided, as we know today, to challenge British trade and the British Navy, to make a bid for Suez and the mastery of the world.

A little while ago, the President went on, we mentioned Roehm. Does anyone remember the unsavory Baron Holstein and the Court camarilla that flitted around Wilhelm before 1914?

My opinion, Winston, is that the strength of Hitlerism is something apart from the strength of the German Army and of German industry. Bismarck married them, of course, but Bismarck was the first to disown the baby when Wilhelm went out for imperial mysticism and a naval race with England. The capacity of the Germans to believe in this mystical nonsense is the measure of their strength. When I say believe in it, I also mean to work for it. The Germans are a magnificent people, as people. They have produced Goethe, Bach, Kant and Einstein, to mention only four of the world's great names. They have produced Dürer and Wagner, Thomas Mann and Schiller. They stand high in the history of art, of science, of literature, of philosophy. By no standard are they to be dismissed lightly.

Yet this German people, whether as the primitive tribes

described by Tacitus or as the highly educated moderns led by Hitler, are capable of tremendous and personally disinterested efforts to achieve some great, mystical ambition. They are not like the lemmings which drown themselves in the Norwegian fjords. They are more like the Crusaders, who go out to rescue the Holy Sepulchre, without knowing where it is, why it is holy or why it must be rescued.

What you have said, Winston, about their industrial and military power is absolutely true but it does not explain why the Germans use those powers as they do. I see in Germany an immense capacity to believe—even in the wrong things—and to work for what they believe—even in the wrong ways. This seems to me the real meaning of Hitler's power. He has, in his day, grasped the German imagination and, like Peter the Hermit, has preached a Crusade against the Jews, the Marxists and the decadent, capitalistic democracies. The more absurd his doctrine is, the more it is accepted. They believe it because it is impossible.

The only way we can destroy this power of German belief is to show them a higher power of imagination, a wider humanism. We must fight mysticism with mysticism, fire with fire. Blood and soil or, as you said, "blood and tears, toil and sweat", must be overcome by a greater faith.

As I see it, Putzi, the real strength of Hitler is not so much that Hitler believes in himself as that Hitler believes in the Germans.

That is very close to the truth, Mr. President.

They believe in him because he believes in them?

Yes.

So what do they believe in?

I shall try to explain or remember it for you.

8

Hanfstaengl paused. It was like a tidal wave, he began, it was like the sea. You remember in Macbeth when Birnam wood came to Dunsinane? Well, this was like all of the Black Forest marching to Berlin. Nothing could stand against us, because we were the German people. Even the cries which seem so silly: the Heil Hitlers, the Sieg Heils, the Ein Volk, Ein Reich, Ein Fuehrer were like the cheer of Harvard! Harvard! Harvard! at a Yale football game. I taught Hitler that.

It has been said that we Nazis were the creation of the Army, but the Army was against us. The Army was with Hindenburg, with the Stahlhelm, with Krupp. Those Prussian officers—they despised us. They are men like your down-east Yankee skippers, Mr. President, or like your Norfolk squires, Mr. Churchill. They have the east wind in their pale blue eyes and they don't give a damn for Munich or Vienna. They were against us all the way through and even now, after nearly four years of war, they are not for Hitler. Yet the Army gave way to us.

How about the industrialists, Hanfstaengl? They contributed money to your movement.

Yes, Mr. Churchill, but do you know how they gave that money? A group of Nazis, with cudgels or brass-knuckles, would call on a factory owner and tell him that he would contribute so-and-so many Reichsmarks to the Party Fund. They stood around, breathing down his neck and bulging their muscles, until he signed the check.

Sheer blackmail, eh?

Natürlich. But why did not the owners send for the

police? It was because they knew we Nazis had the German people behind us. The institutions were against us but the people supported our movement just as here Big Business and the newspapers opposed the people's New Deal. No, the industrialists were not for us until they knew that we must win. Blackmail again. Krupp and Thyssen gave funds but they were converted *in extremis*. The Stinneses and the Hugenbergs were not with us. They were for the Weimar Republic which gave them profits without responsibility. We conquered them as we conquered the Army. And we won by parliamentary means.

Your S.S. and their brass-knuckles were not what we British would call parliamentary, Churchill remarked.

But we had to gain power against frightful odds. We had all of the newspapers against us, all, so we had to have our own Party Press, on about the same intellectual level as the *Harvard Crimson*, Mr. President. We were denied the use of the radio by the Government, so we had to speak on street-corners and train our soap-box orators. The police was against us, so we had to have our own police—bullies who held the ring for us while we said our say. The Masons, the Jews, the Catholic Church and the foreign bankers were all against us. So, of course, were the Allies. Yet we won and we won by majority votes in a series of elections in which every German learned what we meant and what we proposed to do.

All very true, Hanfstaengl. But still you don't make it clear to me what was the real strength of the Nazi movement. Surely not the Black Forest marching. Let's leave out the fairy-tales.

Mr. Churchill, Hanfstaengl said, I know of only one way to measure the strength of any given force. That is to describe what is its working capacity in, say, foot-pounds or horse-power. This Nazi thing is not an ore to be dug up and analysed, it is a dynamic which proved itself stronger than the German Army, stronger than German industry, stronger than the Catholic Church, stronger than Masonry, stronger even than the Lion of the Tribe of Judah. And, having conquered these terribly powerful forces, Mr. Churchill, Hitlerism has absorbed much of their power. England today is not only England. England is India, the Empire, the Dominions beyond the Seas and, for many purposes, the United States. So today Hitler is the German Army, German industry, German Catholicism and all that he has mastered in his struggle for Nazi power. Not only the appetite but the strength grows in eating. And on top of all these, there is the original thing which Hitlerism had that made it an earthquake and not just a tidy political democratic party.

Just the same, Putzi, Roosevelt interrupted, we have to find out what there is in Hitlerism that made it an earthquake. What, in your experience, were the things which are characteristic of the movement that made it different from the other movements? I think that we'll have our answer if we know its characteristics.

I am not sure, Mr. President, that it will be at all easy to agree on the ways in which Hitlerism is different from Sovietism or Americanism or the British way of government. In fact, it is easier to prove the precise opposite, that Hitlerism is not specifically German but is instead generally true of the white races of the world.

9

Whew! I'd like to see you prove that.

Very well, Mr. President. Let us begin by taking the

organization of the Nazi State. Hitler is the single and supreme executive-one-man government. Yet so, in fact, is Stalin in Soviet Russia. Mr. Churchill, in the absence of parliamentary elections which have been postponed until after the war, is also vested with similar authority in England. In theory it could be taken away from him but not in practice. Let us also remember that the Catholic Church is governed by the Pope as Supreme Pontiff, elected for life, and that his infallibility in matters of doctrine is an article of Catholic faith and discipline. There is good precedent for such a government.

But you may object, Mr. Churchill, that Hitler's is also a one-party government. The Nazi Party holds the monopoly of position, power and authority under the Fuehrer. Is this so very different from the control of the Communist Party in Russia? Is it very different from the Democratic Party control in the Southern States of President Roosevelt's America? Could it be argued that for the last two hundred and fifty years the British ruling classes have constituted an effective élite which controls politics, foreign policy and defense, and with Parliamentary government almost a Praesidium of two opposing factions of the one British party? I do not say that such is the case, but it could be argued by a dialectician.

Rubbish! Parliamentary government stems from Magna Carta and the long British tradition of liberty of the subject.

Then I withdraw this suggestion, Mr. Churchill, and content myself with the remark that no Republican has been elected in the State of South Carolina in more than sixty years. Let us proceed to the racial question. The Nazis have persecuted most horribly the Jewish people, as well as other races, like the Poles, deemed to be biologically unsuitable. There are still lynchings, I believe, in free America and it is not so long ago since the British Black-and-Tans applied Storm Trooper methods to the Irish Rebels. As recently as the South African War, which all of us remember, British troops herded Boer women and children into concentration camps where many died, and I recall the Amritzar Massacree where a British general ordered his troops to fire on a crowd of Indians, killing and wounding men, women and children who were unarmed, in order to teach them a lesson. I do not say these things to justify the Nazis, but rather to point out that they are not alone in doing such things. I purposely do not mention Russia where the killing has been done for ideological and not racial reasons.

This racial segregation and discrimination of which Germany is justly accused is not unlike some American policies, Hanfstaengl continued. You do not admit Asiatics on the ground that they are not eligible for citizenship, since you wish to protect the purity of your breed. In many Southern States, there are parallels of the Nuremberg laws. Marriage between whites and Negroes is absolutely forbidden. Negroes must travel in separate and inferior Jim Crow railway cars. Negroes must live in black districts or ghettoes apart from the whites and must attend separate and inferior schools. They are not permitted to vote and they are given the hardest and most disagreeable work at rates of pay below those offered to the meanest white man. And when a Negro man is accused of sex-relations with a white woman, he is lucky if he is only hanged or sent to prison for twenty years, instead of being castrated and burned at the stake.

The Nazis are correctly accused of antagonism to religion, meaning the Catholic Church, went on Hanfstaengl.

Here the American record is good by contrast, excepting always the Ku Klux Klan, the A.P.A. and the mobs which burned nunneries in New England in the 1830's. But it is barely a century since Catholics were allowed to vote or serve in the British Parliament, and even now English Catholics are taxed along with Jews, Moslems and atheists, for the support of the established church of England. And there was a time, under Elizabeth, when freedom from the Church of Rome was a condition of national survival. If Hitler opposes the power of the Church in Germany, he has at least good though ancient precedents. He at least has not had Jesuit priests burned at the stake, as did Elizabeth.

There is yet one other criterion of the truth of which I can personally testify. Hitler is faithless and his government untrustworthy. This quality in political leadership is as old as the Bible, which tells us 'Put not your trust in Princes.' Long before Macchiavelli became required reading among rulers, it was clear that the Prince must often break his word in the interest of the State. England has a formula for breaking her word—the fall of a Ministry or the overthrow of a Party at a general election. America can break her word, by the action of the Senate. The Nazis simply have a Leader whose word cannot be trusted and whose actions must, as with other nations and leaders, be measured by the national interest.

10

Roosevelt laughed. You make a good apologist, Putzi, but you overlook many things.

Natürlich, Mr. President. I merely wish to show that there is not a fundamental difference in kind, only a difference in degree, between the power of Hitler and the power of the Allies.

It's those blasted Junkers and industrialists, if you ask me, exploded Churchill. One time they're Bismarck, the next Wilhelm and now Hitler. They change their shirts but not their nature.

You must be right, Mr. Churchill, but for the life of me I cannot see how German industry differs from British and American industry. Bismarck fostered it with customs union and tariff protection, combined with social security. German miners, for example, are better paid and better treated than Welsh miners. German industry has learned to cooperate and coordinate itself through cartels but so does British industry, as witness Imperial Chemicals, Vickers, Cunard-White Star, and such. American industry doesn't seem to find the anti-trust laws a great obstacle to the consolidation and growth of big business, judging by General Motors, U. S. Steel, Standard Oil, Du Pont and Aluminum Company. German industry has long since learned what American and British industry is reluctant to accept: that it is good business to have satisfied employees and good business to work with and not against the government.

I am not, of course, Mr. Churchill, a financial expert but I do not fail to observe a certain very close resemblance between Dr. Schacht's system of blocked marks and money fiddle-faddle and your British Sterling area and dollar pool. I know that when I was still in Berlin we had British experts studying Schacht's methods and applying them so as to use currency controls to force trade into British markets on a barter basis. Dr. Schacht's money had no gold behind it, but it had plenty of steel bayonets. The pound sterling has been off gold since 1931 but is also backed by steel in the form of the Royal Navy. As for what Mr. Morgenthau has done with the dollar and Lend-Lease I cannot say, but I should be very much surprised if his Treasury had not studied and applied much of Schacht's incredible jugglery.

I'll have to ask Henry about that, Roosevelt said.

Churchill grinned.

Which brings us to the other thing, continued Hanfstaengl, the great German Army. Surely no one will pretend that this is the first or the only army in the history of the world. The Red Army of Russia is much larger in men and, being German-trained, is good in its staff-work. Given equal equipment, the Red Army is as good as the German Army. The British and American Armies are small in time of peace—your navies guarantee your defense—but they do exist and, even in time of peace, they manage to do quite a little fighting, in China, in India, in the Caribbean. Today they are strong, well-equipped, well-led. Marshall and Eisenhower, Montgomery and Portal are strong, able commanders, as good as Rommel and Kesselring, perhaps as good as Rundstedt.

What makes the German Army great is Prussia. I am not a Prussian as you know, but a Bavarian, and I do not like the Prussians but I must admit that they are very good soldiers. They—now I speak of the officers—are men with a high sense of duty, loyalty, service and sacrifice. They are good Protestant Christians. Their military career is a priesthood of national duty. They have a grim, stubborn character which is like Cromwell or Stonewall Jackson. Prussia, under Frederick, stood off the armies of Europe and won the Seven Years War after he had lost it. Prussia and the Army saved Germany from being the world's battleground as it had been for a thousand years before Waterloo.

Mr. Churchill spoke of the Cimbri and Teutones who attacked Rome before the time of Julius Caesar. They were Germans that had been driven from Germany by hordes pressing into Europe from Asia.

Since Prussia and the Army made Germany strong, the pressure from Asia has been held back by Germany. The frontiers of Europe, which once ran a little east of Berlin and a little south of Vienna have been pushed to Leningrad and to the Dneiper. Germany is strong because of the Army but the Army is strong because of its historic mission as the frontier-guard of Europe against an Asia which can still breed Attilas and Stalins. The Mongol ponies once trotted to the shores of the Adriatic. Shall we soon see Soviet tanks at Trieste or on the Rhine? Granted that Hitler's power is great, he carried the Army with him because, by his anti-Communist policy and the Russian War, he recognized the inner purpose and spirit of those thin-lipped, pale-eyed Prussian officers who stand guard on the East, facing Asia forever.

11

How does that explain Hitler's attack on France? asked Churchill.

Mr. Churchill, you may recall that once you sent word to me for Hitler's ears that England would welcome a German attack on Russia. That was many years ago and you may not remember it. In any case, I did not pass the word to the Fuehrer as I do not like diplomatic hanky-panky and perhaps, I thought, the man did not come from you.

He most certainly did not!

So. From the start, Hitler did not wish war with England or France. He did not believe you would fight. He hoped to make an arrangement. That was a mistake against which I warned him but when Hess was sent to England, Hitler still believed that he could purchase your approval for his war of conquest against the Soviets.

Just so. When France and England guaranteed Poland and remained at war after Poland ceased to exist, he or the General Staff did not believe it prudent to attack Russia, leaving an enemy in the West. So France fell and the British escaped from the Dunkirk trap. Then that Mussolini upset the Hitler apple-cart. He attacked Greece and was badly disappointed. For the prestige of the Axis and to have no enemy on the South, Hitler had to seize Greece and Crete and then take Roumania and Bulgaria, in order to have the broadest base for his Russian campaign. You must understand, Mr. Churchill, that from the very beginning both Hitler and the Army knew they must attack the Soviets. That alone offered the political and moral base for the unification of Europe.

Putzi, said Roosevelt, you have talked yourself into a circle. You have shown that the German Army, with its fixation against Russia, is the controlling force in German politics and dictated the course by which Hitler overran most of Europe. Yet earlier you said that the Army hated Hitler and did not control him.

Mr. President, hatred has little to do with politics. Your American Big Business hates you and the New Deal, yet you have found it most serviceable in the conduct of both the New Deal and the war. You have given it direction and profits, by also giving it a free expression of its productive powers.

If Hitler conquered us, he would curb our industry, would he not?

But of course.

Then if we conquer Germany, we must curb the Army.

Without the Army, Germany would not exist.

Nonsense, Putzi. There is no reason why Germany should not be prosperous and happy without an Army.

Is there no reason why England should not be prosperous and happy without a Navy?

It seems to me, I said, that the trouble is with the German mind and not with the Army. Putzi has said that the Army is Germany's frontier, because Germany has no natural frontiers except her armed men. That is his meaning, I think.

Ja, that is what I mean.

So the German Army must expand indefinitely until it rules all Europe and Asia as far as the Urals or must collapse until it is a disarmed remnant in the ruins of Berlin. Now England, France and America have natural frontiers and produce minds which have natural limits. A Frenchman has a hard, firm surface to his mind and personality, good manners, precision, a sense of form. The same thing is true of an Englishman, with minor foggy differences. The American mind is still growing into the wide natural boundaries of North America. But the German mind—and no offense to you, Putzi—must either bully or cringe. It must impose its will on you or submit to your will.

The Hun is either at your feet or at your throat, Churchill quoted himself.

I did not mean to paraphrase you, Mr. Prime Minister. I merely tried to find the reason for German aggressive power in the kind or mentality which makes Germans weep if Senegalese troops are on the Rhine and offer logical explanations of why they themselves had to go into Greece, Norway or Roumania, because naturally they had to attack Russia.

If it is the German mind, Jack, the President said, here we are back at the man who expresses it— Adolf Hitler.

12

Ach! Adolf Hitler. Where have I heard that name before? There is of course nobody else quite like him in the whole world.

Thank God for that! What's he like, Hanfstaengl, close to, among his intimates? asked Churchill. I've read tons of our intelligence reports on him. What's he really like?

Of course he is a parvenu, Mr. Churchill. He was born poor, failed in his work, suffered, struggled and found his first real self-expression in the German Army in 1914, as a corporal. It gave him a sense of security, solidarity, purposes—that Army. There are men like that in all armies and Hitler is one.

Being a nobody, he attached great snob value to the 'right people.' That is why he liked me—hm! because I represented the culture and art of Germany. He wanted to be a painter and the Hanfstaengl firm had been famous as the patrons and the friends of artists. It gave him a sense of security to have the entrée to the intellectual and artistic group in Munich. You have read *Mein Kampf?*

Rather! And a beastly job it was, too.

I agree, Mr. Churchill, and yet that book shows Hitler as he really is, groping for a large pattern for his personal insignificance in order to be comfortable in a world filled with Jews and Marxists and other enemies of the German people.

What do you mean by his personal insignificance, Putzi? asked Roosevelt.

Mr. President, Hitler is personally an insignificant man. He is quiet and unassuming in manner. He works hard, consults experts and keeps records like a shop-keeper. He neither drinks, smokes nor eats meat. He is even unmarried although not perhaps a complete celibate. His taste in music is another example. He is an addict of Wagner—loud, full harmonies which give him again a sense of comfort, of belonging to something bigger than himself. I have known Hitler in time of trouble—mine was the first house to which he came when he was released from the Landsberg Prison after the Beer Hall Putsch—and I have seen him triumph by the will of the majority of the Germans. And he was always the same man—quiet, unassuming, introspective, sensitive, with a sense of inferiority and personal insufficiency.

How do you explain his success as an orator?

He is not an orator at all, Mr. President. You are an orator, a great American political orator, with mastery of your audience. Mr. Churchill is an orator, perhaps the greatest British political orator in history. He makes phrases that ring like swords. His 'blood, sweat, toil and tears' is an improvement on Garibaldi's original. But Hitler is not an orator. He is helpless without a large audience and it must be a friendly audience. He does not know how to deal with hecklers. The S. S. men simply beat them up. His quality is not oratory at all.

What is it then in God's name? snarled Churchill. I've listened to that blasted Hitlerian drivel on the radio until

I thought something had gone wrong with the machine.

Mr. Churchill, Hitler depends on the audience to tell him what to say. It is the same thing in conference. I have attended many meetings of the Nazi leaders. Hitler sits back and lets them talk to each other. Then, when the time comes, he suddenly states his decision and it is the one which unifies all different opinions. You might call that quality 'intuition' if you please.

I can bear witness to what Putzi says, I observed. I heard Hitler speak to a Nazi mass-meeting at Munich in September, 1932. He spoke for hours and he used no script. I do not understand German very well, so I could only follow the main sense of his remarks. The idea he was putting across was that Hindenberg was over eighty years old while he, Hitler, was in his forties and could afford to wait for the Chancellorship of Germany. At the time the opposition said that this speech had finished Hitler because the Germans loved the old Fieldmarshal so dearly. Not understanding all that Hitler said, I was able to see the mechanics or the dynamics of his speech. He was exploring the mind of the crowd by a process of oratorical triangulation or range-finding. He would make a point and there would be a cheer. He would make another point and there would be another cheer. He would make a third point and there would be no cheers at all. Silence. A miss. He would then start to make a fourth point and you said to yourself, 'This is it!' It was. The crowd went wild. He did that not once but several times in the course of a long, long speech, delivered without notes. That's quite a different approach from your Fireside Talks, sir.

That's mighty interesting, Jack. What is your conclusion?

My conclusion is that it was not the German people who

were subject to hypnotic suggestion by Hitler. It was Hitler who was intimately controlled in his utterances and policies by the German people. They only recognized their will when he managed to express it for them. He had to hunt for it and find it first.

13

Oh, come now, Jack! What about all his rages and rag-chewing. That can't all be invented.

I've never heard, sir, that hysteria was a sign of strength of character. It simply bears out Putzi's statement that Hitler has an insignificant personality.

Then, Putzi. Suppose you tell us what there is that has given the Nazi movement this enormous power.

Mr. President, it is not easy to explain. The fact is that Nazism is a kind of political cocktail—a wry Martini!—two parts of Prussianism and one part of Plato.

Plato! What has poor old Plato got to do with it?

You have read Plato's *Republic,* Mr. President?

Yes.

Did it ever strike you that Plato's outline of the Perfect State is remarkably like Hitler's Nazi system?

I can't say that it did.

I did not see it either until John Carter pointed out two things. First, that Plato's *Republic* was an intellectual booby-trap set to blow up anyone who tried to apply it literally; second, that Hitler's Third Reich was the Perfect State as ironically described by Socrates in *The Republic.* Perhaps Carter can explain it better than I. It is his idea.

Go ahead, Jack.

I refuse to believe, I said, that any man who held the spiritual views of Plato could represent a man like Socrates, who came so close to the spirit of Christ, as believing that you could grow a city of good men the way you grow asparagus or produce justice the way you produce wine. Behaviorism and Platonism don't mix. In the end—and I admit I read the book hastily—Plato seems to come to his real conclusion, that the Perfect State is inside the soul of every man. Every man is the captain of his own city. Like Christ's "The Kingdom of Heaven is within you." And all the elaborate description of a mechanically organized Perfect State is really a reductio ad absurdum. Plato had a way of arguing in circles and his spheres, moving in circles, made music. Later generations, trained in the logic of Aristotle, who moves from point to point like a surveyor, made the mistake of taking Plato literally. It was Hitler's colossal error that he believed the simple-minded German scholars and tried to build the Third Reich on what Socrates, according to Plato, admitted was a lie.

How's that?

I wish I had the book here, sir, and I could point out the passage. The argument began over the nature of justice and then the Perfect State was described in terms which made one of the characters call it 'a city of swine.' Socrates starts off by proposing that, while every citizen must tell the truth, the State shall have a monopoly of lying. Page Dr. Goebbels. There shall be a complete reform of nursery songs and tales and, of course, a complete change of religion so as to condition the citizens to their duties. Page Dr. Rosenberg. There shall be a special group of so-called Guardians whose life-long duty shall be to protect the State. This is very like the S. S. There shall be a complete reform of marriage, with controlled breeding and parents separated from their children, and communized mating. Page Hitler's biological program and the unwed mothers of Germany. There shall be a military education for boys and a special training for girls. Page the Hitler Jugend and the Hitler Maedel organizations. Above all, racial purity must be maintained and music shall be purged of all effeminate Asiatic influences. Page the purge of Jewish influences in German art, literature and music. Page the Nazi pogroms against the Jews and the search for Jewish ancestors among presumed Aryans. I haven't made a profound study of it, Mr. President, but I don't think a profound study is needed to show where the Nazi movement found its characteristic ideas.

By George! That's fascinating. Drunk and disorderly on too much Prussia and Plato! Well, they've got to be locked up and brought before the beak in the morning, said Churchill.

So where Plato makes his music of the spheres strike a chord which is not unlike the song of the Christian angels, I said, Plato in Hitler's hands is like one of those stones on the end of a string that small boys twirl around a stick. The wind whistles and the stone spins faster, but the string winds itself around the stick until it comes to a dead stop.

I always said, Franklin, give Hitler enough rope and he'll hang himself.

How about it, Putzi? asked the President.

I agree with John Carter. Perhaps what we are seeing is the death-throes of Europe, as the Continent in its last moments lives through scenes of its childhood.

14

That's somewhat too Teutonic for me to grasp, said Roosevelt.

Mr. President, let us again remember Harvard and our Class reunions. You know how the older the graduates are the more they talk of their undergraduate days. Well Europe is an old grad and this is its fiftieth reunion.

When Europe was young there was one great political problem which it tried to solve. This was the question of whether citizenship depended on blood-relationship and birth—once an Englishman, always an Englishman, so to speak—or whether it depends on some common agreement, what the Romans called the public thing, the res publica which gives us our name Republic.

At first there was no question at all. Every State was composed of a tribe who spoke the same language, came of the same stock, worshipped the same gods and lived in the same place and manner. This is still the rule for millions of primitive tribesmen in Africa and the Pacific Islands. Even Athens, the most progressive and civilized of the Greek city-states, never solved the problem of citizenship. Only Athenians could be Athenians. Others were allies, slaves or resident aliens, and only native-born Athenians had the power to make political decisions. The Spartans, who conquered Athens, were even more of a tribe. The Asiatic Kings of those days were simply superimposed on the tribes they had conquered and ruled. There was no uniform citizenship, not even a uniform degree of subjection, rather like the British Empire today . . .

Get on with it, Hanfstaengl, and leave the Empire out of it, please.

Very well, Mr. Churchill, but this is important. It was not until Rome that the new idea came that citizenship need not be based on blood but on common allegiance and common ideas—like the United States.

I've read Ferrero, too, Putzi, said Roosevelt.

Guglielmo Ferrero is a great historian, Mr. President. At any rate, it was only after Rome won its great series of wars against Carthage that the old racial ideas declined. They never really died. The Jews, for example, never abandoned them and Rome itself fought a series of civil wars before Italians were admitted to Roman citizenship. It was not until the Caesars that Roman citizenship began to spread to other parts of the Empire. It was a privilege which included the right to appeal to Caesar from local magistrates. St. Paul was a Jew from Tarsus but he was also a Roman citizen. I do not wish to bore you with philosophy, Mr. President, but it has seemed true to many Christian theologians that it was the common citizenship of Rome which prepared the way for the idea of the equality of souls under Christianity. The Christian religion never spread easily outside the Roman regions. The Semitic races in particular—the Jews and the Arabs—clung to their belief in the tribe and the tribal God.

That's not quite true of the Arabs, Putzi. They had Mohammed.

Ja, you are right about that, John, but it is a fact that Christianity and Rome have marched together and it is of interest that the first great attack on the Church comes from outside the Roman orbit, from Russia which never knew the Legions, and more recently from Germany, which Rome invaded but failed to conquer.

Where does this bring you? I asked.

The question is rather, where does this bring Europe? Again I say, Europe in its old age and perhaps on its death-bed is living through once more its early struggles over race and citizenship. It has turned its back on the idea of the Rights of Man, which is a true expression of Roman Christianity, in order to go back to the old tribal idea of the rights of Germans, the rights of Nazis, or of Fascisti, Falangists, or Communists. It is absurd, of course, to argue that a man is a bad composer of music if his name is Mendelssohn—a Jew—and a good composer if his name is Mozart—an Aryan. Both happen to be good.

Yet I say to you, Mr. President, and to you, Mr. Churchill, that the racial purity idea is the strongest force in the whole Nazi system. To America in particular it is very dangerous, because it could not be applied in the Western Hemisphere without exploding your melting-pot so as to shake the stars. It is not so long since that your Supreme Court provoked a Civil War by ruling that the black man has no rights that the white man is bound to respect. That was the Dred Scott decision, as I remember, and it cost you four years of agony and thousands of lives and gave my ancestor, General Sedgwick, a reputation. Think if the Nuremberg Code should be applied to New York City or even in Washington.

15

What about London, Hanfstaengl?

London would be no worse than Berlin, Mr. Churchill, and it would not be so bad in England. The British people are a sound tribal stock and could survive racial purges. It would be easier for England, even with the Dominions, to adopt Nazi race-policies than for the Western Hemisphere to permit them to exist. That is the dynamite that Hitler borrowed from Plato, to whom it was not dynamite at all but a commonly accepted fact—the idea of racial purity and racial citizenship.

So you really think that the pogrom is Hitler's secret weapon?

Yes, said Hanfstaengl, although Germany itself could not pass the Aryan test—it is half Slavic already. When the Nazis wanted real Nordic brides—with blonde hair and blue eyes—do you know what they did? They sent to Sweden for them, as though they were importing bananas.

I'd heard that, said Roosevelt.

Did you also hear, sir, I asked, about the time one of Himmler's men showed Goering proof that two of his assistants were non-Aryans? Damn it! he roared. "I'm the man in Germany who says who's a Jew!"

Poor old Italy couldn't pass the test, Roosevelt remarked, with their mixture of Arab and Negro and Greek blood in Sicily and around Naples and with the traces of all the slaves that Rome dragged in from all over the world.

No, Mr. President, Hanfstaengl agreed. Nobody could pass. That is why Hitler's racial policy is really a policy for export. That he is wiping out the Jews is true. That he is also exterminating Poles and Russians is also true. But he does not exterminate the Czechs and he spares the Magyars who are descended from the yellow race, while he confers upon the Japanese the peculiar honor of being known as Honorary Aryans.

What does this racial policy do for Germany, Hanfstaengl, if it simply serves to infuriate decent people elsewhere? asked Churchill.

46

Mr. Prime Minister, Hitler's race-policy gives to the Germans the very great advantage of having their own system of tribal ethics. They can make their own morals. They do not need to justify their actions in the eyes of God or man so long as they are justified in the eyes of Germans. They are living on a lie, like the citizens of Plato's city of swine. They are trained, as Plato suggested training human swine, by music and gymnastics. Goebbels and Rosenberg supply the music in the form of propaganda. Goering, Hitler and the Army supply the gymnastics in the form of military training. Whatever they do is right, because they do it. My country right or wrong, but with this morality the Reich can never be wrong.

As the Eyties say, "Mussolini is always right!"

Just so, Mr. Churchill. You can see, then, what a great practical advantage it is to a statesman or a regime never to be forced to apologize or explain.

The divine right of nations?

The divine right of Nazis, at least. Here again, it must be admitted that they carry to a logical German conclusion what other nations already practice. It is the nature of sovereignty that it is absolute and is its own justification. The British blockade in the last war cost more lives than the U-boats or the Zepplins. Yet it was the German Government that had to explain, justify and defend its actions. Many more Germans are being killed by the Liberators and the Flying Fortresses, Mr. President, than died at Guernica, Warsaw, Rotterdam, Coventry or in the Blitz on London. Yet you do not feel compelled to apologize whenever a block-buster kills fifty German babies. Hitler is still more free than either you or Mr. Churchill, almost as free as Stalin, to do whatever he thinks may win the war for Germany.

That has a great weakness, Putzi, the President remarked. The danger of tribal ethics is that they blind a government to what may or may not help them succeed. They shut themselves into their own prison and end by believing their own propaganda. They alienate forces which might befriend them or at least refrain from injuring them. As soon as these forces realize the complete moral irresponsibility of the Nazis, they are compelled to oppose them by the instinct of self-preservation. As the whole world knows, including the Kremlin, my friend Winston has not been particularly partial to the Soviet Union. But as Britain's war-leader he is careful to do nothing which can prevent Russian and British military cooperation against Germany.

Do you believe that this cooperation will continue after the war against Hitler has been won, Mr. President? asked Hanfstaengl.

Why not?

Perhaps it will but I would be surprised to see it happen. In any case, it was an error to believe that Hitler could ever remain on terms of friendship with Moscow. It was like a porcupine in the marriage-bed, that Nazi-Soviet Non-Aggression Pact.

16

Yet as late as the spring of 1941, Russia and Germany were negotiating for the extension of that Pact, right up to to the moment when Hitler invaded the Soviet in June, Churchill objected.

The Fuehrer had to attack Russia. His whole career and regime compelled him to attack Russia. Most of all the racial policy. God knows how many races there are in

Russia, perhaps hundreds. They are of every color; they speak any number of horrible clicky, squashy, slithery languages; they worship several different kinds of God, including the Holy Trinity of the Communists—the mummy of Lenin, the name of Karl Marx and the Fordson tractor. These races are again on the move. They threaten to spill over into Europe. Perhaps before this war is over there will again be Cossacks on the streets of Paris, as in 1815, and Stormovik planes based on the Pas de Calais.

So long as there was a Tsar in Russia, Hanfstaengl went on, Europe was moderately safe. For the Tsars used the Russians to rule the other races and they exalted the Orthodox Church above the other religions. Russian was the official language. The language in which you bribed the Tsarist officials. Tsarist Russia was itself an ally of Germany in holding back the peoples of Asia. After Bismarck, Kaiser Wilhelm made the horrible mistake of driving Russia into the arms of France and England.

The Russians fought jolly well in the last war, Churchill pointed out, and it was Ludendorff who sent Lenin and the Bolsheviks into Russia, to break up the Russian Empire.

You are right, Mr. Churchill. Like a plague bacillus in a sealed railway-carriage, as you wrote. That, too, was a mistake. The Communists first Judaized and then Asiaticized Russia. That is Europe's great danger today. In the eyes of the Third International, a Negro, a Hindu, a Chinese or a Scot can be a good Communist. All Communists are equal in the eye of Marx, so long as they follow the Party line. The Orthodox Church was disestablished, though now Stalin has revived it, which was a distinct improvement in the opinion of the Russian Moslems, for example. Russian is still the official language but the Communists have granted cultural autonomy to regions like Turkestan, so that they no

longer are compelled to Russify themselves. That is why
Hitler's racial policy is a strong weapon against Russia,
since Russia—as Asia—has been the enemy of Europe—
the womb of the great invasions—since the dawn of time.

Don't you overlook the Catholic angle in the Soviet
religious picture? I asked.

But that is vital, John. It is the essence.

Here is the story told me a good many years ago by Alex
Gumberg, I said. Gumberg was by origin a Russian Jew
attached to the American Embassy as an interpreter in the
last war. Later he worked with Colonel Robbins and the
American Relief Administration in Russia. He came over
here to work for Amtorg and wound up with Floyd Oldum
in Atlas Corporation. Gumberg knew Lenin quite well and
knew what was going on. He told me that the Vatican sent
Father Walsh of Georgetown University to Moscow to
negotiate a Concordat with the Soviets. Pope Benedict believed that the liquidation of the Russian Orthodox Church,
which had become a corrupt and oppressive political machine, as witness the Rasputin affair, offered a unique mis-
sionary opportunity to the Catholic Church. There had been
a difference of opinion at Rome, with the Jesuit Order
objecting to the whole idea. The compromise was to proceed
with the plan but send a Jesuit to administer it. Gumberg
said that Lenin was entirely willing to sign a Concordat
with the Vatican. Why not? The Bolsheviks were fighting
a dozen campaigns against Tsarist generals and Allied interventions, and it would have helped them to come to agreement with the Church, especially as there were few Catholics
in Russia to begin with. According to Gumberg, Father
Walsh ignored his directives and reported back to Rome that
no agreement could be reached with the Soviet regime, that
it was essentially godless and anti-religious and that a Con-

50

cordat would be what Garrison called a 'a covenant with hell.' So the Church passed up its chance and committed itself to a course of political hostility towards a country which was then ready to admit Catholic missionaries.

I'd heard that story but not in the same way, Jack, the President said. It's an interesting question. I've done my best to persuade Stalin to grant greater freedom to Catholics in Russia but it's almost as difficult as persuading the Ulster Presbyterians to come to terms with the Catholics of South Ireland.

17

The Vatican is against Hitler, Churchill said.

But the Vatican is still more against Communism, Mr. Churchill, countered Putzi. Why does Franco send his Blue Legion to the Russian Front? Why does Mussolini send Italians to the Russian Front, and Vichy-France, too? It is because the Catholic Church hates Communism more than it hates Hitlerism.

But Hitler's racial policy is dead against the Catholic idea, Putzi. Christianity has this at least in common with the Third International, that a Negro, a Jew, a Hindu or a Scot can be an equally good Christian in the eyes of the Church.

I agree, Mr. President, most heartily I agree, especially is that true of the Catholics. The Protestants believe it, too, but they seem to prefer to wait until they are all in the eyes of God. That is why you have the nice rich people of this country Episcopalians like you and myself, and the nice poor people Methodists, and the foreigners Catholics and the Negroes Baptists or worshipping in Jim Crow churches.

There's too much truth in what you say, but we can agree that the Catholics really practice the equality of souls.

That is why Nazi racism and Catholicism cannot live happily together ever after, Mr. President. The Church does not forget the Nazi persecutions of priests and nuns, the beastly charges and other nasty things which violated Von Papen's Concordat. It is most important to remember that in spite of all this there are millions of good Catholics in the Third Reich, Catholic churches are open for worship and Catholic priests are free to administer the sacraments. The Army above all has kept its chaplains and its Christianity. That could not happen in Soviet Russia. It would not, be allowed to happen. The authorities would put a stop to it. The Catholic Church knows that this is so and, knowing it, submits to the fact of Nazi rule because of the fear of extinction by the Communists.

But don't you agree that Communism and Catholicism have many things in common?

Of course they have. So do all religions and Communism is a religion even if they bend the knee to the Fatted Tractor. Yet there can be only one Pope, not two, not Pope Pius XII in Rome and Pope Stalin I in Moscow. What a scandal! It is because they resemble each other so greatly, especially the Society of Jesus and the Communist Party, that their differences are insurmountable.

Isn't that true of Hitler and the Church? I asked. Can there be Pope Pius at Rome and Pope Adolf at Berlin.

Yes, *mein lieber* John, because there is so great a difference between the Nazis and the Catholics that it is not too difficult to find some points of agreement for a Concordat. The Church in any case cannot consider the Nazis a serious rival so long as the Nazis believe and practice their racial doctrines. At most there are perhaps 200,000,000 people who could claim to be racially true Aryans. That leaves 2,000,000,000 people for the Catholic Church. That is enough to win any election—is it not, Mr. President?—and in the long run the Church knows that it will swallow up those silly 200,000,000 Aryans, with their talk of Blood and Earth, their Neo-Wotan worship and their belief that they have been chosen by a completely non-Jewish God to be the Master Race and rule the world for a thousand years.

18

I can see that, said Roosevelt. Our job is to speed up the process and knock the Nazi race policy out of the way. How can we do that, Putzi?

You overlook the most important part of that policy.

What's that?

You propose to try and punish the Nazis for their crimes against humanity, do you not, Mr. President?

Certainly we do!

That's Britain's policy, too, Churchill added.

You are prepared to follow the rule of law, namely that judicial process shall first establish personal guilt, in order to prevent the confusion of personal vendetta. Just as you hang your murderers in order to spare society the ancient blood-feuds? Hanfstaengl asked.

Exactly, Roosevelt agreed.

And you are determined to follow this policy so that no guilty man shall escape?

Yes.

Then you are not going to punish only a handful of

leaders and allow the smaller murderers and torturers and robbers to go free?

No.

Not even if it means executing two or three or even ten million Germans? Not even if they plead that they acted only in obedience to orders which they could disobey only at the risk of their own lives?

Churchill snorted. Hanfstaengl, you know perfectly well that we could never accept such a defense. Otherwise they could all blame Hitler, and Hitler would undoubtedly be dead and in hell.

Lord Lothian told me in 1940 that he expected Hitler to commit suicide at the end, I said.

Not so, John, Hanfstaengl objected. He will contrive to die a soldier's death in battle against the Russians so as to preserve the Nazi mythos, like Barbarossa in his cave.

In any event, Putzi, the President said, even if, after the war, we should decide to spare all but a few hundred of the top-Nazis we could not make such a decision now without offending the people of the occupied nations, not to mention the Russians who have suffered horribly. The morale of the Underground depends on their conviction that the Germans are going to be punished thoroughly.

Just so, Mr. President. That is why you cannot destroy the Nazi racial policy without destroying all the power of the German people in battle first.

What rot!

No, Mr. Churchill, it is not rot. It is the truth. Hitler persuaded or compelled the Germans to adopt a system of tribal ethics under his race policy. This system encouraged the Germans, millions of them, to commit what the world rightly regards as crimes which must be punished. That is why even the millions of decent Germans—and they do exist

—dare not stop fighting. It is because they fear complete national destruction in the form of Allied punishment for the Nazi crimes. They would rather die in battle than before a firing-squad. They have burned their boats and you do not dare build them a bridge. Even if you built that bridge, they would not dare trust themselves to it. They would not believe you if you offered them a peace of mercy.

19

Well, Putzi, we seem to have come full circle and still we haven't reached a conclusion, said Roosevelt.

Perhaps there is none.

Wait a minute! Let's see what we have established. The strength of the Nazi system and Hitler seems to lie in no particular department. Their conduct and their institutions are different in degree but not in kind from what exists in the different Allied countries. Hitler himself is not a powerful personality and the secret of his influence lies in his ability to grasp the combined will and instinct of the German people.

He is a bar-tender, said Hanfstaengl, not a distiller.

A damned bloody bar-tender, added Churchill.

That's right, Winston, but the brew he dispenses is mainly composed of Prussian military efficiency, including the efficiency of German industry and German science, with the old idea that there is such a thing as a Chosen People and that the Germans are it. As a result, Germany is drunk and disorderly and is resisting arrest because the Germans know that they are going to be punished, perhaps hung, for what they have done while under the influence of Hitler.

Mr. President, you have stated it clearly. I could not have done better myself. Hm.

Very well, then. The problem still remains: How are we going to find the formula which will persuade the Germans to stop all this killing and submit to justice, tempered with mercy.

Perhaps, Mr. President, it is also a question of persuading the Germans that Russia is not Asiatic, that Asia is not the enemy of Europe, and that Russian Communism is not the enemy of Roman Catholicism.

We'll just have to keep on bombing and burning until they submit to the might of Allied arms, Churchill said.

There must be some shorter way than that, Winston, the President replied. Let's see if we can't get at it another way. Let's see if we can't establish the principle of difference.

What do you mean?

I mean, let's try the scientific method of analysing a substance by determining what it is not. Let's test Germany the way you test a metal, to see if it reacts to the different chemical tests for copper, zinc, lead, gold and so on.

You mean to apply the acid test to the Hun? I'd drop it on them with considerable relish.

We're both doing that, aren't we? What I propose this evening, though, is to try to find the essential way in which the Allied nations differ from Germany. Perhaps in that way we can find a key to the puzzle at Berlin. Let's see what we ourselves are like and then we may see the pieces that are missing from the German picture.

Quite easy, Franklin. They're Huns and we aren't.

All right, Winston. You've asked for it. England is closer to Germany than we are. You haven't said much so far. Suppose you tell us what the British Empire is that the Third Reich is not.

II

Mercury

1

I MUST say, said Churchill, that I feel more at home in an English garden than in the Black Forest of Teutonic philosophy. I am in full agreement with much of what Hanfstaengl said but yet I am forced to repeat that we British are at war with the entire German people—their Hausfraus and Frauleins, their Gauleiters and their Fuehrers and their unspeakable Master-Race ideas.

You have asked me, Franklin, to try to establish the vital points of difference between the Empire and Hitlerism. If you were an Englishman you would not ask. This is an old story. We humbled the power of Spain at its greatest and beastliest. It was my ancestor, John Churchill, Duke of Marlborough, who warred down the proud might of Louis XIV. We utterly defeated France under Bonaparte, who was possibly the greatest European political leader since Julius Caesar—

With German help, Hanfstaengl observed.

With the help of all Europe, including Russia, and in spite of the fact that the United States were arrayed against the cause of freedom. Again, in 1914, we met and, in four bitter years, defeated Imperial Germany under Wilhelm. And I would urge you not to forget that for one entire year we stood alone against the power of all Europe under Hitler.

Hanfstaengl, you spoke of the German part in the defeat

of Napoleon. That is my precise point. As one wicked man after another has found a nation strong enough and stupid enough to attempt the conquest of the world, England has always found allies to resist him. Why? Because we stand for freedom under authority, for order and obedience for more people than ever before in human history.

Franklin, in spite of America's long, exaggerated and historic grudge against the British Empire, twice within our own lives, when England was threatened, the question was not whether America would move to our support but when America would intervene in behalf of the right.

That's true, Winston, and we'd do it again.

You must also remember that England has the longest organized memory of any government in the world. Not for close to nine hundred years has a foreign enemy set foot in England. I say this humbly, for it is thanks to the providence of Almighty God that England has remained free: the home of freedom and the mother of orderly self-government and law. Our experience of Government and our record for peaceful self-rule have grown together. We do not believe that it is necessary to set everything down in black-and-white. We believe that the rights and dignity of free men are best defended in their own hearts and lives, not in written constitutions or the courts of law.

You Americans became a nation in the age of reason and the Rights of Man. French philosophers tutored Jefferson but the French who aided American independence were themselves the children of English freedom, students of Locke and Hobbes, of Pym and Cromwell, men who saw northward across the Channel a nation which kept its kings but kept them in their place, even to the scaffold.

The truly vital point at which England differs from Hitlerism and, indeed, from all the world, Churchill included, is the sure, steady instinct for freedom which runs through all our history. Our freedom, which we have shared with all the world, is such that even Hanfstaengl here, a convinced Nazi and co-founder with Hitler and his gang of that monstrous tyranny, turned to England for asylum in his hour of need and reproaches us only that we knew our classics too well to require such aid and such defenders.

2

Will the right honorable gent yield for a question? asked Roosevelt.

Churchill grinned and nodded.

Granted that what you say is true of England and the self-governing dominions, how do you reconcile the British instinct for freedom with British domination? How do you mix freedom with empire? Many Americans, myself included, like and admire the British and their free institutions and still question their readiness to bomb Iraqi villages or machine-gun the natives in Indian bazaars.

Franklin, all my life in one form or another I have been asked that question: in home politics, in foreign policy and in my own studies. The only possible answer is based on hard, simple facts.

Is it simply a matter of law and order? asked Roosevelt.

Yes. Woodrow Wilson once admitted to Cecil Spring-Rice that his Mexican policy involved 'shooting men into self-government.' We do it in the general interest in law and order, which are vitally important in themselves. In fact, I almost believe that even tyranny is better than anarchy: it costs less in life and property.

Here are the facts: under British leadership the Western

Europeans have developed a highly advanced technology. Other parts of the world, excepting always the U.S.A., did not even approximate Europe's technical and industrial development. The task fell upon England—as ruler of the seas, a role forced upon her by the mere necessity of self-preservation—to be the agency through which technical skills and industrial progress were spread among primitive and backward peoples throughout the world.

That is what England accomplished in the Nineteenth Century. This has led to the extension of British sovereignty, particularly in Africa, since it became necessary to combat destructive customs abhorrent to decency and human freedom—such as suttee and thuggee in India and slavery and cannibalism in Africa.

What about the Opium Wars against China? asked Roosevelt.

A Roosevelt, whose fortune was founded in the China trade, should be the last to raise the issue of opium, Franklin. Yes, even the Opium Wars fall into this pattern of liberation, for they ended the humiliations and difficulties which all foreigners, Americans included, suffered at the hands of Chinese officialdom. The result of even those sordid wars was an increase of trade and welfare in the Far East, such as Asia had never known in all history.

What about Japan? I asked. The modernization of Japan was another result of the spread of European techniques among backward peoples. Was that a good thing?

Let me see, Carter, Churchill replied. As I remember it was an American named Matthew Perry who opened Japan to the wonders and the thunders of Western Civilization. Granted that Japan was too apt a pupil for our comfort, I will point out that, had it not been for Japan's successful war against Russia in 1904-5, the German War of 1914 would have been lost by the forces of freedom. Imperial Germany would have been free to concentrate against France and England, while America must have been committed to hostility toward Russia in the Far East. This would have debarred her from the grand alliance which destroyed Wilhelm's power.

Just the same, Winston, Roosevelt remarked, your case has been weakened since the last war. Industrialization has spread to all the world and British economic policy has been less liberal than in the Nineteenth Century. Especially since you established the Sterling Bloc in 1931, it has seemed that the Empire is committed to a policy of repression in order to safeguard British trade and investments. This has been disturbing to the rest of us.

It is still better than any economic catastrophe to the Empire.

3

Do you mean to tell me that the suppression of free trade relations between the Empire and the rest of the world is consistent with British sponsorship of freedom?

Most assuredly I do!

I'll bet you a box of those Havana cigars against a carton of Camels that you can't prove your point.

Franklin, I wouldn't trust you for a package of fags on this question. However, I'll take Hanfstaengl's word for it.

Unfair! He's your prisoner.

Very well, I'll take Carter's word.

All right. Jack, you have to decide whether the Prime Minister or I get the better of this argument.

Very well, said Churchill. Let's get down to first principles on this issue. I'll begin by stating that there is an immense difference between the American conception of freedom and British freedom.

How so? Roosevelt asked. Isn't freedom more or less indivisible?

You Americans conceive of freedom as a right to be enjoyed by all, no matter how unprepared for it, no matter how unable to take advantage of it. We British consider freedom to be a privilege which must be earned and deserved. We respect freedom so highly that we are not disposed to cheapen it, as you do.

I don't follow you there, Winston.

It cheapens freedom to thrust it upon people who are unable to appreciate or use it. For example, after your Civil War, you gave freedom to the Negro slaves. Where is their freedom now? They were not prepared for it, they did not understand it, they abused it and they lost it. In my opinion, many generations must pass before the American Negroes get real political and civil rights in the United States of America. Take another example: You stand pledged to grant national independence to the Philippines in 1946. Are the Filipinos prepared for it? Do the Moros even want it? Will the Islands become a sovereign, independent nation or will your grant of freedom simply confer upon a handful of Manila lawyers a temporary monopoly of political office and commercial advantage?

Without the grant of independence to the Philippines, the President answered, we would have lost the war against Japan. It was that which made the Filipinos fight a successful delaying action, while the Javanese and Malays collaborated.

That's a sound policy but it is only one of expediency.

If you defend the grant of Philippine independence as a military move against Japan, that is one thing, but we are discussing freedom in principle.

Very well.

The British position is that freedom and independence must be earned. We prize it so highly for ourselves that we do not concede that it is a right or a gift. We are willing, more than any other nation in history, to confer freedom on those who prove their will and ability to maintain it but we are damned if we will hand it over to every Zulu, Hottentot or Kanaka who parrots about freedom. As our long history as an independent nation shows, freedom is not a matter of natural right but must be defended.

Have you ever paused to consider, Franklin, how reasonable we are, judged simply as conquerors? We do not habitually put our enemies into concentration camps. We do not systematically torture or enslave them. It is not our idea that the purpose of empire is to kill all those who have opposed us or to impose harsh and oppressive systems of police on the vanquished. Instead, we state—and our record supports our words—that we stand ready to welcome any real national movement and to yield our sovereignty, as with the Irish Free State, rather than impose our will and power on a subject race. But we do not regard cannibalism, slavery, anarchy or savage cruelty a better thing than the liberty of the subject under the law of the realm. You Americans have a different theory. You proclaim your belief in liberty but deny the ballot to as many of your citizens as your very clever politicians can contrive to disenfranchise. You set constitutional terms on the authority of those whom you do allow to vote. You distrust democracy. We do not. We do not, however, believe that you can enact self-government or improvise representative institutions. We confer the franchise only on those who insistently demand it, but, once granted, we place no limit on the sovereign power of the people to direct their own destiny.

4

Winston, your eloquence and logic are unanswerable, the President said. Yet the same arguments could be used to justify the cruelest tyranny. If you say that freedom is granted only to those who can effectively insist on it, you also admit that freedom can be denied by those who have the power to suppress those peoples who demand it but lack the weapons with which to get it. Translated into foreign policy, this leads straight to power politics and war.

That's a good point, Churchill admitted, but only for purposes of debate. I assert that a candid scrutiny of the record would not place us in the same category with Hitler or Stalin.

If you were, you wouldn't be here tonight, Winston.

All I need say is that we would long ago have been obliterated by an indignant world if we were really oppressors. It is a fact that the British Empire has been so vast a—shall I say, convenience?—to the nations of the world that it has never occurred to any of them, save for Germany and Japan, to challenge our authority or defy our power.

For my part, Winston, I think it was feeble of you to return the Irish ports to the Free State. We would both be safer if we held Queenstown today.

No matter how appetizing the prospect, let's not be diverted into a discussion of Mr. Eamon De Valera and the

Irish Free State, Churchill said. At great cost to ourselves, we have scrupulously respected the neutrality of Eire and have tolerated his disregard of our own security rather than insist on our legitimate rights.

The Irish are always with us, Roosevelt admitted. Especially here we've always been hypnotized by the Irish question and do not see that your general policy has always been much larger than Dublin Castle or Phoenix Park.

As you know, Franklin, we have charted the seas and established light-houses and other aids to navigation throughout the world. We have put down piracy and suppressed the slave trade. We have established fair and useful systems of freight-rates and insurance throughout the seven seas. We have gone into unhealthy, dangerous and savage countries, where we have combatted disease, built roads and harbors and established order. We have founded plantations and developed mines. We have encouraged systems of production and exchange.

That is entirely true, Winston. The world is better for the Empire, which is one of the reasons we are your allies.

Naturally, said the Prime Minister, we did these things plainly in our own interest. We do not pretend to be complete altruists. But we have acted in the general interest of decency and orderly development, on terms which did not unduly discriminate against any other nation. Nobody, not even the Irish, would expect us to incur the vast expenditures, the political inconveniences or the diplomatic embarrassments of colonial conquest and then turn the benefits over to the exclusive advantage of others. However, we have not prohibited foreign imports, we have not forbidden foreign investments and we have allowed great freedom of travel and residence in our possessions to the citizens of nations which have not lifted a finger to create the opportunities of which they take advantage.

What you say is true, Mr. Churchill, said Hanfstaengl. Yet it is a fact that you have opposed the spread of German colonies. Why?

We did not oppose the German colonies at first. On the contrary, we made many agreements with Berlin about Africa. It was only when we saw that German colonies were designed to serve as military bases from which to attack the Empire that we opposed German colonial expansion. By contrast, we have allowed Spain, France, Portugal and Holland to share the burden of colonial administration, because we know that their aims are not hostile to the peace and security of the civilized world.

Is it not a fact that you also control these countries? Hanfstaengl asked.

It didn't look as though we controlled France at Oran or Dakar, did it? In fact, President Roosevelt might have much to say about Vichy's policy in Indo-China, since it was Pétain's supine abasement before Tokyo that actually launched Japan's attack upon the United States. The truth is that we are an empire because we must be, because no other power can be trusted to develop these backward countries and still refrain from using their resources in wealth and manpower for their own aggrandisement.

5

Just the same, Winston, said Roosevelt, your wars haven't all been for freedom. Neither have ours, for that matter. Take the Boer War. That was fought to establish

British sovereignty over South Africa, but when it was over it seemed that the war had actually been fought for the London speculators who owned shares in De Beers. Gold and diamonds were the real issues, and dividends.

Surely that is not the first time when blood has flowed because of money or jewels, Churchill answered. I grant that the war was originally a piece of stock-jobbery organized by Rhodes and his speculative friends, just as Hearst organized your war with Spain. From the imperial aspect, the South African War was a disaster in that it advertised our military incompetence to the world. Even so, the aftermath of our victory was a settlement which gave to the Boers more liberty than they had enjoyed under Oom Paul Kruger. Jan Smuts, who made me prisoner in Natal, is today the wisest adjutant of Empire policy. Where our weapons conquer, we not only spare but enrich the vanquished so that those who opposed us become our firm allies and the enemies of yesterday are the friends of today.

And the other way around, too, Mr. Churchill, Hanfstaengl said.

Unfortunately, yes. The Germans, most of all the Prussians, had been our allies for better than a hundred years. There was no time when the German people would have found us hostile, had they wished to reconcile our respective interests, but they were unwilling to discuss terms. They declined agreement or else proposed settlements which were manifestly inconsistent with our interest and dignity as a sovereign state. Even so, it was not England that invaded Belgium in 1914 and it was not England that attacked Poland in 1939.

Yet a wiser or a firmer policy could have prevented this war, said Hanfstaengl. Hitler asked only one thing for Germany, to be allowed to support its national interests in Eastern Europe, without interference from the Western Powers.

That is what Goering told me in Berlin, in 1932, I added. Locarno in the West, a free hand in the East, was what he asked for Germany.

He asked England to betray Poland, as the price of peace, after Chamberlain had sacrified the Czechs on Hitler's assurance that this was Germany's last territorial demand in Europe.

Yet you had no obligation to the Poles until the late spring of 1939, Hanfstaengl objected. You made Poland your official chip on the shoulder. This condemned the Poles to loss of freedom and national extinction.

Hanfstaengl, Churchill said, I absolutely refuse to accept a British responsibility for Hitler's monstrous deeds. It was he who attacked Poland, not Britain that attacked Poland. He had been offered terms of appeasement, yet he wanted war. Had he kept the peace, all Europe would have peacefully fallen under German control within ten years. Whatever history may say of England, it cannot say that in 1939 we betrayed either the freedom or the interests of Europe by refusing to condone the premeditated larcenies of that gang of Nazis who took Hitler as their prophet and Germany as their God. And since you spoke of German hostility to Russia, as defender of Europe against Asia, let me remind you that it was Hitler himself who let the Russians into Eastern Poland and Finland and Roumania, and broke through the wall that held the Asiatics back from what Hitler pretended he was defending.

6

Winston, Roosevelt said, when you hit your "blue water" school of oratory, it takes the rest of us a little time to get our sea-legs. But I agree with you one hundred per cent that England's record in 1939 was one of honest desire for peace. And your magnificent stand alone in 1940 has entitled the Empire to the eternal gratitude of mankind. Now how about Russia? How about the Empire and Russia, the two powers that fought Hitler until Pearl Harbor.

In every great struggle for human liberty, Franklin, the Russians have been England's allies, against Napoleon, against Wilhelm, and now against this monstrous Nazi menace.

That is a proper Parliamentary answer, Winston, but we are not addressing the House of Commons. We are talking in confidence in the Catoctin Mountains.

Thank Heaven for that, Franklin, otherwise I might even doubt our final victory.

This Russian question is the most important issue we have to meet. I want to help in any way I can. Historically, England and Russia have been at loggerheads for more than a hundred years—in Greece in the 1820's, in the Crimea in the 1850's, in Turkey in the 1870's, in Persia and the Far East in the 1900's, and pretty generally everywhere in the 1920's and 1930's, right up to the day when Hitler invaded Russia. You yourself, the President pointed out, took a leading part in the interventions against the Soviets after the last war and even Hitler believed he could count on some form of passive cooperation from you in his attack when he sent Hess over to England in 1941.

71

Right.

Now what I want is a general line on British policy towards Russia, once Hitler is out of the way.

That depends on Russia's policy. If Russia wants certain things we shall not object. If Russia wants other things we shall certainly oppose her. If Russia tries for Suez, the Low Countries or the Straits of Denmark, England will fight.

How about the Dardanelles? I asked.

The world forgets, Carter, that our battle for the Straits was fought because we strove to open the Dardanelles in order to bring aid to beleaguered Russia. We had promised the Tsars Constantinople in the Treaty of London and we suffered grievous losses in an effort to make good our pledge.

But you did not deliver Constantinople to Russia at the end of the war, I said.

We most assuredly did not. The Bolsheviks proceeded to break the Treaty of London by signing a separate peace with the Germans. That infamous separate act enabled Ludendorff to mass troops in the West and launch the March 1918 offensive which cost the lives of thousands of British soldiers and almost lost us the war. Could we, humanly speaking, be expected to fulfill a treaty which the Russians themselves had violated at our expense?

I think the verdict of history will fully justify that decision, Winston, the President said, but after this war won't the Russians again demand the Dardanelles?

Naturally.

And won't British policy oppose them?

Only if they demand exclusive control.

How about the Near East?

The Turks hate the Russians and the Arabs are with us.

I have noticed on the short-wave radio, Hanstaengl said,

that you are already beginning to back the Arabs instead of the Jews. I said, "Aha! London is now riding the Arab stallion!"

What about Asia? Roosevelt continued. Doesn't all this boil down to a struggle by the British Government to hold India and a series of Russian attempts to reach India? I've always thought it was more than a coincidence that the Sepoy Rebellion of 1857 followed so closely after the end of the Crimean War. The Russians are half-Asiatic anyway. Doesn't that give them an advantage in their drive into Persia, Afghanistan and India? They seem to have had no particular trouble in Outern Mongolia.

When I was a cavalry subaltern in India, said Churchill, we all believed that some day soon we would be skirmishing with Cossacks in the Khyber Pass. But somehow it never happened. Always something occurred to distract the energies of the Russian people and the attention of their government. I see no reason why matters should change. India is British and India is safe.

7

How long will India remain safely British? the President asked. And how do you justify to enlightened American public opinion your holding "millions of poor, peaceful Hindus in colonial subjection." I quote from almost any resolution by almost any American woman's club discussing "the Indian Problem."

American ignorance of India is almost as vast as India itself, observed Churchill. India is not a country, it is a sub-continent as large as all Europe and with a larger population—over four hundred million of them. These millions speak more and different languages than do the peoples of Europe and they follow more and different religions. Europe, even Germany, is mainly Christian, but over one-fourth of our Indian population is Moslem. Between the Moslems and the Hindus is a fiercer and more sanguinary feud than ever divided Protestant Ulster from Catholic Ireland, and you will recall that in 1914, Ulster was ready for armed rebellion rather than accept Irish Home Rule. I shall not mention the Sikhs, who have their own religion, or the Jains or other strange votaries of stranger gods, but the task of administering a United India in the face of the Moslem-Hindu rift makes Hitler's New Order in Europe look like a simple game of bowls on the village green. Only the British could have done it.

I'm inclined to agree with you as to the past tense, but could not the Russians do it in the future?

Nonsense! They are Asiatics and the secret of our Indian Raj is that we are not Asiatics at all. We blundered into our Indian Empire almost by accident. When the old John Company established its trading-posts, the Mogul Empire was falling to pieces. The country was in a turmoil of war and disorder, while the French—and in those years we were fighting the French—were intriguing as usual. Men like Clive and Warren Hastings were forced to become conquerors against their will, to the horror of the Company's stock holders and to the vast displeasure of the Home Government. In less than a century, these circumstances forced us to assume the responsibility for the whole huge region and its monstrous problems. And it is good for the world, as well as for India, that we did not flinch from the burden.

Elihu Yale, I said, was one of the nabobs of the East India Company and some of the loot he brought back from India was used to found Yale University. At least that is what I heard old Arthur Twining Hadley tell Rabindranath Tagore when I was an undergraduate.

Our nabobs founded more wine cellars than universities, was Churchill's comment. One forgotten debt the world owes to British India is the fact that it was as commander in the campaign against the Mahratta Confederacy, that Arthur Wellesley got his training. It was there that he learned the tactics and logistics which helped him to defeat the whole crew of French marshals in Spain and later to thrash Bonaparte himself at Waterloo. Where else but in India did men like Kitchener and Haig learn their trade? Without such generals and their habit of command, the war of 1914 would have been lost at the First Battle of the Marne.

Granted, Winston, that India is a good-sized West Point for training British commanders, isn't it a bit hard on the Indians to serve as a drill-ground? asked Roosevelt. You know yourself how much the American troops in England get on your nerves.

Any time that the four hundred million Indians really want the fifty thousand British to leave India, we shall leave. The truth, in spite of all that is said by chaps like Gandhi and Nehru, is that they would go mad with fear if we threatened to go. Not fear of Japan or Russia, mind you, but fear of themselves. Their caste-system is an invitation to the Hindus to prey on each other and to the Moslems to attack the Hindus. We, as a strange, remote people, happened to fit into the caste system we found in India and we rule only in the way in which India expects to be ruled, by a superior caste whose role it is to maintain order, protect property and avoid direct contact with the mass of the people. India want us to leave? No fear! We are the only force which stands between the pack of babbling Hindu barristers and merciless money-lenders and their own destruction, just as we are the only force which stands between millions of Indian coolies and plague, pestilence and famine on a scale never seen in America and unknown in Europe since the time of the Black Death. These are facts which your American women's clubs ought to understand before they pass judgment.

God knows that we don't want India, said Roosevelt. I've never been there but as soon as the war is over I'd like to take a trip. You and I ought to take a tour around your Empire, and you can show me the sights.

I'd like that, said Churchill. The Empire is well worth seeing and so long as the Navy controls the seas it will still stand and prosper. Trade is the real bond of empire.

Will the seas still serve in the future? the President asked. This trend towards what the Nazis call 'autarchy', economic self-sufficiency, has got pretty strong roots in science. Take rubber. We used to buy raw rubber from the East Indies. Today we are making it out of oil, alcohol and God knows what. Both Germany and Japan, behind their iron walls, are making the most extraordinary articles without imports. Even before the war, we developed nylon and got rid of our reliance on Japanese raw silk or Siberian bristles. Perhaps the future will find the seas almost as deserted as the old stage-coach routes after the arrival of the steam-engine.

I doubt it, said Churchill. Why should people build monstrous and costly factories, in time of peace, to turn alcohol into rubber when they can buy rubber from the place where it grows naturally and the sun does most of the work.

All of this beastly autarchy, the Prime Minister continued, is simply a tribute to the power of the naval blockade. Do you suppose that Hitler would make cloth out of birch-

76

bark if he could buy virgin wool from Australia? Would you spend millions to make artificial rubber if the Japs would let your ships get to Penang?

Probably not, Roosevelt agreed. Yet as a result of these blockade conditions new discoveries have been made. Not all of them will die with the war. The rule of the seas may defeat itself by teaching the nations how to produce everything they need within their own borders. In the case of Russia, that might be dangerous. I still think it would be prudent to encourage the Russians to use the seas, give them their warm-water ports, and teach them the solid advantages of trade and exchange.

Russia doesn't understand the first thing about sea-power, Churchill said. They seem to think the second front can be established as easily as they would start a land-offensive.

In any case, the President continued, are you sure that the Royal Navy still rules the waves. The American Navy not only is stronger in fleet-units but is gaining more modern battle-experience than you are.

Franklin, naval power depends not only on ships and guns but on the steady will to rule the seas. You have a magnificent Navy, considering ships and men, and it is winning and will win battles which will be imperishable glories in your national history. Yet we shall continue to rule the seas because with us it is a matter of life-and-death. Even now, with all your strength afloat, you could not move a single ship east of Gibraltar or Iceland without our consent. You cannot even approach the Indian Ocean save as we agree. And that is in time of war, mind you, when we are your allies and when our fleet is numerically weaker than yours.

We shall continue to control the seas, said Churchill,

because we shall continue to control the vital points past which sea-borne traffic must pass. We control the narrow seas from England. We control the Mediterranean from Gibraltar, Suez, Malta and North Africa. We control the Indian Ocean from South Africa, Australia, Malaya, Ceylon and India. We control Cape Horn from the Falklands. We can hold the passes of the South Atlantic from West Africa, Asuncion and St. Helena. You will never contest our control because to you the seas are only a convenience. To us they are life itself. Every man, woman and child in the United Kingdom knows this to be true and will submit to arduous labors, to incredible sacrifice and to every form of ingenuity to assure for themselves the control of England's seas by England's power.

What about the airplane, Mr. Churchill? asked Hanfstaengl. Has the Luftwaffe made any change? I refer to their bombing of your ports—London, Liverpool and Plymouth—and the crippling of your harbors.

8

All that was rather annoying, Churchill admitted, and it took us a bit of time to get things sorted out but it was no worse than the magnetic mines and not nearly so bad as the U-boats in the last war. On the whole, I should say, air power strengthens the Empire.

I wonder, said Roosevelt. With the present range of aircraft the Channel isn't a barrier. Even before this war, Stanley Baldwin said that your frontier lay on the Rhine. Won't it have to be the Vistula or the Volga after this one?

After this war, our frontiers are world-wide. The Blitz

was at its worst in 1940, when the Germans held the French coast and the R.A.F. was numerically weak. Today we can fly the Atlantic and from the practical point of view, can assemble and train our air forces in Canada, the States or South Africa—well out of hostile range—and bring the pilots and machines over when and as they are needed—and where they are needed.

Does not that mean that England becomes an advanced base, instead of the heart of the Empire?

Quite the contrary, Franklin, said Churchill. If you take a look at the map, you will see that England is the center of an arc which extends from the North Cape, through the Baltic and Central Germany, through Southern Italy, Spain, Portugal and out west of Ireland. That gives us maximum striking power with great economy of men and equipment. It enormously expands our blockading power. Our patrol planes can sight hostile shipping a thousand miles at sea or before it leaves European ports, so that our surface craft can intercept them. With radar and all the other gadgets the scientific chaps have worked up, it is not difficult to defend an area the size of England. Think of the task of defending all that part of Europe which lies within the range of our Lancasters and your Fortresses!

Crete and Malta suggest, sir, I said, that airpower has altered the control of the Mediterranean.

In our favor, Carter. For a time the Nazis and the Eyties had it pretty much their own way but they still couldn't stop our convoys from getting through to Valetta. They couldn't block the Suez Canal, even from Rhodes, and they weren't able to give Rommel decent air-support in Africa. Now we control the entire southern shore of the Mediterranean, from Palestine to Casablanca. With a couple of advanced bases in Sicily and the Peloponnesus, together with our Navy, we can deny its waters to any other power and protect our shipping against hostile attack.

Will not the Dominions, asked Hanfstaengl, when they find that it is their air-bases rather than the shipyards on the Tyne which give England the means for blockade, tend to become more independent?

Why should they? Considered merely as air-bases, every part of the Empire needs every other part of the Empire. Canada and Great Britain between them are needed to patrol the North Atlantic. West Africa, the Azores and the British West Indies control the narrows between Africa and Brazil. East Africa, India and Australia, not to mention South Africa, are needed to control the Indian Ocean. Australia, New Zealand and Fiji are needed to control the Southern Pacific. Aircraft have given British naval power and British land bases far greater range and control than were dreamed of when Nelson and Rodney laid the foundation of our naval supremecy.

What about the new types of aircraft? I asked. I have heard reports of pilotless planes and such things. Might it not be possible for some enemy to launch air-bombardment of your cities from ranges equal to the present range of aircraft?

The Nazis have been beavering away at a number of damnable gadgets, Churchill admitted, but our people have spotted them from afar and moved in to drop a few helpful bombs at the critical moment. I don't say that something of the kind may not ultimately happen, but I see no reason why our scientists should not get there firstest with the mostest. After all, the Nazis have no monopoly on these things. Here and in England there are first-rate men who know pretty much what can be done and who are working hard to see that we win the race in fancy airplanes.

David Harum, Roosevelt said, is quoted as believing that you should do to the other fellow what you know he is going to do to you, only do it first!

Quite so. The issue simply becomes a matter of knowing what the other chap is going to do and stopping him from doing it or, if he is unreasonable, doing it to him.

9

I think I see where this is leading us, said Roosevelt. We've been over this ground before, Winston, and I'm still not convinced.

Yes, Franklin, said the Prime Minister, I am back to the old question. I say that there must be, from now on in, the closest, most intimate, most fraternal association between the Empire and the States. We must have a common staff, a common strategy, a common defense, and a common sovereignty. I do not talk of alliances. That is for nations which distrust each other, while we must walk together in confidence and fellowship.

Does that imply a common policy? Roosevelt asked.

Why not?

And where will that policy be formed, in London or at Washington?

I'd say, in London after conference with Washington.

How would you work it? the President asked.

We should consult together, of course, said Churchill, but London is the place which possesses the information, the experience, the traditions, the habit, the institutions to maintain a workable foreign policy. I am not criticizing your officials, Franklin. They are most friendly and helpful, particularly at the State Department, but I think that you will admit that we have a far better intelligence service than yours and the habit of acting on information received.

It didn't look like it in 1939, the President replied.

The Service was all right. It was the Ministry that ignored the intelligence reports.

Well, I must admit that if I had to choose between your secret service and Bill Donovan's, I'd take yours.

That is generous praise indeed, Franklin. And I think that you must also admit that our Foreign Office and diplomatic service is better organized, better trained and better paid than your own.

I won't argue that.

You must remember that our foreign policy is already a world policy. We are used to fitting together the needs and demands—often most discordant ones—of the Dominions and India, together with our relations with the United States, with the Continental powers and with the other independent sovereignties both in your and our spheres of interest. We are used to team-play, with the Admiralty, the Board of Trade, the Bank of England, the India Office, the Colonial Office, the Dominions Office and the Foreign Office all working together to manage the affairs of one-fourth part of the two billion people in the world. You have nothing to match this. You yourself will not be President forever nor will your Party remain indefinitely in power. There is no reason to expect that your and your party's successors will follow your policies. There is no prospect here of that firm continuity which is necessary if the world is to be wisely governed and its forces held in balance.

What you propose, said Hanfstaengl, is then to make the

Foreign Office a political Vatican for the English-speaking world?

I wouldn't call it a Vatican, though some of those old boys like Curzon and Vansittart would have been ripping in Cardinal's hats. Still, that is somewhat the idea.

Rubbish! said Roosevelt. I'd like to see how it would work. What I want to know is, whether this idea means that all American foreign policies should first be cleared with London. Would that apply to Latin America?

By no means. We are not such fools as to trifle with the Monroe Doctrine.

How about Canada? Roosevelt asked.

Your relations with Canada and Canada's relations with the Empire constitute a very special arrangement. There is no formula which precisely fits the circumstances.

What about Australia? I seem to remember that when I wanted last winter to send Ed Flynn to Canberra, some of your political friends among the Southern Democrats opposed him most successfully.

That was a purely domestic affair in which the British Government was not interested. However, I do not envisage the same kind of relationship between the States and Australia as between you and Canada.

So I gathered at the time, the President laughed. What about France and Italy? We have close historic ties with both of them.

And both are essential to Britain's European defenses.

The same is true of Germany?

Quite.

Let's see! That seems to leave only Russia. What about our relations with the Soviet Union? They've been pretty distant so far but remote relations are often the easiest to get on with.

We should deal with Russia first, said Churchill.

Does that mean that we should deal with Russia through your Foreign Office? Roosevelt asked.

Not at all. I think you should consult the Foreign Office because British interests are deeply affected by Russian policy and power.

Don't you think, Winston, that we could do a better job of protecting your interests, as well as our own, if we dealt directly with Moscow instead of going through London?

10

I honestly doubt it, Churchill said. First thing you know, your State Department would begin bartering away our interests against your comfort and convenience.

Sumner Welles would not agree with you, said the President.

You have no direct relations with Russia because you have no direct interests in Russia. We have. If you value our friendship, as I think you do, it would be friendly of you to take our interests into account before taking matters up in Moscow.

That makes sense so long as it is a two-way proposition, the President said, but we can't be expected to give the Foreign Office a blank check. Congress would never stand for that.

No reason why they should be expected to, said Churchill.

And then there are the Russians to be considered, the President continued. Will they understand that they are allowed to deal with us only through London? I don't think your plan will work well in the long run, Winston. Our public opinion would doubt your disinterestedness and the Russians would conclude that we were ganging up against them. We'd both be safer and happier if all three powers felt free to deal with each other without first having to clear matters through London or, for that matter, Washington or Moscow.

Mr. Prime Minister, I said, I've been disturbed by the growth of anti-British feeling during the war, especially among the G.I.'s. Won't that prove an obstacle to cooperation in time of peace.

And I, said Churchill, am sitting on the lid of growing British resentment against the American troops in England and, generally, throughout the Empire. These are only trifles. They will pass. The friendship will remain after the irritations have disappeared.

As a matter of fact, the President said, there are probably no two nations in the world that get on better than the British and Americans, and no two that have less in common than the Americans and the Russians. Yet there would be more violent opposition to a political alliance with England than to an alliance with Russia. It's curious, isn't it?

That's what makes me fear a post-war revival of isolationism here, I said. It's too much of an American tradition to have disappeared completely and it is fed by all this grumbling about the British.

I don't doubt that our people rub some of your people the wrong way, Churchill agreed.

I do not entirely agree with John Carter, Hanfstaengl said. As a German, many things that are English are to me not easy to understand. I cannot understand how your King can go to the Derby while British troops are at Dunkirk. Yet I am pro-British and I do not forget that the English have learned to make learning a graceful burden or that they were very kind to me when I needed friends. No people likes another people, yet after the first shock of discovering their differences, they can become firm friends.

Just so, Hanfstaengl. Judging from the way the American soldiers got off with our English girls, I doubt that you could say that the two peoples don't get on together. Altogether too well, at times.

Roosevelt laughed. I'll never forget the consternation in the Pentagon when you cabled to send no more Negro troops to England.

That was Liverpool. Far too many English girls were turning up with coffee-colored babies. It threatened to become a scandal.

So you see, Mr. Prime Minister, Hanfstaengl exclaimed, you too have a racial policy, *nicht wahr?*

On the contrary. We had none. Hence the babies. What we feared was that Goebbels or your American Southern senators might take hold of it and make propaganda. But that's a bit far from the point. Where were we? Russia and America. No, Franklin, we do not propose to end this war face to face with a powerful Russia and an America which is disposed to work with Russia. I did not become His Majesty's Prime Minister to preside over the liquidation of the British Empire and I intend to see to it that when Germany falls, England and America stand together as joint guardians of Western civilization. Russia has a sixth of the world's land area already. That ought to be enough for even Comrade Molotov.

England has a fourth, said Hanfstaengl.

11

Winston, the President observed, there's every reason why we should work together and only one obstacle. Jack Carter mentioned the growth of anti-British feeling here. It might become dangerous if our people got the idea that your Foreign Office was running our policy. The best way to avoid that is to let us establish our own relations, good, bad or indifferent, with Moscow. In any case there's a big hole in the fence you're trying to run around Russia.

Where is that hole, Franklin?

In Asia, with more than a billion Asiatics. Russia occupies the whole north half of Asia and you can't run your fence far from tide-water. When the war ends we'll be in control of the Yellow Sea and the Sea of Japan and have a direct contact with Russia in the Far East. How do you propose to hold the Asiatics in line?

As we've always done, Churchill said. By trade, by strength, by being shrewder than the Asiatics, by giving them a good show and good value for their money. You see, Franklin, bar the Australians and South Africans, we don't worry about color the way your people do. Jim Crow is an American institution, not British. We are not worried by the fact that there are colored races in the world and they know it.

Our own ideas on color may be modified by the war, I suggested. There's something quite attractive about the American G.I.'s—naive as they may be—that is appealing to all races. I'll gamble that after we take Japan, we and the Japs will suddenly start finding reasons to like each other. The Chinese also get on with us well. Most of our color attitude applies to the Negroes rather than the Asiatics.

The Chinese think that·the Americans are either fools or crazy, the Prime Minister replied. They know that we can handle ourselves. They flatter you and they respect us. And they'd sell us both to the Russians quick as a wink if they thought it worth their while.

That's just what I'm trying to say, the President observed. You can't run your fence around Russia with China in the way, and if anybody thinks that we'll take on the defense of all North China—Communist China, at that—along five thousand miles of Soviet frontier, he's crazy.

You'll have to keep the Russians out of China proper, Franklin. You fought Japan because Japan took Manchuria, most of China and threatened to take the whole Far East. The moment the Red Army moves south of the Great Wall, you must react.

How about the European colonies in Asia, Roosevelt asked. They'll be all stirred up when the war is over and they are expected to return to the old colonial status. Granted that they now find the Japs worse than the Europeans ever dreamed of being, don't you agree that Communist propaganda will have a field day in southeast Asia when the war is won?

Possibly. But we appoint, train, pay and control the police. If we stopped shipping and buying goods and labor lots of those people would starve. There is no real problem of control there, as you'll see when the time comes. They may attempt some monkey business, as the Afghans did after the last war, but they'll soon learn to give Russian agents up to the police.

"When all is said and all is done, we still have got the gatling gun," I quoted.

88

What about the countries which aren't your colonies, the independent, sovereign nations under British influence? Persia, say, or Turkey or Mesopotamia? Roosevelt asked.

Franklin, we're going to organize the United Nations, are we not?

Of course.

That will be better than the League? It will have longer and sharper teeth, eh?

We hope so.

Why should not Iraq and Iran and the Turkish Republic become charter-members of the United Nations which must, if it means anything, include a pledge of armed defense of its weaker members against aggression? Otherwise, why have any League at all, if the small nations are to remain at the mercy of the big nations?

So the United Nations will be, among other things, a device to keep Russia away from the sea and the oil-fields.

It will also be a device to keep Germany away from France, Japan away from China, ourselves away from Mexico and you away from Suez, if it's a case of armed aggression, Churchill answered.

Do you think that Russia will agree to that?

I believe that Russia will sign anything while the war is going on and they need our help. Let's see that they do sign the pledge.

That is a very sensible idea, Mr. Churchill, said Hanfstaengl.

12

I agree, said Roosevelt, but it seems to me that the defense of the Empire against Russian imperialism and Asiatic nationalism requires a completely inconsistent policy.

How inconsistent? I asked. Any more so than our own policy of intervention and isolation?

The Empire will defend Asiatic nationalism against Russia in Persia, Turkey and Iraq, and will suppress it in India, Southeast Asia and the East Indies. As you know, Winston, I have tremendous respect for the grand job the Empire does. I'd like to see its policy clear-cut enough so that our public opinion won't get self-righteous jitters.

I think this is the way to put it, the Prime Minister said. What we are defending is something much older and more fundamental than nationalism, which after all, is only of recent growth and means little or nothing in Asia. We are defending the ancient principle of sovereignty based on accepted possession or prior conquest. It is the rule by which the whole world is governed.

13

Here is one problem, Mr. Churchill, said Putzi. All sovereignty is based on conquest, is it not, in fact?

Naturally, conquest or discovery and settlement is necessary, provided it be confirmed by treaty or accepted by common consent.

Then joint conquest would create a joint sovereignty, *nicht wahr?* Like the Anglo-French Condominium in some of the Pacific islands. That has been a workable policy, not so?

Not so describes it, said Churchill. No, Hanfstaengl, joint sovereignty is nearly always a failure.

Could not Russia or the U.S.A. argue that the liberation of Axis-occupied countries is a joint conquest and that all of the United Nations should have a voice in settling these colonial issues? Will not the Soviets ask for a voice in the Italian colonies in Africa. Could not the American State Department say that the U.S.A., having made the major contribution to victory over Japan and to driving the Japanese out of the former European colonies, has acquired an equity in their future status?

Churchill grinned. That's pretty legalistic, he said. The same argument could be applied to the American oil-fields or to our own raw materials.

Well, why not oil? asked Roosevelt. Oil and other things. Tin, rubber, quinine, jute, copra, that stuff from Burmah they use to make phonograph records. Markets. Chances to invest. Chances to bid on public works. Call it the open door. If we get the Japs out of Java and Malaya, why should we pay three prices to Dutch monopolies or have the price of raw rubber jacked up by London? If we help save the Empire, why should we have it locked in the Sterling Bloc, so that your subjects can't buy from us unless they first get the permission of the Bank of England. Our contribution to the final victory should entitle us to the open door in trade all over the world and when we set up the United Nations I think it would be fair to call a halt to a lot of this economic nationalism.

Churchill smiled. That depends on whether the States carry their share of the load, he said. Sometimes to us it seems that you want to have the run of the resources of the

European empires, leaving to us the trouble and expense of their administration and defense.

That's partly true, Roosevelt admitted, but, as you know, up until the end of the last war, we had no real complaint about any of these things. You had done the conquering, you had done the development, you allowed other countries to trade freely with the Empire countries. If you gave yourselves the breaks, you were entitled to them, as your fee for services rendered. We got on very well together all over the world on that basis.

Not so well in Venezuela on in the Mexican oil business, in 1915, sir. The House papers show that there was a real duel over Huerta in Mexico, I said.

Of course we've had squabbles, Jack, but they never cut deep or lasted long. What worries me, Winston, is that since the last war, you have started to apply exclusive British policies throughout your Empire, including this sterling control and Empire tariffs. This means that we are losing our stake in the Empire and it may even lead to a condition in which we shall have to start competing for empire trade. When the Spanish Empire built a trade wall around itself, it compelled the British and the Dutch to break Spain's commercial monopoly.

You don't propose to send an American Drake to the Channel to raid British shipping in Plymouth, do you, Franklin? If so, we'll give him a hearty welcome.

Quite seriously, Winston, Roosevelt replied, one of the great dangers I see to Anglo-American cooperation lies in just these matters of trade-policy. Exclusive commercial policies, as we learned for ourselves in the 1920's, make for trouble between nations. Give us a fair voice and a fair break —the Open Door—and we can take a lot of the load off your shoulders.

14

What you propose, the Prime Minister said, is a policy which would, if actually applied, destroy western civilization.

Roosevelt cocked his cigarette quizzically.

A while ago I mentioned, continued Churchill, the principle of sovereignty on which British policy in Asia is founded. This is only part of a broader policy, which can best be described as the maintenance of established rights.

The trouble with established rights, said the President, is that they became chronic wrongs long before they cease to be established. Just as tariff protection for our infant industries soon became monopoly rights for our trusts.

The great need of the world after this war will be peace and security, Churchill said. To have peace and security, Franklin, you must establish some firm principle of stability. I know of no other place to begin than with the recognized established rights of commercial groups, religious organizations and national governments throughout the world.

Is not that what Metternick proposed at the Congress of Vienna in 1814? Hanfstaengl asked.

Right! said the Prime Minister and the Treaty of Vienna gave Europe as a whole one hundred years of peace, during which it prospered as never before in history.

It blew up at the end, I said, and is still exploding.

That was not the fault of the policy. During the entire period, we worked for established rights, including constitutional monarchy. The opposition to that policy came, oddly enough, from one of the victors—the Russian Empire. The Russians were all over the map of Europe during the sixty years after Waterloo—in Greece, in Roumania, in Turkey, in Hungary and in the Balkans. It took much to hold them in check, but we succeeded and we did not deal any grave injury to Russia in the process of restraining her aggression.

I am glad to hear you say that, Mr. Churchill, said Hanfstaengl. That too is my opinion.

After this war, Churchill continued, it is clear that the great challenge to established rights will again come from Russia. Russian policy, as well as threatening boundaries and nations, will be engaged in combating the Catholic Church, combatting private British and American industry, combatting the British Empire, and combatting democratic self-government in America and everywhere. The conflict of interests is too great and the gap between Soviet and Western institutions is too wide for it to be otherwise. Do you agree, Franklin?

Yes, said Roosevelt, but—

Exactly. But . . . Now I do not propose that British policy shall oppose Russia's national interests except where their expression collides with Britain's vital concerns.

Who will define your vital interests? Will we be consulted? asked the President.

Any nation must define its own vital interests, Franklin. I'll trust the Russians to define their own national interests. I do not propose to facilitate the Soviet advance into our vital zones by causing additional upheavals ourselves.

How will that work out in practice, Mr. Churchill? I asked.

Among other things, Carter, it means that we shall probably back the Vatican to the hilt in restoring orderly religious life to the Continent.

Will that also apply to Spain, Mr. Churchill, asked Putzi.

The same applies to Spain. Why should we cater to the Spanish Reds and uproot the Spanish Catholics, simply because Franco is a bounder and a Fascist.

Spain is one point on which all Americans see red, I said. They were all one hundred percent pro-Franco or one hundred percent pro-loyalist. It knocked the bottom out of the New Deal in 1937.

We should maintain and expand our pooled economic and industrial operations, Churchill continued. The system is working well now and it will provide the goods and the foods with which to finance the peace faster than they can be delivered by the Russians.

Won't that cost a lot of money? the President inquired.

Certainly, but not nearly so much as another year of war.

Who will supply the money?

America ought to help us in that, said Churchill. Otherwise, we'll somehow manage to squeeze it out of the Sterling Bloc. This policy means that we shall maintain established political institutions, including the sovereignty of states and the sanctity of treaties and the general principle that agreements are to be kept and contracts are to be fulfilled. This is the keystone to peace.

15

Now we are in the Roaring Forties, Roosevelt remarked. Fifty-foot waves that shake the screw out of the water.

I'm surprised, Franklin, to see you draw on sea-scapes for your oratorical effects, the Prime Minister observed. You usually rely almost exclusively on the New Testament or the Twenty-Third Psalm, don't you?

Now, Winston! Suppose we leave these great sweeping generalities of yours that break in foam and thunder on the foredeck, and get down to cases.

That is where I am. Both feet on the ground, while you've been reaching for the stars, like most of your countrymen. Well?

Suppose you tell us, in so many words, what you, as Prime Minister of Great Britain, propose to do with, to or for conquered Germany. Some day you'll have to deal with conquered Germany and you can't tell me that you and the Foreign Office haven't your plan worked out to the last decimal-point.

That's what we keep the Foreign Office for, Franklin. But we are dealing with variables. When Germany falls we don't know whether the Red Army will be on the Vistula, the Oder or the Elbe.

The British policy must adapt itself to the facts in that case, Churchill continued. Western Germany is the most densely populated area—and I use the word 'dense' advisedly—of the Reich and also the most highly industrialized region in Western Europe. Taking account of Nazi dispersal of industry in the east, you cannot transport coal mines or iron deposits, and the Ruhr will not be moved to Saxony or Silesia. The Ruhr will be under Allied and not Russian control.

What about the French, sir? I asked. Won't they have a strong claim to take over the Ruhr when the time comes?

We'll have to cross that bridge when we come to it, Churchill said. In any event, about three-fifths of the Germans and of German industry will be linked to the West. I think that I would agree with Hanfstaengl, that the interests of Western civilization require that Western Germany shall serve as buffer against the semi-Asiatic power which will occupy Eastern Europe.

You do not mean that Germany shall be partitioned like a pie among the conquerors? asked Hanfstaengl.

More like a sausage. Only we'll have the mustard.

Ach Gott! And Russia will slavify and sovietize the East.

Quite, replied the Prime Minister. That's where the peasants and the food stuffs are to be found and the Russians will try to use the food supply of the East to control the politics of the West.

Then this Hemisphere must feed Western Europe in the post-war period, said Roosevelt.

Exactly. Unless you are ready to see Europe ruled by men whose chief instrument of government is organized hunger.

The British Blockade is also a form of hunger-control, said Putzi.

That is quite different. We don't starve people after we have conquered them. In any event, after we have conquered Germany, we shall have to annex Western Germany to Western Europe and hold the old Roman line against the Eastern peoples.

What about the Germans east of the Elbe? I asked.

They may become a political salient behind the Russian lines—I cannot call them a Fifth Column. Russia cannot afford to let us occupy all Germany. Russia cannot afford to liquidate or deport the Eastern Germans. On the contrary, she will try to woo them, and quite cleverly, too. But all the time it will be Teuton against Slav, and the Germans in the Russian Zone will be heart-and-soul with us in the West. As Hanfstaengl pointed out, they are historically anti-

Russian. We shall not need to propagandize or indoctrinate them. Thus we shall save all Germany.

Henry Morgenthau wants to have Germany dismembered and deindustrialized, said Roosevelt.

And I, replied Churchill, wish that I had wings, a halo and a golden harp.

16

Well, Roosevelt continued, we come back to the real question, How are you, Winston—meaning the British Empire—proposing to deal with Russia.

If you back us up, said Churchill, Russia can be held in line. It will not be easy but it will be possible.

I wonder whether you have any idea of the terms on which the Empire can obtain American support against Russia.

Why should there be terms between friends who think alike and have a common interest? Britain and America must march together in the future, said the Prime Minister.

The Senate will say that we ought to march together on equal terms into British markets and British oil-fields, Roosevelt said. That's their idea of cooperation.

Those are minor issues, Franklin. The real test of the relationship between our countries—whatever we may think or say—is what Kipling called "the bonds of common funk." If you want Stalin to control Suez, North China or France, you need not support us after the war. And if you don't support us we may be forced to come to terms with Russia and leave you really isolated. Would the Senate like that?

Now you're getting back on your quarter-deck, said the President. Let's see what you really propose as a means to restrain Soviet power from aggression against your interests.

Monarchy, constitutional monarchy, is the solution. That gives stability and security as no other political institution can do. It is the complete opposite of the Communist idea. It gives people a good show for their money. It does not interfere with real democratic government. It is irrational and traditional and rather dear to the hearts of people.

Where do you propose to set up your monarchies, Mr. Prime Minister? Hanfstaengl inquired. In Germany? I hope not, although I am a monarchist, because Germany monarchy has been discredited by the Hohenzollerns. Perhaps later the Wittelsbachs, but not yet.

The Allies will be strong enough in Germany to need no monarchy just yet, Churchill explained, except perhaps in Austria with the Hapsburgs. Behind our lines, in Western Europe, we shall support the ruling houses. The British Monarchy is as strong as Gibraltar. Holland and Belgium will follow our lead, although Belgium may make some difficulty over Leopold. Norway, Denmark and Sweden will remain kingdoms. We must keep the House of Savoy in Italy, after we drive out the Fascisti, and we shall work for the restoration of monarchy in Spain and Greece.

Isn't the real danger area in the Middle East? I asked. How will the system of tide-water kingdoms work out in the danger-zone between Athens and Bombay?

Persia is a kingdom, Churchill replied. So is Iraq. Turkey is a Republic but it retains the tradition of the Sultans. Egypt is a Kingdom and the various Arab principalities adhere to monarchy.

It will take more than the average Arab potentate to hold the line, the President insisted. Arabs, like other Asiatics, are always eager to jump on the bandwagon as was shown by their encouragement to the Nazi before Alamein.

The R.A.F., the Navy and British garrisons, as well as Lend-Lease goods, are at hand to help maintain Arab loyalty to their rulers.

Let us suppose, Mr. Prime Minister, that the Soviets should raise the issue that British forces in the Middle East constitute aggression on the sovereignty of Egypt or Iraq, Putzi said.

The proper answer is that, in every case, British troops are there in conformity with treaty rights.

What, asked Roosevelt, would you do if the Egyptians asserted that your garrison in Egypt obtained their treaty-status under duress?

The sanctity of treaties is the corner-stone of international law, the Prime Minister insisted. No question of their validity is admissible after they have been accepted as binding between two sovereign governments. Of course, they can always be modified or abandoned by mutual agreement, like any other contrac⁺

17

Since we are trying to remove causes of friction, the President remarked, let's consider the most irritating question—after sterling control—outstanding between England and America.

The Argentine? asked Churchill.

Yes, the Argentine.

Well, what of the Argentine? Haven't things gone better since we changed our Ambassador?

That's just it, Roosevelt replied. Why should it be necessary for you to change Ambassadors at Buenos Aires in order to make a fair adjustment of our interests in

South America? What are you up to in South America, anyway?

It is not necessary for me to remind you that a great sum in British capital is invested in Argentina, Churchill said. A substantial portion of our food and overseas income is derived from the River Plate. There are many British subjects there, far more than there are United States citizens. And we have every interest in maintaining friendly relations with the Argentine Government.

My State Department friends tell me that the Foreign Office interprets good British relations with Argentina as meaning anti-American activities, I said.

Churchill chuckled. What does the State Department expect from Downing Street? Plasma? It's well-known that the Argentine is a rival of the U.S. for leadership in the Western Hemisphere. American trade, banking, interest and influence are supreme from Canada to Cape Horn. That is a fact. It is also a fact that the Argentines are jealous of your position. It is good business for us to deal with them on their own ground just as it was good business for you to deal with the Irish in terms of their feud with England.

We can take care of ourselves in South America, said Roosevelt. The only thing that worries me is the chance that some senator will start yelling about the Monroe Doctrine if the Foreign Office isn't a little more careful.

We have put a stop to it, said Churchill. We have changed Ambassadors. New instructions have been issued.

Isn't part of the trouble, Mr. President, I asked, that our businessmen complain that British competition in South America is an attack on our trade.

Naturally we wish to hold our trade, Carter, said Churchill.

And we don't grudge you your trade, Winston, the President insisted. What worries me is the encouragement the Foreign Office has given to an anti-American bloc in the Western Hemisphere. This helps the Axis.

How so?

For all practical purposes, Argentina is part of the Axis, the President said.

Have they given aid to Germany? asked Churchill.

They didn't dare to and weren't allowed to.

Are you going to prosecute them for what you say they were not allowed to do?

Of course not, said the President. But it is just one more point of friction and misunderstanding and I'd like to clear it up.

So would I, said Churchill, but we've learned by experience that it does no good to interfere in the internal affairs of an American Republic. It always works out the wrong way. Your State Department will learn that too, in time.

18

How about your sterling area and exchange controls? I asked. Speaking as an economist—and I was one once—that seems even less defensible than our own protective tariff.

You Americans understand production but you don't understand exchange, said Churchill.

"You Americans". You're half-American yourself, on your mother's side, said Roosevelt. We boast of it.

I, too, am half-American, said Putzi. My mother was a Connecticut Yankee, a Sedgwick. It is strange that not only do you not boast of it but that Harvard refused my German scholarship.

You couldn't be more German, Putzi, and you, Winston, couldn't be more British than if neither of your mothers had been American.

Quite so. But as I was saying, *we* Americans understand production while we *British* understand exchange, because we live by it. Napoleon called us a nation of shop-keepers and as usual he was absolutely right, so far as he went. At all events, we do most thoroughly understand the exchange of goods and all the banking and ancillary arrangements necessary to the process of exchange.

There is no question about that, sir, I said. I remember that it took the State Department three years to understand what it meant when you went off the gold standard in 1931. Hoover never understood.

You—we—Americans, on the contrary, fail entirely to understand that you can't sell if you won't buy. The States produce and export fantastically but American ideas of finance are rather peculiar. You prefer to lend money in order to let people buy your wares, so as to save yourself the trouble of buying their wares in return. You—hanged if I'm going to argue on an Anglo-American basis!—simply do not realize that commerce is the exchange of goods rather than money.

In England's case, said Roosevelt, it looks as though the reverse were true. Your sterling area countries pile up enormous sterling balances in London which you refuse to convert into other currencies, thus tying up their credit and their capital without selling them stuff in return. That doesn't look like commerce to me. It's more like imperial tribute.

It is a tribute to our reputation for commercial compe-tence, the Prime Minister said. We do not compel our ster-ling countries to sell to us. They could quite as easily sell to you, if you wanted their goods. We are their traditional market and best customer. They are content to let us carry these balances on our books against future orders rather than turn to you, who are willing to sell but afraid to buy.

How about the empire preference tariffs, sir? I asked. I was in the State Department when they started. Now, the British countries penalize our imports. This means that they render the price of our goods artificially high and put an artificial premium on British goods. On top of that, your Dollar Pool means that even when we do buy their goods they are not allowed to buy ours without your permission.

Churchill laughed and slapped his knee. Carter, I never expected to hear an American rebuke tariff protection. Where, if not in Germany and America, did protective tariff policies reach their highest level?

That's one for you, Winston. Yet there is another angle. We—that is, Cordell Hull and I—as you know, have been working for ten years to reduce tariffs and have done so, more than any other country in the world, your own included. British protectionism has steadily increased in that period and shows no sign of disappearing after the war.

Why should it? We do not deceive ourselves as to America's willingness to supply us indefinitely on credit.

We learned from the Smoot-Hawley tariff, I said, that, as you increase your protectionism and impose your exclusive trade policies, you lose friends. It has always seemed to me that the Empire has been a convenience to the world as well as a benefit to British subjects. How long will the world regard you as a convenience if you become totalitarian in trade? How long will the Egyptians for instance, be content with British control if they cannot buy from you what they want and are forbidden to buy it from us?

I believe these things can be adjusted without too much

bother, said Churchill. But aren't we straying away from the subject?

Perhaps we are, the President answered. After all, you haven't yet told us in what particulars the British Empire differs from the Nazi system. All you have done is give us a very persuasive hop-skip-and-jump description of British policies.

19

I am like Hanfstaengl, said Churchill. I can describe the Empire's nature only by depicting it in action. After all, it is a fair-sized enterprise—close to 600,000,000 human beings with a common center is foggy, bombed old London.

Are you still growing as an empire, Mr. Prime Minister, or have you stabilized? asked Putzi.

Of course we are still growing, Hanfstaengl. Since the onset of the war, we have taken over the Italian possessions in Africa. We have established a protectorate over all of the Arab countries, while the United States, despite past quarrels and rivalries, is for many important purposes intimately associated with us.

Do you expect that the Empire will continue to grow until, under one form or another, it includes the entire world? I asked.

We have no plan or desire for world domination, Churchill answered.

What about that Western Bloc that old Smuts talks about? asked Roosevelt. Welles thinks that this is a scheme to bring all European colonies under British control after the war. Holland, Belgium, Spain and France are all to be in the Western Bloc and they also happen to be the only

Continental powers with colonial possessions. Is that the idea?

That proposal is linked to the Russian problem, the Prime Minister answered. If there is to be any pith in Western Europe to counter-balance Russia, we must pool our resources and consolidate our interests.

Our people want to know whether this means that raw materials will be monopolized, Roosevelt said.

Their distribution will be controlled, of course. However, the Empire is the subject of discussion and not any set of imaginary policies to be followed in Europe's colonies after the war.

The chief point at which we differ from the Nazis, Franklin, is where we differ from all other peoples. Our empire has been created and defended, in slow growth, throughout the centuries, by the endless expenditure of blood and toil, treasure and thought. Nobody planned it. It is as though Providence itself had decreed that such an organization should come into being to serve the needs of men and had chosen the people of our islands as its instrument.

You Americans, he continued, are like the Nazis and the Russians in that you believe that everything can be planned and that everything must be planned. You pay no heed to the slow, instinctive, inarticulate forces which move behind the paper of written constitutions and the amateur theatricals of totalitarianism.

We British do not pretend to know what we are doing and it embarrasses us to be told why we are doing it. We have too much respect for the great silent force that shapes history to pretend to speak for it. We are agents of destiny and the thing which destiny has chosen us to create—the

Empire—is something which we respect, even when the weight of our burden is almost unbearable.

We took India. We did not plan to take India. Even after it was unquestionably ours, we did not know why we had taken it or what to do with it. We have now taken most of Africa, and we do not know what to do with it. We shall develop its wealth, undoubtedly, and try to administer it with some consideration for the natives.

The Nazis say that God created the world in six days and in the seventh an Englishman came along and asked whether the natives made good servants, Hanfstaengl remarked.

Let me see how I can state it most fairly, Churchill said. If the people of the world are destined to have one system of rule and one set of administrators, which I doubt, I do not see that they could do better than turn to the British Crown and the British people. Personally, I hope that nothing so appallingly difficult will be imposed on us. It is difficult enough now to persuade the Australians that the Kanakas have any more natural rights than a pearl oyster or a kangeroo. We make pretty good policemen—but, as you know from Gilbert and Sullivan, the policeman's lot is not a happy one, and there are other careers which seem more worthy of our talents than telling others to move on quietly, please.

20

Winston, said Roosevelt, what I honestly wish is to take some of your people off the world's police force and set them free to make their real contribution to the world. You have given the world so much—Shakespeare, Milton, Keats,

Masefield, Dickens and Thackeray—that I am haunted at the idea that there may be some more inglorious Miltons condemned to silence as magistrates or administrators in East Africa or the Trans-Jordan.

The difficulty is that most of those who urge us to turn over the police-beat have their eye on the silver, said Churchill. No, Franklin, if the Empire exists it is because Providence needed such an organization for the preservation of the human race.

In other words, the President said, the Empire exists because of the Will of God or perhaps I should say Act of God.

The Empire, Franklin, is much vaster than anything that you may think about it or I may say about it. There it is! Close to 600,000,000 human beings, all under the sovereignty of His Majesty King George the Sixth, God bless him! They are black and white, yellow and tan. They are Hindus and Arabs, they are Chinese and Canadians. They are Zulus and Boers, Irish and Maoris. They are everywhere. They hold title to four-fifths of Africa. They hold India, the darling of all the conquerers since the dawn of time. We have Malaya and Borneo and Hong-Kong, as soon as the Japs move out. We are established in North America, in Central America, in South America.

The whole South Pacific is ours from the Falkland Islands to the Cape of Good Hope—Fiji, New Zealand, Australia. We hold the Mediterranean from the Rock to the Ditch. There is not a race or creed or color that is not represented among His Majesty's loyal subjects. I do not say this in evidence that the British way is possibly the way which Providence has chosen for the peaceful governance of the human race.

And so, said Roosevelt, after a long, rough voyage we at

last cast anchor in the Thames. Ahead, gentlemen, is the dome of St. Paul's and that dark mass of masonry is the Tower of London. God's in His Heaven, all's right with the world, and the crowds swarm to guard-mount at Whitehall and Buckingham Palace. Winston, what you have told us is this: You hold a world-wide empire for which you have not planned, and you do the best you can with what you have. The chief difference between you and the Nazis is that they would dearly love to take that Empire away from you.

Who would not? asked Churchill.

Not I! exclaimed Roosevelt. Can you see some of our 'white supremacy' Southern senators confronted with the problems of the Matabele or grazing-rights in Swaziland? It's hard enough to keep Millard Tydings and Tom Connally from Jim-Crowing the Virgin Islands, as it is. You keep your Empire and don't imagine for a moment that we want to take it away from you.

I honestly believe, I said, that we want the British to run the Empire and give us the free use of it.

Some one must run it, said Putzi. I believe that it is better for us all that it is not ruled by the Nazis or the Soviets.

So do I, said Roosevelt.

Then you are prepared to support us against the others?

So long as we are consulted about the policies we are asked to support and have an interest in what we are expected to defend.

If you are not with us you are against us, said Churchill. Here we are, the Empire, an army of nations marching side by side into the future. That is the true difference between us and the Nazis. They are nothing but Germans, and bad ones at that. We are the British, the Scots, the Irish, the Canadians, the Australians, the South Africans, the Hindus, the Arabs, the Sikhs, the Burmese, the Egyptians, the

Sudanese, the West Indians, the West Africans—Catholics, Moslems, pagans, Presbyterians, atheists and animists—but all together, all one, all marching in a common allegiance towards a common future.

Mutatis mutandis, Hanfstaengl observed, the same might truly be said of the Soviet Union under the Communist Party.

Well, Jack? asked the President. Who wins the bet? Does the Prime Minister get his cigars or do I get the cigarettes?

It seems to be a stand-off, so far, sir, I replied. I can't tell which of you is getting the better of an argument like this. Russia seems to be the key to the whole problem and so far in this discussion Russia has not been heard from.

III

Jupiter

1

THERE WAS a knock on the door and Colonel Starling entered.

It's getting on toward midnight, Mr. President, he said. The sandwiches and coffee are ready.

Grand! We won't wait for Harry and Bernie. Serve 'em right if they find them all gone. Wonder where they've got to.

I heard them say, sir, that they were going for a long walk, Starling replied. Perhaps they'll get some food at the village.

Hold out a couple of cheese sandwiches for Mr. Baruch, will you? These others are ham from my Georgia place.

They're jolly good, the Prime Minister remarked. I was about to say that Russia is—

Wait a minute, Roosevelt urged. Let's get some fresh opinions before you appear as spokesman for the Soviet Union.

I've been there, which is more than you can say, Franklin.

That's true, Winston, but I suspect that you're always in Merrie England wherever you set foot. Like Marlowe's Mephistopheles. How does it go? "Why, this is Hell nor am I ever out of it". You're always in England, Winston.

I should hardly describe the Empire in such lurid terms,

113

said Churchill, but you must admit that it's a bit difficult to get out of it, since it's practically everywhere.

You're right on that, the President conceded, but I still doubt that Comrade Molotov would regard you as qualified to express the Soviet point of view. If Harry gets back, we'll ask him to give us his slant. He's been to Moscow. We really ought to have the Commissar for Foreign Affairs here, though he needs an interpreter. Frankly, Winston, I know your point of view on Russia and I'd like to get some fresh slants before you state it for purposes of discussion.

Some of my State Department friends call Molotov the Samovar for Foreign Affairs, I said. They say that there are three good reasons for this title: First, he hisses, steams and splutters; second, you don't get any action until intense heat is applied to his bottom; and third, if you're not careful, when you do get action you'll find yourself in hot water.

I must say, Jack, that when he was over here last year I found him a good man to deal with. He's tough but he's fair. Just the same, I can't imagine him sitting around with the Prime Minister and myself talking things over. He'd have diplomatic agoraphobia. Why don't you give us an outline of what you think Russia is all about? Have *you* ever been there? You have the reputation of being rather radical.

That's because I supported the New Deal, Mr. President. The nearest I got to Russia was Constantinople, in 1919. I traveled from Brindisi to Salonika on a transport loaded with British officers on their way to help General Denikin fight the Bolsheviks in South Russia. They each carried cyanide in case they were captured. I went to a few heavy drinking parties with White Russians at the Pera Palace in Constant and when the *Arizona* was anchored off Seraglio Point, I went to a dance on board and drew as a partner a Russian girl who claimed she was a sister of Pavlova. She weighed tons and stepped on my foot. And I did some work for an M.A. degree on Russian policy in the Eastern Mediterranean after the Napoleonic Wars but left Yale before I finished it. I don't pretend to know anything about the Soviet regime. For example, I've never read *Das Kapital*.

Mein lieber John! Putzi groaned. *Es ist unglaüblich!*

Putzi has made it clear where Germany and Russia stand, the President observed. The whole world knows where the Prime Minister stands. I want to try to keep Stalin friendly while there's a war on, so I can't afford the luxury of personal opinions on the subject. Jack, until Harry gets here, it looks as though you would have to carry the torch for the Kremlin.

I think that the Kremlin would be worried if they knew it. I don't read, write or speak Russian and have never set foot in the country.

Neither have I, neither has Putzi and neither, really, has the Prime Minister. You're a pretty good devil's advocate, Jack. See what case you can make for the Soviets.

Perhaps it would be more accurate, sir, to call me the devil's disciple, since I got my bad reputation by supporting you and your policies.

The President roared with laughter. Good for you, Jack. I deserved that. Now come on. You are the Commissar of Foreign Affairs. Where do England and America get off?

You won't object, Mr. Churchill, I asked, if I try to express myself as frankly as I think Molotov feels about these things?

Not a bit, Carter. The Empire has survived some strong language in the last thousand years.

The worst that can happen to me, I said, is to be interned, along with Putzi, until the end of the war. So here goes.

2

Russia, I said, no less than England, has its own destiny and regards itself as an instrument in the hand of Providence. The chief difference between the two countries is that, whereas Russia has never thwarted England's destiny, England has repeatedly blocked Russia.

What about 1918 and the Bolshevik desertion of her Allies? That jolly near cooked our goose?

The worst that can be charged against Russia in that case is that, after an exhausting and unsuccessful war, she made a separate peace with Germany. That peace was harder on Russia than on any other country. Marshal Pétain did the same thing in France in 1940, yet nobody proposes to damn France to eternity on that account. We don't even propose to deprive France of her colonies.

That's a good point, Jack, said Roosevelt.

The Russian people believe that it is their mission to unite the peoples of Europe and Asia in a single system of life and government. Today, the Nazis and some Western politicians call the Russians Asiatics. They are, instead, the only white race that has ever been conquered by Asiatics— the Golden Horde—and then thrown off the Mongols and become an independent nation. Since then Russia has grown steadily and slowly. Their territories are not as far-flung as the British possessions but they are in impressive variety of races, colors and creeds.

Unlike the Germans, I continued, the Russians have

never complained that history was unfair because they came late on the international scene. They came much later than the Germans who, as Mr. Churchill pointed out, were strong enough to topple the Roman Empire some fifteen hundred years ago. It was not until the time of Peter the Great, two hundred odd years ago, that it was known that Russia was stronger than Sweden. Since then the Russian Empire has expanded until today it includes about one-sixth of the land in the world with about 200,000,000 inhabitants. At the end of this war, I assume that Russia will get back the Baltic States, some of Poland and Germany, and will get control of Hungary and Rumania, with influence over Bulgaria, Jugoslavia and Greece.

Not Greece! Churchill exclaimed.

I won't object to having Greece in the British Zone, I said, since even Molotov must recognize history and strategy. At the same time, it is worth remembering that it was Russia that fought for Greek independence against the Turks while it was Britain that resisted Russia's attack on the Ottoman Empire.

That's not quite historical, Carter, Churchill objected. We supported the Greek revolutionists and we have supported the independence of the Balkan countries. What we opposed was the substitution of the Russian Empire for the Ottoman Empire.

Russia might well take the same attitude toward British control of the Arab countries which formerly belonged to the Turks, I said. After all, it was Russia and not Great Britain which wore down the power of the Ottomans in a series of wars which lasted about two hundred years. The only time that England fought Turkey was the war of 1914-18.

Churchill grinned. That one was enough, he said.

Then, sir, I asked, can you blame the Russians for making a clean sweep of their government if the result of their long struggle was to be despoiled and invaded by their allies, while the British Empire befriended the Moslems and got control of the trade-routes and the oil?

Bolshevism was introduced into Russia by the German General Staff in 1917, said the Prime Minister. It was an act of war against Tsarist Russia. It caused Russia to forfeit all of the advantages which would have been rightly hers if she had kept her word.

3

Mr. Churchill, I said, when Colonel Robbins told Lenin that the Russians had never voted for peace, Lenin said, "Oh, yes they did! They voted with their feet. They ran away." The truth is that Russia had been defeated long before the Bolsheviks made a separate peace. History alone can decide who was using whom when the Germans sent Lenin into Russia. The Communists say that Lenin used the Germans for the purpose of the Revolution.

England kept her word, observed Churchill. We were loyal to the terms of the Treaty of London until Lenin and Trotzky betrayed the alliance.

I have read your account of the Gallipoli campaign, I said, and I noted that the British Government never sent enough troops at the right time to force the Dardanelles. Did you never ask yourself whether the British Government really wanted to take Constantinople and turn it over to the Russians?

Thousands of gallant Britons died in the attempt, the Prime Minister replied.

That is the final answer but Soviet suspicions remain.

When the Bolsheviks took control there was a new life in British Near Eastern policy. General Dunsterville managed to fight his way up to the Caspian. British intervention became vigorous. It seemed to Moscow that the support which was denied you at Gallipoli was on free tap for the Tsarist generals who were fighting the Red Army.

We had no obligations towards the Bolsheviki, who were admitted German agents, said Churchill.

Sir, I said, I have read in the State Department the minutes of the Allied Supreme War Council at Paris. Even ten years later, the British Government was reluctant to have them published. The record shows that England, France and Japan were eager to send their armed forces into Russia while only America acted as a brake on this anti-Soviet policy.

Yes, the President agreed. When Litvinov came over here in 1933, he had a long list of claims against us on account of the intervention. When I showed him the record he tore up his bill and we arranged for recognition. Until then, Moscow had never known that this country had tried to prevent the Allied invasions of Russia in 1918.

Under these circumstances, I said, I can understand why Moscow is suspicious of the British Government.

Today we are Russia's allies, Churchill replied. The war is going on *now*. Russia is invaded *now*, by the Germans. Whatever our differences in the past, *now* we both depend on each other.

Quite true, sir, but that doesn't mean that Russia trusts you or us, for that matter.

Why not?

Because it is England which has thwarted Russia for more than a hundred years. It was England that hailed the Battle of Navarino, in which the Turkish fleet was destroyed and Greece liberated, as an unfortunate event. It was Russia that freed Greece, but England that inherited Greece. It was Russia that freed Serbia and Bulgaria, it was England that blocked Russia at the Congress of Berlin. After the last war, British troops invaded North Russia and occupied the Caucasus and the oil-fields. The Royal Navy sank Russian warships off Leningrad and the British foreign office ignored the findings of the Bullitt Mission and supported Clemenceau in establishing the Cordon Sanitaire against Soviet Russia.

Quite so, said Churchill, but what does that matter in the face of Hitler and his Nazis?

It matters to Russia, which will not trust England's intentions but only England's necessities. It means that in the future Moscow will pay no attention to British pledges but will depend entirely on what the circumstances will permit.

Well, why not?

Because, I said, England's whole position depends on legality and the binding power of treaties. If the Russians force you to deal with them on the basis of expediency, the Empire's position will be hard to justify to our public opinion. That, as I see it, is what Moscow will do as soon as Germany is defeated.

4

Jack, the President said, what you have said tells only part of the story. This country is in a position to mediate between England and Russia in most of these problems, none of which seem to be insoluble.

Molotov would probably reply that he trusts you personally but has no confidence in this government's disinterestedness.

Why do you say that, Carter? asked Churchill. Doesn't the President represent your country in foreign policy?

When it comes to foreign affairs, he is about fifty years ahead of the country, I replied. Just imagine what would happen if the President retired or were defeated. The Solid South, with their fear of popular government and of the Negro, would try to identify reform with Communism. The Irish Catholics would grab control of the Northern wing of the Democratic Party and start preaching a holy war against the Soviet Union. The Republicans, with their backing from big business, would say that minimum wages, collective bargaining and price-control are all communistic and the whole country would go anti-Russian with a bang. The newspapers would start labeling as a Red anyone who had an idea above the belt or an aspiration higher than the pocket-book.

I don't agree with you at all, Jack, the President remarked. It might be like that to begin with but as soon as the mass of our people got the notion that all this might lead to war with Russia, there would be a change. Just as we started looking cross-eyed at the Jews when it seemed likely we might have to fight the Nazis, so we'd begin to be anti-Catholic if we thought that the Church was getting us into war with the Soviet Union. Labor is strong enough to defend its rights and to try to tie collective bargaining and fair labor standards or decent treatment of the Negroes with Communism would boomerang faster than the Klan. I don't say that a lot of Americans wouldn't try it but I do say that it wouldn't work. Why! that would mean that fellows

121

like Ham Fish or John Rankin would run the House and that Bilbo or Taft would run the Senate. The people wouldn't stand for it.

Mr. President, I said, the people of this country will stand for anything, so long as they eat regularly and can choose between strawberry and vanilla. They stood for Harding and the Teapot Dome Scandal and it wasn't until they lost their jobs under Hoover, nearly ten years later, that they voted Democratic. They stood for Prohibition and by the time it was repealed they had broken down most of civil and criminal law. I remember one case in South Carolina where a Federal Judge directed the acquittal of a moonshiner on the following grounds: accused made good licker, he charged fair prices, and he refused to sell to the niggers.

I never heard that one, the President said.

Still speaking as involuntary representative of the Third International, I'd say that we trust President Roosevelt. We think he's on the level. We believe that he's trying to help us beat the Nazis. We know he would like to fix things so that we can get an outlet to the sea without being forced to fight the British. But we have no reason to trust America.

Why not?

It was America that joined Britain in egging on Japan in 1904, I said. Later still it was America that seized on the anti-Jewish pogroms to break off commercial relations. After the last war, it was America which maintained a moral and financial blockade of the Soviet Union for ten years after the British dropped their naval and commercial blockade.

I changed that as soon as I came into office.

That's what the Russians think is the point. It was you and not America. Don't forget, sir, that Russia has been under blockade for nearly thirty years. In that period, the Russians have formed ideas, policies and institutions which would never have been possible or necessary if the world had been reasonably friendly toward the long overdue change in Russian affairs. That's why the Russians trust nobody but themselves.

5

They don't trust each other, said Churchill. Look at their police and spy-systems.

Whether Russia trusts other nations, she needs them, said Roosevelt. Without Lend-Lease and without the British convoys to Murmansk, Hitler would have won.

That's what gives Moscow the jitters, Mr. President, I said. During his series of Five-Year Plans, Stalin built up Soviet self-sufficiency at the cost of millions of Russian lives. Living in a state of blockade, including a self-imposed foreign trade monopoly, it was clear that Russia by itself lacked the resources for fighting a great war. Now she has two choices. The first is to trust her war-time associates to admit Russia on fair terms to the trade and raw-materials she needs. The second is to reach out and grab for what she needs before war-time friendships are forgotten in traditional rivalries.

Stalin knows that America has never grudged Russia a legitimate outlet to world-trade, the President said.

Neither has Britain, said Churchill.

But Stalin knows that you, Mr. President, will not be President indefinitely and the Kremlin must know how deeply we distrust Soviet intentions.

In spite of past rivalries, said Churchill, it is a fact that Moscow got better terms and fairer treatment in trade at London than anywhere else in the world.

Of course, sir. But Soviet jitters extend to other things than trade. There is Fascism. Russia has been sandwiched between two tough Fascist countries—Germany and Japan. We may laugh when the Russians claim that they are true democrats but it is no laughing matter when they define democracy as opposition to Fascism. They mean it. They have learned the meaning of Fascism the hard way and are definitely the world's greatest experts at detecting it in other countries.

They're pretty blasted totalitarian, if you ask me, Churchill remarked. As a matter of fact, they're an absolute government, more so than in the days of the recent Tsars. Stalin is not unlike Ivan the Terrible.

Would you say, then, I asked, that Russia is really a semi-Asiatic autocracy? Then there's hope for Russian democracy.

That's a good point, Winston, the President said. Autocracy can develop into democracy but Fascism leads straight to chaos. That's because autocracy needs a set of general principles to make it work, while Hitlerism knows no law at all.

Coming back to my main point, sir, I continued, Russia has seen Fascism at close range and from the wrong side of the tracks. Russia considers that Fascism, as a political system, is corrupt, cowardly and cruel, and lacks a scientific basis. Moscow sees in Fascism the rule of gangsters whose only bond of unity is their fear of punishment. The Nazi Party is more like a military organization than a political body and does not bear comparison with the Communist Party in morale, discipline and self-sacrifice.

124

I can agree with you there, Carter, Churchill admitted, without acknowledging that either the Nazis or the Commies are desirable neighbors.

I heartily agree, sir, I said. But this means that Moscow is forever detecting signs of Fascism in other countries, including the democracies. The Kremlin regards itself as a skilled diagnostician when it comes to spotting the first signs of this political disease.

Rubbish, Jack! The President was emphatic. What do they think we are, hypocrites or idiots?

Neither. The Russians simply do not understand our system of checks and balances in government any more than they understand British self-confidence and self-restraint towards dissenters. In Russia, the Kremlin considers that elementary self-preservation requires the prompt liquidation of even semi-Fascists. When they see that we do not deal drastically with our Coughlins and Moselys they conclude that we are secretly encouraging Fascism. This in turn makes them believe that we nourish dark, deep designs against the Soviet Union. So there is bound to be a distinct reserve in their attitude towards us, to put it mildly.

That seems a little far-fetched, Jack.

No, Mr. President, said Hanfstaengl. John Carter is right.

As I see it, I concluded, the Russians feel pretty much as though we were training and equipping an army of, say, anti-Soviet Polish troops within striking distance of their borders, when they see that we do not suppress those whom they regard as American Fascists. Why do it at all, if not to attack them? they ask.

6

Molotov and Litvinov know better, said the President.

And you know better about Russia than most Americans, sir. Don't forget that Stalin, too, has to reckon with public opinion, even if it is confined to the Soviet bureaucracy and the Communist Party. Every statesman has to be wiser than his own country if he is to handle foreign affairs.

Right! said Churchill, but Soviet statesmen need only push the correct button to achieve the desired results. Ten years ago they called me a war-monger. Today they almost call me their Little Father. Tomorrow I expect they will call me a Fascist.

What exasperates the Russians in dealing with the democracies, I said, is that, according to them, we are decadent.

Not too decadent to fight jolly well, with or without the Red Army.

It is our political and business system that they consider decadent. They contend that we are not democracies at all but plutocracies hiding under the forms of popular sovereignty. To them, plutocracy is by definition decadent since it cannot select its rulers and administrators on the basis of ability.

How so? I should think that Beaverbrook or Henry Ford could refute that argument.

Not in the least, Mr. Churchill. They would begin by asking where Beaverbrook got his money and how he got it and would imply that the Empire is simply teeming with mute, inglorious Max Aitkens who are denied the right to publish the *Daily Express* because they lack the right financial connections.

God forbid!

They would also make short work of Ford. They would simply ask whether Ford, with his genius for production and his grasp on public demand, was welcomed by the bankers and manufacturers who controlled our business system. They could probably tell you, far more accurately than anybody here, every move that was made to freeze out Ford and take his business away from him, from the fight over the patents to the Michigan bank crash that touched off the panic of 1933. They would then state that a real system of democracy would extend to economic opportunity. They would point to all the patents which are suppressed or locked away in corporate controls, in order to protect existing investments, and they would make caustic Marxian remarks on the opposition of our railways to trucks, planes, river and lake transportation, and the Panama Canal tolls.

Doesn't that show that our industrial system, far from being weak, is, if anything, too strong? asked the President.

That would admit the Russian argument, that our democracy is decadent and that the real rulers of the United States are the bankers and industrial managers.

They wouldn't be far wrong, would they, Franklin?

Deponent sayeth not, said the President. Go on, Jack.

Then the Russians, who like to think that they are truly scientific, would ask how our managers and bankers got their power, what training they received for their jobs, to whom they are responsible or whether they are responsible to anybody. They might ask what arrangements we have for finding and training unusual talents among poor, average people. They would ask about the kind of recognition and reward the democracies offer for outstanding intellectual or moral achievement. They might ask whether Thomas Edison or the bankers made the money out of the electric light. They might ask what happened to Durant, who organized General Motors. They would certainly ask why Marian Anderson is not allowed to sing in Constitution Hall.

All those things may be black marks against us, Jack, the President agreed, but they don't begin to tell the whole story.

The trouble is, sir, that the Russians think that they *do* tell the whole story. They honestly believe that our elections are just like theirs, fixed so that the right man always wins.

How do they explain 1932? asked Roosevelt.

I don't know. I imagine they'd say that it was all fixed by the New York bankers in order to take the dollar off the gold standard.

They must find British politics rather confusing, Churchill said. I know that I do at times.

To Moscow, British politics seem very simple. They know that when the opposition wins, it has all been fixed in advance. Even if you were defeated in a general election, they'd suspect that it was a typical Churchill trap.

7

They are a simply incredible lot, said the Prime Minister. Our intelligence chaps tell me that Stalin isn't the real head of their government, at all; that behind him is a group of four of five inner circle merchants who really run the U.S.S.R. and that the Marshal is only a figure-head.

What sort of a man is Stalin himself, Winston? You've met him.

Simple, reasonable, well-informed, pleasant, and all that.

Joe Davies once said, I remarked, that the Kremlin kept two or three Stalins on tap: one to review parades, another to preside at Party meetings and still another to deal with foreign envoys. He swore that the Stalin he saw reviewing the troops in the Red Square was not the Stalin he met in the Kremlin.

Quite so, Churchill remarked. The man I saw in Moscow was extremely well-informed and seemed to be both reasonable and fully responsible.

Who are these people behind Stalin? Roosevelt asked.

God knows, Franklin. They might be the inner circle of the World Revolution or they might be a secret sub-section of the German General Staff, for all I know. My job was to see the supposed head of the state and arrive at some practical decisions. I must say that the Russians have lived up to the arrangements we made.

When we see him this summer, Winston, you tell me if it is the same Stalin you met in Moscow.

It will be.

Then what's the idea of these inner and outer circles? Jack, have you any information on the subject?

No, sir. If any one here knows, it is the Prime Minister.

What about it, Winston? It sounds childish to me.

It's part of their idea of defense, I imagine, Churchill answered. They begin by assuming that the whole world is against them and behave accordingly. They remind me of these chaps who complain to the police that they are being followed by little black men who hide in corners and make nasty remarks behind their back. Quite probably, the Russians imagine that if they conceal the real head of their government they can thus thwart the wicked capitalists.

Mr. Churchill, asked Putzi, has it not occurred to you

that perhaps the Soviet Union is itself the bastard child of Plato?

The Prime Minister 'raised his eyebrows. I never call anyone a bastard inadvisedly, he said.

What I mean to say is that perhaps the Third International also took over Plato's ideas, like the Nazis, with extensive borrowing from the Society of Jesus, and established in the Communist Party a kind of anti-religious order which would be more Marxist than Karl Marx himself.

That's quite possible, Hanfstaengl.

Bill Lewis tells me that in his old age Karl Marx said, "You can call me anything you like but don't call me a Marxist!" I said.

But Putzi, Roosevelt asked, you don't seriously mean to compare the Communist Party with the Catholic Church, do you?

That is what I say, Mr. President, answered Hanfstaengl. The idea is so much the same. There is a small, central, highly-trained, well-disciplined organization, which has cut itself off from worldly considerations. It is true that the Communists pursue the proletarian revolution instead of the redemption of mankind. But it is easy to see how they can despise the Nazis, who can be bribed, bullied or seduced, and regard themselves as a superior order of being with a mission.

I don't know that there is much choice between a Gauleiter and a Commissar, Churchill observed.

There's no doubt, though, said the President, that the Communists have both fire and discipline. I'd bet ten to one that if Moscow announced that the Soviet Union needed air and naval bases in New England, Earl Browder and *The Daily Worker* would solemnly come out in favor of ceding Maine and Massachusetts to the Soviet Union, with Rhode Island as an autonomous Republic.

You'd be lucky, said Churchill, if they didn't insist on placing a bronze bust of Lenin on the Plymouth Rock.

That's going a bit too far, Winston, said the President. They'd be much more likely to make it a statue of Karl Marx.

I have one idea about the Soviet system, I said, which might help explain it. That is: it is much easier to divide too little than it is to divide too much. It seems to me that the bankruptcy of the Russian Empire in 1918 gave the Bolsheviks the greatest chance in history. I wonder how they will behave when they face real prosperity in Russia.

I would say, Carter, said Churchill, that they have a sure thing. To the bottomless pit of Asiatic poverty, Russia's poverty is great riches. No matter how stupid and disastrous their policies might be, the result is bound to an improvement over what previously existed. The Soviet mission in Asia, of which they talk, is based on two facts: first, the truly appalling destitution of the peoples of Central Asia, in which a frying-pan or a shovel seems like a fortune; and second, the complete ignorance of the peoples of Central Asia concerning the produce of the West. They believe that the Soviet Union did it all themselves.

But Winston, Roosevelt objected, that might be true before the war but now the Russians are up against the Germans, who are industrially proficient. You can't tell me that the Red Army is ignorant that German weapons are better than their own or that Lend-Lease supplies are saving the Russian forces from disaster.

Franklin, I'll ask you just one question: Does the Soviet Government advertise to its people or to the Red

Army that the Lend-Lease supplies are coming from us and not from Stalin's factories in the Urals.

No.

They most certainly do not advertise our sacrifices in running supplies around the North Cape, the Prime Minister continued. If I were you I'd tell Admiral Standley to raise a row over this. I'd have him take it up with Molotov.

Molotov couldn't help, said Roosevelt. He's tied hand-and-foot to Soviet red tape. Jack, he continued, do you remember last year when you sent me some strawberries from your farm? Well, I served them to Molotov and he ate them. I had planned to tell him the joke about Communism and strawberries but at the last moment I decided that he'd have to ask Moscow for permission to laugh.

What story is that? asked Hanfstaengl.

It's an old one, said Roosevelt. The Communist agitator is addressing a meeting of the faithful. "Today," he cries, "only the rich can eat strawberries. Comes the revolution, we shall all eat strawberries." A guy in the back of the hall yells, "But I can't eat strawberries. They give me a rash." "Comes the Revolution, Comrade," roars the Communist, "you'll eat strawberries and like them."

I agree, Franklin, said Churchill, that Comrade Molotov would not have been amused. That does not mean that some day, Moscow will not suddenly introduce the strawberry plant into Turkestan as a unique achievement of Soviet science under the all-wise direction of the Third International. As long as Moscow can keep all knowledge of the West from the mass of its people, I can even imagine the Turkestan Young Communist Club organizing to send strawberries and other forms of proletarian culture to the poor oppressed wage-slaves of England and America. It's a mug's game, Franklin, and we simply must break through to the Russian people and show them that Stalin did not invent the strawberry, the steam-engine or the electric-light.

8

Oh, come, Winston, said Roosevelt. The Russians may be ignorant but they can't be that dumb!

Mr. Churchill is right, sir, I said. I remember that when I visited the T.V.A. in 1938, there was much the same situation. The private utilities had made a secret of their operations but Dave Lilienthal, as part of his public relations program, encouraged visitors to inspect the dams and dynamos. As a result, a surprisingly large number of Tennessee mountaineers came to believe that the New Deal had invented the dynamo and developed electricity.

Really, Jack. That's a new one to me.

Just so, said Churchill. You have the Kremlin mounting guard over some 200,000,000 odd Soviet citizens—some of them most odd—all across Asia. The Communist regime has really improved their lot, quite a bit, by introducing the rudiments of modern technology. So the simple moujiks believe that the Party is really leading the world in science and industry. Do you believe that Moscow would dare admit Western goods? Would Stalin permit you to show American films across Asia?

When we turn over our planes to the Red Army, they insist on "modifying" them up in Alaska so as to camouflage them as Soviet products.

Quite. That's why they have such stiff censorship. It is not because they are afraid of political propaganda against their system. It is because they fear the spread of knowledge of Western goods, particularly consumer goods, among their people.

By George! That gives me an idea, Winston. When the time comes for us to make propaganda in the Soviet Union, I won't talk about democracy or the Bill of Rights. I'll simply send them the Sears, Roebuck catalogue, with the text in Russian and the prices in roubles.

So the Soviet policy of anti-imperialism in Asia is really to protect the markets and peoples of Asiatic Russia from Western goods, said Putzi. That is very interesting. It had not so occurred to me.

That's why they've fought the Germans like mad, said Churchill. They didn't dare contemplate what would happen if German industry found an outlet in Russia.

In one way, said Roosevelt, you can't exactly blame them. They had to spend twenty years getting organized for defense. That meant that they couldn't spare much effort for consumers goods and had to neglect light industry. Once Germany and Japan are licked, they'll be able to relax and start enjoying life.

They dare not relax, Franklin. Their whole political existence depends on keeping their people convinced that the Party leads the world in promoting the welfare of the average man. To do so successfully, they have to persuade the Russians that, except for a few sinister millionaires and jingoistic generals, the people of the capitalistic countries live in a state of horrid degradation.

Won't they get a shock when they roll into Central Europe and see what some of those wonderful cities are like? I asked.

They'll be jolly careful to smash everything first, Carter,

the Prime Minister said. And if any of their troops are tainted by such evil devices as uncommunistic wrist-watches they'll never be allowed back in Russia where they might undermine morale.

After the Napoleonic War, said Putzi, it was much the same. Only then it was the Russian officers who had seen Paris and Vienna who tried to make a revolution. They wanted a constitution but the peasants thought that Constitutya was the name of the Tsar's wife, and they were shot down. Any Russian regime must protect its people from knowledge of the world if it is to survive.

9

In that case, Mr. Prime Minister, I asked, wouldn't it be smart to encourage the Russians to get access to the sea? For a long time they've tried to get warm-water ports. Once they have them, they'll establish commerce, luxury will grow and the whole rigid system will begin to melt.

You have something there, Jack, Roosevelt said.

Churchill shook his head. That would be true of any other nation but not of Soviet Russia. They have been blockading themselves for the last generation and their greatest anxiety in the post-war period will be to prevent large-scale smuggling and freer trade. German and Japanese industry will be wrecked, leaving England and America as the only powers which could undermine Communist austerity with sewing-machines and stockings. They will move heaven and earth to maintain their complete monopoly of their own markets, for reasons of internal security. Once their people suspect that Russia is industrially backward and denying

135

them things they want, the Commissars will be done for.

That reminds me of another story Alex Gumberg told me, I said. It was during the first big Russian famine after the last war. Herbert Hoover's relief organization had sent Colonel Robbins to Russia to arrange for the distribution of food. Gumberg translated for Robbins when he asked Lenin's permission to supply food to the Ukraine. Robbins explained that his men would steer absolutely clear of political activities and limit themselves to feeding the starving peasants. Lenin laughed. Food, he said, *is* politics.

Quite so, Churchill agreed. They not only blockade their own country against the world but blockade their own people internally. They want the Dardanelles, the Persian Gulf, the Danish islands, Port Arthur and the Kuriles for the same reason.

How's that, Winston? the President asked.

They don't want to expand their trade. They want these bases so that they can tighten their trade-controls and keep out foreign goods. Every single port which they demand is a point from which history shows Russia can be blockaded.

Oh come, Winston! Since the last war they've imported plenty from you and from us.

Naturally they have, but none of it is manufactured goods, aside from plant-equipment, tools and machinery. They'd rather build bad tractors and inefficient harvesting-machines for the peasants than let first-class British and American articles increase their food-production. They'll buy oil and steel and copper and raw cotton and other stuff that doesn't carry a trade-mark. Have you ever been able to get them to agree to patent and trademark protection for your goods.

No, said Roosevelt.

Neither have we, said Churchill.

But what are we going to say to Stalin when he asks us to agree to Russian outlets to the sea? He's bound to do so and Russia has earned the right to our consideration.

Mr. President, Putzi suggested, why do you not give him what he asks for and not what he wants?

How's that, Hanfstaengl?

It is my thought, Mr. Churchill, that the Russians will ask for trade-outlets for Russia and not for blockade bases against Russia. Could you not propose arrangements which would be suitable for trade but a guarantee against blockade?

By Jove! Churchill exclaimed, I believe you have it.

In other words, Winston, if the Marshal wants an outlet to the Persian Gulf or the North Sea or the Mediterranean, we'll have a plan which guarantees international control and freedom of transit for Russian trade but no power anywhere to blockade Russia.

A jolly good idea. Thanks, awfully, Hanfstaengl. But how will you handle that in the Far East, Franklin?

I'll let 'em have Port Arthur and the Kuriles. But we'll have Japan and can reach Korea and North China. Through China we can keep the Open Door in Asia and keep on saying it with sewing-machines and lamps.

And we'll keep on with piece-goods through Hong-kong and Shanghai. The Kremlin won't like it but there isn't much they can do about it.

I will tell you what the Kremlin will do about it, said Putzi.

10

The Soviet will borrow its policy from Japan, just as they borrowed their industry from Germany, Hanfstaengl explained. They will preach "Asia for the Asiatics".

That won't be so easy, said Roosevelt. Once they get a grip on Korea and Manchuria, the old Tsarist imperialism will stand in their way. The Chinese won't swallow it.

The way that the Soviets will do this thing, Mr. President, is to preach against white domination. They will try to turn the colored races against the whites. In many parts of Asia that will not be very difficult. It will be most troublesome for America to combat this propaganda, with the treatment of the Negroes in this country.

If they try that game with us, Churchill observed, they will find that they are fighting the colored races who are our allies.

I do not think that you understand what it is that the Nazi race-policy has done to the world, Mr. Churchill. It is quite as dreadful as Ludendorff's introduction of Bolshevism into Russia. It made Germany a battle-field for the Chosen Races. Two chosen peoples in one country, that does not work.

There aren't many Jews left in Germany today, poor devils! said Churchill.

Nein, Putzi agreed. Hitler tried to make of the Germans another Chosen Race which had borrowed in their most extreme form the worst qualities that they charged against the Children of Israel. This war cannot end except as a victory over the idea that any race is chosen.

And that will be all to the good, Putzi.

Ja, Mr. President. It will be to the good, especially of the Soviets. Mr. Churchill has already said that perhaps the English people have been chosen by providence to manage the world. For myself, I think that perhaps it is so. The Jews call themselves chosen, the Nazis think that the Germans are chosen, but the British take it for granted that *they* are chosen. After the war, if the British restore order in Asia, the Soviets will profit.

I don't agree with you, Putzi, I said. That kind of thing doesn't last. Take the Ku Klux Klan here in the 1920's. Native-born, white, Protestant Nordics. We soon knocked that on the head.

Ja, John, you did knock it on the head but not until it had gained great political power for ten years, *nicht wahr?* Much can happen in ten years.

We're dropping the Chinese Exclusion Law, Putzi, said the President. That will help us in Asia, where the struggle will be.

It will help but it cannot change one very big fact. That is, that nowhere in the world does a colored race rule a white race. Nowhere in the world is there an Asiatic or African colony. All the colonies are white. All the empires are white.

You see, Mr. President, Hanfstaengl continued, that this race and color question is where the Soviets can most easily attack the British Empire and the U.S.A. It is good propaganda, not here perhaps, but in China, in India and in the colonies where Japan has been preaching Asia for the Asiatics. The Commintern has been disavowed but it will begin again after the war and it will not be difficult for the Communists to turn against the white races much of the feeling that propaganda has built up against the Nazis and the Japanese.

It would have some effect on our own public opinion, the President admitted. The North is always ready to criticize the South on the Negro question and the whole country, God knows, is always ready to criticize the British for what they are doing to the poor Indians. For some reason, we don't worry about the French or Dutch, who treat their colonies much worse than any Anglo-Saxon country does.

11

Haven't you left the Jews out of your equation, Putzi? I asked. Won't they be under attack from the Soviets as another of the chosen races? Yet the Nazis claim that the Jews are Communists.

They aren't in England, said Churchill. Both in England and here the leading Jews are anti-Communist.

They are always pro-Russia, Hanfstaengl answered. They must be. It was the Tsars who made the pogroms against the Jews. The Bolsheviki had many, many Jews among them, such as Trotzky and Litvinov.

You aren't going to give us the Protocols of Zion, are you, Putzi? asked Roosevelt.

Nein, Mr. President. They were forgeries which were believed only because they resembled the facts. At first, the Bolshevists were mainly Jewish. Stalin has changed that. Today there are few Jews left in high Soviet office. Too many of them supported Leon Trotzky to escape the purge. Yet there are still many Jews in the Russian Government and they are most active in the Communist Parties all over the world.

That is Jack's point, the President argued. If the Soviet Government starts attacking us as a chosen people they will run the danger of being themselves attacked on the same basis.

They would be only too happy, Mr. President, if the U.S.A. should start a pogrom against the Jews. That is all they would need for their purpose. England is much wiser and has already taken a better course.

How so, Hanfstaengl?

Palestine, Mr. Churchill. That is the lever by which you can turn the Arab world against the Soviet without yourselves making an attack on the Jews.

Palestine is a frightful problem, the Prime Minister said. We're attacked by the Arabs because we protect the Jews and we are attacked by the Jews because we protect the Arabs.

But you have already decided to back the Arabs, not so?

Not precisely, said Churchill. But there are millions more Arabs than there are Jews in the Near East. They have weapons, armies, and governments and they have lived in Palestine for over a thousand years. We can't be expected to push them off the map to make room for all the Jewish refugees in Europe. Palestine is not the solution of the Jewish problem, in any case.

What Putzi is trying to say, sir, I remarked, is that the effect of the British policy in Palestine is to line up the Arabs against the Russians.

Yes, John, that is it. The Jews are to be sacrificed in order to create a strong military Arab League against the Soviets.

The Jews are not being sacrificed by us, said Churchill. It is Hitler who is killing them, not we. It is a curious fact that there is all this agitation for allowing the Jews to swarm into Palestine—

And into this country, too, Roosevelt interjected.

Quite true. And all the time there is one of the largest countries in the world, underdeveloped and underpopulated, with an official policy of friendship for the Jews and a deep quarrel with Hitler. Why doesn't Russia take them in? Why do these Black Sea shiploads of Jewish refugees always head for Palestine and not for the Caucasus?

The Russians maintain a special Soviet republic for the Jews, in Birobidzhan, wherever that is.

Jack, said the President, if you look at the map you'll find that Birobidzhan is way the hell and gone across Siberia on the borders of Manchuria, a little north of Vladivostok.

A sort of Jewish National Home from Palestine, said Putzi.

I think I can guess why Russia doesn't welcome the Jewish refugees, I said.

So can I, John, said Putzi. It is because they are too well-informed and too good at business. If the Russians wish to blockade themselves from the outside world it will not do to admit Jewish blockade-runners who understand values and cannot be bamboozled about trade.

I was going to say, Putzi, that the Kremlin feels it to be a good idea to keep the British in trouble over the Jews in Palestine, I said. Among other things, it keeps our public opinion stirred up—just read any issue of *PM*—and it makes it that much harder for England and America to work together. For example, when the time comes, some of the Jewish financiers may not be eager to help finance England after the war.

By George! the President exclaimed. I wish Bernie Baruch were back. I'd like to hear what he has to say on the subject. There's a wise old philosopher for you, Winston.

Pity your country can't make use of him the way we did

Disraeli and Rufus Isaacs. A man like Baruch ought to have been President at least once in his lifetime.

The American people, which believes in racial tolerance, social equality and religious freedom, said Roosevelt, wouldn't elect Bernie as dog-catcher. He knows too much, he has too much money and he is Jewish.

12

That kind of attitude may put America at a disadvantage in post-war trade, Churchill said.

No less than England.

Far less than England, Franklin. We depend on our trade for our daily bread. We could be Fascist, Socialist or Communist and we would still have to trade with the world for our living. Every Englishman knows that if we do not trade, England will go under. Whatever our system of government, we still have to find a fair way to divide what we earn by trade. We could discount radical attacks on our foreign policy by going Socialist.

Would Moscow believe that you meant it? I asked.

Probably not. They are after our empire and our power and even if we went Communist they would still criticize us unless we accepted their direction.

Whatever this country may do, the President said, it will never go Communist.

That's rather a pity, Franklin. I can imagine nothing that would baffle and infuriate Moscow more than to have the States join the Third International. Short of that, the Communists will make propaganda against your institutions and confuse your decisions.

If they attack us on the race-issue, said Roosevelt, they will make trouble. We treat our Negroes better than they treat their factory-foremen bu: that won't matter. They will play up every lynching and prove that we systematically kill and torture Negroes every day of the week.

If the Communists take up race-equality, I said, they will simply unite America against them. I remember about ten years ago when Whitney Seymour defended a Negro Communist before the Supreme Court. They had caught him distributing radical race-pamphlets in Georgia and gave him the works. Seymour got him acquitted in the Supreme Court but it was clear that the Negro's crime was not Communism but teaching social equality in the Deep South.

They can also make trouble for us in South America, Roosevelt added. The Latin Americans, as Catholics, are anti-Communists but they are also anti-Yankee and most of them are distinctly not lily-white in complexion.

Isn't it also because we are anti-greaser? I asked. Our race-prejudice doesn't stop at the Negro but extends to the Asiatics and the Mexicans.

Yes, Jack, but they would be against us anyhow, because we are powerful and they are not. That's human nature. In fact, it wouldn't surprise me to see Argentina making eyes at Moscow, after we've won the war, simply because they couldn't bear to think that the Colossus of the North had guessed right again.

What will you do, Mr. President, if Buenos Aires marries Moscow? asked Hanfstaengl.

Nothing, Putzi. That marriage would be without issue. England buys most of Argentine's food. We control the Western Hemisphere. If they want to tie up with Stalin it can't make any real difference to the way the world is run and in any case the Church would stop it.

But will not Moscow begin to raise the color-question in South America in a way which will really injure you? Putzi insisted. Will they not arouse the Indians and the Negroes and the café-au-laits to cancel oil-concessions and nationalize foreign investments?

South America doesn't need the Russians to teach them *that* trick, the President said. Our position is always that they can do as they like provided they pay compensation, but that we can offer great advantages in return for cooperation—including public health, transportation and aid to education.

Back in 1934, Mr. President, I said, Sumner Welles told me that our Good Neighbor policy was designed to keep Latin America in line against the coming storm.

Of course it was, Jack, and the storm is not over. When it was clear that Hitler was hell-bent on war, we made sure that we wouldn't be faced with trouble on this side of the Atlantic. I think the record speaks for itself. Only in Buenos Aires, where they have always hated us, has there been any real trouble, and there Winston and I have kept it from getting out of bounds.

That won't help you in Asia, Churchill said. The issue will be decided across the Pacific, not here. If the Russians raise the race-issue, you can handle any trouble in this Hemisphere just as we can handle India and Africa, but it will make it hard for you in the Far East, won't it?

Of course it will, Winston, but there the Russians will have troubles of their own. In Europe, the Catholics, the Germans, the Poles and probably the Turks will keep Moscow worried for quite a few years.

Might I suggest, sir, I asked, that we still haven't got far in establishing the points where the Soviet system differs from Hitlerism. It is clear that they are opposed, for reasons

of their own, to racism, but so far that is the only distinc-
tino between the two set-ups.

There is another very important difference, John, Hanfstaengl said.

13

You mean their economic system? I asked.

Germany is highly industrialized, while Russia is still
largely agricultural, Roosevelt remarked. That makes a
difference.

It is not that their economies are different, Putzi replied.
It is that Russia is full of tremendous riches. What Russia
has that Germany has not is raw materials. The Russian
people are terribly fertile and most energetic. You have
mentioned the famine and civil wars of a generation ago.
Yet Russia recovered from these losses so easily that it is
fantastic. Russia has timber, flax, wheat, potatoes, caviar.
There is gold, platinum, oil, coal, iron. There are fine furs
in Siberia. It is the last frontier in the Northern Hemisphere.
That is the great difference between the Soviet Union and
Nazi Germany.

That was why Hitler attacked, said Churchill. The
Russians had what Germany needed, just as the victim
has what the footpad needs.

Garret Droppers, our Minister in Greece during the last
war, I said, used to say that self-determination always
seemed to break out in the neighborhood of coal-fields and
oil-wells.

The Romans said it better, as usual, Putzi remarked.
During the Great Proscription of the Dictator Sulla, it was
ruled that the properties of the proscribed traitors should be

given to the informers. A Roman gentleman who had taken no part in politics, one day learned that his name was on the list of those condemned. "My Alban farm has informed against me!" he cried.

In other words, Putzi, said the President, you say that it is Russia's wealth—Lebensraum—and not the Third International which is the real issue between Hitler and Stalin.

Ja, Mr. President. That is what I say and it has been true for two hundred years. Without Germany, Russia is Asia. With Russia, Germany is the world.

Don't you think, Putzi, I asked, that the Russians made their greatest mistake in assuming that the Western democracies are simply greedy materialists?

I do not think that I understand what you mean, John.

Well, I can give you one example. At the Washington Naval Conference in 1922, the Russians were very anxious to promote a war between us and Japan. Lenin believed, as he was bound to believe according to Marx, that what we wanted was oil, gold, timber and other forms of wealth. Idealism? Of course not, that was simply to befuddle the bourgeoisie. So Lenin baited his trap with a Far Eastern Republic, with its capital at Chita, supposed to be entirely independent of the Soviet Union and in a position to grant capitalistic concessions. Just to make sure that there was no mistake, the Russians hired a New York lawyer—

Was it Morris Ernst? Roosevelt asked.

—I never heard the name, sir. I was told that it was a New York lawyer. Period—to draw up a constitution for the Chita Government that would pass the eye of old Iron-Whiskered Charlie Hughes in the State Department. The lawyer took the American Constitution as a model and reworded it a bit and brought it into the Secretary of State, along with a request for American recognition. Hughes looked it over and said that it was all right—surprisingly good, in fact. But Lenin never got us to recognize the Chita Government and never understood why we wouldn't rush into a position which would expose us to the full hostility of Japan for the sake of a few mining-concessions.

That's it, Carter, Churchill said. They do not understand the imponderables in Moscow, even when the imponderables have saved them from Hitler. I confess that I find it terribly difficult to reconcile their blasted dialectical materialism with their successful appeal to generous Russian patriotism. What do you make of it, Franklin?

I think that the Russians have been tripped by their own arguments, the President said. They contend that men are moved only by self-interest—that is what materialism means—and they are compelled to be ascetics for a generation of short-rations followed by three years of tremendous sacrifices by the Russian people. They've stopped the German Army, but haven't they also stopped the Communist revolution? I'm hanged if I can see how you can make mystics out of materialists or materialists out of mystics—which is what Stalin has to do if he is to win his war. Once you have tied yourself to materialism you open the door wide to bribery, corruption and treason, and so far in this war Russia seems to have escaped them on the whole. It would take a better theologian than I am to explain it. What do you think of it, Putzi?

14

I would say that Moscow's only escape is to destroy or annex Germany, Hanfstaengl replied. That is because Germany has both a more successful mysticism and a better materialism than Russia. Let me illustrate. The Germans make good soldiers. That is because they understand discipline and sacrifice. That is a mysticism based in part on the Master-Race idea but also on the long training in Germany idealism. In spite of all the passion of self-defense in Russia, this would be strong enough to have conquered Stalingrad and Moscow if it had not been for Lend-Lease.

That is also because, Mr. President, the Germans are also the most successful materialists in Europe. They know how to make excellent guns, explosives, automobiles. They can run railways better than any other nation. They are frightfully good chemists. Compared with Russia, Germany —even under Hitler—is a paradise and I promise you that I would rather be a German under the Nazis than a Russian under Stalin. I would live better and I would enjoy greater solidity and support. The old spirit of duty and service of *der alte Fritz* is still strong in Germany. In Russia it is still Ivan the Terrible.

But Ivan is beating Fritz, said Churchill.

No, Mr. Churchill, it is not Ivan who is beating Fritz. Fritz was beating Ivan until John and Sam helped Ivan and are now beating Fritz. This means that Moscow can never again permit an independent Germany on its borders. They will insist on Soviet control of as much of Germany as you let them occupy. If they could, they would also occupy France and Italy and England.

Why in Heaven's name? asked Roosevelt. Molotov told me that Russia wanted only freedom from attack in the west.

I refer you back to your Sears, Roebuck catalogue, Mr. President, Putzi said. The real threat to the Soviets is not democracy or fascism. Russia will always have a different system of politics from other countries. It is the cheaper and better goods of the West that is the real enemy of Communism. I can assure you that you have no idea of the poverty of the Russian people even before the war. Yes, the regime builds steel-mills and tractor factories and exports caviar and vodka. But the people live on black bread and cabbage soup. Salt and needles and calico, that is real wealth in Asia. Buttons? A treasure! Shoes? A fortune! Send to Russia your zippers and nylons and you will have a revolution that would curdle the mummy of Nicolai Lenin.

So you believe that Russia will take over a lot of Germany in order to stop competition?

Ja, Mr. President. They will ruin German industry and even Polish industry. They will try to make peasants out of the Germans even as Hitler would make farm-slaves out of the Russians, but not because they want the German market for themselves. It is because they know that the Russian people, who are a fine people, will not follow them when it is clear that foreign goods are better and cheaper than Soviet goods.

Do you want to try propaganda in Russia, Mr. President? I asked.

Not especially, with the war on. Why, Jack?

If you want to undermine Communism in Russia, sir, do not argue politics with them. Just send plane-loads of nylons, perfume, lip-stick and cigarettes, with the compliments of the U.S.A., and you'll see a revolution.

Stalin wouldn't allow it, said Churchill. They are too shrewd to expose their people to that brand of temptation.

15

As a matter of fact, Roosevelt remarked, the end of this war should favor the Communists.

I should say that our record in war-production favored capitalism, I said.

You are right so far as this country is concerned, Jack. We have seen what capitalism can do. What I'm thinking of is most of Europe and Asia. When the fighting stops, there will be millions of people—Chinese, Koreans, Poles, Czechs, Germans, Danes, Greeks, French and Italians—who will have gone without anything but the bare necessities for three, four and five years. They will have forgotten, if they ever knew, the benefits of a good industrial system. Moscow will move in and be first on the ground with something better than starvation.

I can see how that would work with the mass of people, I replied, but I believe that the upper classes, even the remnants who have survived the Gestapo, will be able to remember better times and offset the Communist theory that it was the Third International which invented fire, the wheel, the lever, the loom and the internal combustion engine.

They will liquidate that sort of person, Carter, Churchill said. They will call them collaborators. The Reds have already started that against the Chetniks in Jugoslavia.

Mein Gott! Putzi exclaimed. Now at last I understand this Soviet system, why it is they are always killing the upper classes. It is because the upper classes can bear witness against Russian industry, not because they are against Karl Marx.

How about religion? asked Roosevelt. In other dark ages it was religion that carried on civilization.

All I know is that Marx called religion the opiate of the people, I observed.

Do you believe, Mr. President, said Putzi, that the Church can keep alive air-conditioning and vacuum cleaners in the Soviet night?

I would say, Putzi, that now that Stalin has decided to work with the Orthodox Church instead of against religion, it will be hard for him to keep Russia atheistic. The Russians have always been a most religious people.

They are anti-Catholic at Moscow, said Churchill.

Yes, Winston, they are, but it is only fair to point out that in pre-war Russia there were very few Catholics. In Tsarist Russia, the Catholic Church in Poland was the rallying-point for Polish revolution, but since 1918 Russia has not had much of a Catholic population. It is easy for them to oppose the Vatican, on the ground that it is a Western organization, but it is not easy for them to suppress the Orthodox Church. And now they have reestablished it.

There are also many Russian Moslems, said Hanfstaengl. I have heard that the Soviets plan to send Moslems as their consuls in the Arab countries. They seem to forget that the British Empire itself is not Christian.

How's that? Churchill asked.

I said, Mr. Churchill, that the Empire is not Christian. It is true that the Church of England is Christian and that the Foreign Office supports the Catholic Church in Europe, but in the Near East, England is a great Moslem power and is giving its firm support to the Mohammedans.

What does that prove, Putzi? I asked.

My dear John, it proves that Russia will have some trouble in posing as a Moslem power against England in

152

those precious countries that produce polygamy and petroleum. And that is doubly the case because Moscow has never really understood the *Koran*.

Surely the Kremlin has studied the Moslem system, said the President.

They have, no doubt, read the *Koran* but they have not understood that, thanks to the *Koran*, every Moslem can be bribed with the promise of houris in Paradise. Least of all, have the Russians understood that a Moslem stays bribed only if he has been bribed to do what he wants to do.

Sometimes I think the same applies to other creeds, said Churchill.

Ja wohl! Putzi agreed. That is true. Hitler knows that Christians could be bribed but never knew how to keep them bribed. Moscow, being against all religions, makes the mistake about the Moslems. It is as Carter said, when they invented that Chita Government as a bribe to you. They never understood that it is possible to reject a bribe, not because it is too little, but because it is too expensive.

16

The door swung open and a slight, pale man entered, followed by a tall, eagle-nosed old gentleman.

Bernie! Harry! Roosevelt exclaimed. Where have you been? This is Putzi Hanfstaengl. You both know Jack Carter.

We were down at the road, said Hopkins. This fire is good. It's quite cool outside.

Bernie, said Roosevelt. There's a tray of sandwiches over on the table. Of course you won't be interested in those made with that ham from Georgia, but there are some sandwiches made of sanitary Wisconsin cheese, just for you.

153

Mr. President, Baruch said, I am a Southerner and a Democrat and I do not believe that Wisconsin has voted Democratic with any degree of regularity.

Once. In 1936, the President replied.

In that case, Baruch remarked, there can be no choice. I'll take a sandwich and no questions asked.

Bernie, the President continued, take your ham and we'll all swear it's cheese. I wish you'd been here a while ago. We've been arguing about Russia and Hanfstaengl here claims that Russia's post-war policy will be to oppose all of the Chosen Races, including the Jews.

I'm afraid he is right, Mr. President. When things go badly in Europe, they always start pulling the whiskers out of the old Jews. Is Hanfstaengl your expert on Russia? I thought he was a piano-player.

I stopped the music when I discovered what kind of a house I was playing in, said Putzi.

No, we had Jack Carter giving us Molotov's point of view.

Mr. President, I object, said I. I was enticed, lured and seduced into arguing the case for Russia in the absence of Harry Hopkins. My chief qualifications were that I am completely ignorant of Russia. The Prime Minister was the only one here who had been there but the President insists on regarding him as a prejudiced witness.

Harry! exclaimed the President. That's who we've been waiting for. Harry spent two or three days in Moscow. He can tell us all about the Soviet Union.

Don't let him bully, you, Harry, said Churchill. You ought to go to bed. You must be done in. You need rest.

Hopkins smiled. I can catch up with my sleep after the war, he said. Boss, you have promoted me to the post of expert on Russia. After my lengthy study of the country, I deserve better than that. What is it you want to know? About the liquor or the girls. They're both wonderful but much too strong.

No, Harry, the President replied. You can't dodge this one. Tell us in one-syllable words what it is that Russia has that other nations, especially Germany, have not.

Guts? asked Hopkins.

Germany has guts, said Putzi. That is about all she now has.

No, Hanfstaengl, I was joking. Russia has something and I'm hanged if I know what it is. The nearest I can come to it is to say that they have almost licked the problem of ecónomic distribution without destroying production.

Not at all, Harry, Churchill interrupted. They have merely licked the problem of distributing too little to a lot of ignorant people. They have police, secret police, machine-guns and the rest of their infernal flub-dub, to make sure that nobody can interfere with their distributing too little.

Maybe so, Hopkins agreed, but they've got it down to a science. If you don't work in Russia, you don't eat and the only way you can work is for the State. When you work for the State, you draw your pay and your ration-books. That's something. It's a damn-sight more than we were able to do here with the W.P.A. How about England and the dole? he asked Churchill. You didn't make much of a success in feed-ing people for not working. That's where Russia has the edge. She's figured a way to distribute what she produces, so that everybody works and everybody eats. That's some-thing.

What about that, Bernie? asked Roosevelt. You're the only man here who has made a fortune in business. Is Harry right?

Having missed the previous discussion, Baruch replied,

I refuse to serve as cannon-fodder for your oratory. If you want my advice on Russia, you are welcome to it and probably won't follow it.

I'll give you a rough summary of what's been said so far, said Roosevelt. Winston has said that England understands the art of exchange, just as we understand the science of production. Now Harry says that Russia understands the art of distribution . . .

Of too little, Churchill insisted. If it was enough or too much, it would be easier for us to deal with Russia.

Harry, said Roosevelt, you really ought to go to bed. I'll need you first thing in the morning and it's after midnight.

Not until I've pulled Bernie out of the hole you're pushing him into. I don't see that we're much farther ahead, since each branch of economic art requires its own chosen instrument. For Britain's system of commercial exchange, the Royal Navy.

That's correct, said Churchill. It's indispensable. Without the Navy the roof falls in on world trade.

For our industrial production, Hopkins continued, the Federal Constitution as interpreted by corporation lawyers and supported by Republican businessmen.

Oh come, Harry! objected Roosevelt. Plenty of good business men are Democrats.

For revenue only! Boss, I bet if you took a Gallup Poll of manufacturers, they'd vote three-to-one Republican.

I guess so, but that's not—

Passing on to Russia, Hopkins concluded, the science of economic distribution requires a very well organized police-force, State controls, identity cards, ration-books, job-books and bureaucracy. If you have licked the problem of distribution that means that you have an agency that controls distribution. In Russia, it is the police, just as it is the police power with us in war-time rationing.

Just like the Nazis, said Churchill.

No, not like the Nazis, Hopkins answered. The Nazis see that they and the Germans get fed, and they starve the others. The Russians hitch the ration-book to the time-clock. That's different.

Harry, said Churchill. Do go to bed, like a good fellow. You'll be done in tomorrow if you don't get some rest, and we'll need you.

I think I'll stick with the party, said Hopkins. I want to see Bernie get his teeth into the argument. He's the man to tell you about Russia. You tell 'em, Bernie.

Mr. President, Baruch remarked, I am perhaps the only man in the world who will refuse to tell you about Russia. I can only tell you how to deal with Russia.

That's the same thing, said Hopkins.

How would you deal with Russia? asked Roosevelt. They are so suspicious that they don't want to deal with anybody.

I would show myself just as suspicious as they are, said Baruch. If I were to make an agreement with the Russians, I would leave absolutely nothing to chance. Every "t" must be crossed and every "i" must be dotted and there must be no room for misunderstanding. You can't deal with Stalin as you can with Mr. Churchill. They are all Doubting Thomases and must feel the wounds. Then, when you have agreement, you must live up to its terms, literally, punctiliously, unimaginatively, and you must insist that the Russians do the same. They do not understand give-and-take in a contract. They are peasants who will take and not give. You must not make the mistake of generosity, or they will conclude that you are weak or afraid of them. Only in this way will it be possible to build up real confidence.

What if they don't keep their agreements? Churchill asked. Take a matter which we British are interested in. Suppose that they don't get out of Persia at the end of the war?

You must handle matters so, Mr. Churchill, that they must either get out of Persia or publicly break their word. They are peasants and parvenus. They are fanatics is their fear of being cheated or laughed at. If you are shrewd, they can only keep their word or cheat themselves. Even a peasant can understand that.

17

Bernie, asked Hopkins, do you think that they will have any strength left after the war to cheat anybody? It seems to me that they will be damn near down and out. Their human losses are enormous and most of their factories have been smashed by the Germans.

Earlier in the evening, Mr. Hopkins, Putzi pointed out, it was said that Russia had been down and out after the last war and the famine and the revolution made it worse. Less than ten years later the Russians were again formidable.

This time their recovery won't be so easy, Hopkins said. They have drained men into the Army from all Siberia and they have put their women into the war-plants. That's a big biological revolution for Asiatic peasants.

That means, Baruch said, that they will face us across a wider gap of industrial deficiency and will be doubly on their guard. Behind them they will have the wilderness of Asiatic poverty, as well as a ring of poverty around them in the war-ridden countries of Europe and Asia.

Would you say, Bernie, asked Roosevelt, that Sovietism was the rationalization of poverty?

What else could it be, Mr. President? How else explain the tenacity with which the Soviets cling to their second-rate factories and their third-rate ideology?

With Germany, Putzi said, it was much the same after the last war. The Nazi movement found its start in the fact that Germany had lost the war and with it the foreign trade, the colonies, the ships, the investments and some territory. Hitlerism was in part an heroic rationalization of the lower standard of living which these unpleasant facts imposed on Germany.

Wasn't it much the same with your New Deal, Franklin?

No, Winston. We had an entirely different problem: a standard of living and production much higher than we knew what to do with. Thanks to machinery and resources, we could make much more than we knew how to distribute. The old spur of hunger failed to satisfy our business system and we had a nervous breakdown.

As a matter of fact, Hopkins said, it always seemed to me pretty important that the first time we took Communism seriously was after the Panic in 1929. With millions unemployed, breadlines, bankruptcies, evictions, suicides, we suddenly became interested in the Soviet Union, where there was work for everybody and where State Planning took over the risks of business enterprise.

In the early 1920's, I said, the slogan was: Free Love and the State takes care of the children.

They dropped that, Roosevelt said. They're getting pretty conservative on marriage and divorce.

What Harry says is close to the point, Churchill observed. We say that the tables will be turned as soon as the Russians realize that a Welsh miner on the dole or a Southern field-hand is better off in terms of food, clothing, shelter and security than the average Soviet factory worker.

You forget that the Russians pay their men higher, Hopkins said.

They do nothing of the kind, Churchill insisted.

Yes, they do. They pay them with pride or honor. The Soviet worker is told, not that he is slaving at starvation-wages in a badly-run assembly-plant, but that he is building a wonderful new world for the working class, that he is a hero of the Soviet Union, that Stalin himself may confer upon him the Order of Lenin for his achievement in making three rivets grow where only two grew before.

Honor is all very well, Churchill said. We understand that in England quite thoroughly but since the days of Falstaff we have been skeptical concerning honor as a substitute for skittles and beer.

"A kiss on the hand is very nice but a good diamond bracelet lasts forever," I quoted from *Gentlemen Prefer Blondes*.

Just so. Men die gallantly for honor but few of them care to live for honor in time of peace. Our excellent Civil Service is proof. They are well-trained, expect to go where they are sent, obey their orders and do their work competently, often under perfectly appalling difficulties. We give them Michael and George when they live long enough, but we are also careful to pay them well and provide them with generous pensions on retirement.

The Soviets rely on Communist zeal to take the place of that kind of security, said Hopkins.

They'll run out of zeal before long, Churchill answered.

The revolutionists who made the days that shook the world are a full generation older now. Who will be their successors? A group of bureaucratic politicians? Or will it be the Red Army leaders who want much more than the Order of Suvarov with Hammer and Sickle for having saved Russia at Stalingrad?

18

There is one way in which Russia is much closer to us than to the Nazis, the President said. The subject's been touched on several times this evening. That is that the Soviet system or the Communist Party is based on the idea of human brotherhood.

Provided, Mr. President, observed Hanfstaengl, the comrades are always able to pass a good examination on the latest meaning of Karl Marx as interpreted by the Kremlin. Some of the great revolutionists of 1917 faced the firing-squad twenty years later, as Trotzkyites or right deviationists or saboteurs of the Soviet Fatherland.

Joe Davies's reports of the Moscow treason-trials stated that to him, as a trial-lawyer, the evidence against the accused was overwhelming proof of their guilt, I said.

I'm sure it was, Carter, the Prime Minister interposed. Their guilt was a necessary result of their whole monolithic regime. All the jobs were filled by loyal Party members who took orders from the Kremlin. There was no hope for promotion, no room for plain, unregenerate ambition in such a system. The only road to political change was through revolution or foreign intrigue.

Speaking as a man who worked hard for your renomination in 1940, Mr. President, I think that the same thing is partly true with us, I said. Thanks to the special circumstances of the war, our political system was closed at the top and the old shift of parties and candidates has been suspended. A lot of the irresponsibility in Congress and in the newspapers, is due to this fact, I think.

I'm afraid you're right, Jack, though God knows I've leaned over backwards to give the Republicans power in the Administration. I've sacrificed some necessary policies in order to keep them happy.

There's nothing like personal ambition, especially for the Presidency, to keep a politician steady, Baruch said. That's why I mistrust men who say that they are disinterested. It's just another way of saying that they are irresponsible.

I don't agree with you at all, Bernie, the President replied. There are plenty of able and patriotic men who have no personal ambition and no selfish axe to grind. Like Harry or yourself.

We are personally ambitious for you and for the success of your administration, was Baruch's answer. You trust us because you know that our chips are down on you. What I say is that any government depends on harnessing the ambitions of powerful men to the public welfare. Once they lose ambition, they become intriguers, courtiers, connivers or elder statesmen. That's the trouble with Moscow today as it was with Robespierre in France. Once a politician is supposed to be incorruptible, people get worried, because they know that he has fallen to the subtlest corruption of all—the sense of power and influence.

I doubt that Stalin or Molotov are in that category, old fellow, the President insisted.

No, Stalin is too busy and Molotov is too ambitious. I'm

thinking of the Soviet group as whole, not its head or the heir apparent. Every Russian knows that Stalin will be head-man as long as he lives. They all know that when Stalin dies, Molotov is the choice of the bureaucracy. That means that far down the line, Soviet decisions are based not on what is good for Russia or even good for the Party, but on whether they will please Stalin and Molotov.

That's human nature, Bernie. We can't change that.

The whole purpose of political systems is to use human nature for society and not to let it control society. Russia may be based on human brotherhood and Russia may stand like a rock against racism. But the fact remains that Russia has its own set of political dissenters and treats them about as tolerantly as the Nazis treat the Jews. There's not much human brotherhood in evidence when the Communist is told that the capitalist is also his brother.

I still believe, said Roosevelt, that the idea of human brotherhood will save them, in spite of themselves, just as it was Christian brotherhood that destroyed slavery in spite of its economic and political advantages for the slave-owners.

That might happen in time, Baruch replied, but in the meantime a lot of people would die.

What do you propose, Bernie? How would you deal with the problem?

I propose that we all have a drink of Scotch. I brought some bottles along in my car and since Harry insists on staying up after his bed-time, I think we would all be much happier for a drink.

Sound man! said Churchill.

A splendid idea, said the President, and if we give Starling a drink, too, perhaps he'll rustle us some ice.

It's all ready, Mr. President, said Colonel Starling from the shadows. Mr. Baruch turned the Scotch over to me with full instructions before he came in.

A very sound man! Churchill insisted.

Not sound, only foresighted, Baruch replied. Now that I have you drinking my Scotch and the President's soda, perhaps he'll forgive me if I tell you why I believe that this conversation, from what I've heard of it, has got off on the wrong foot.

This is good whiskey, said Roosevelt, and I'll have to listen to your ideas, Bernie, though I won't promise to agree with them.

You never did, did you? asked Baruch.

IV
Venus

1

I AM an American individualist, said Baruch, as well as a descendant of the Prophet Baruch. I do not pretend to be a prophet myself. I have been the friend of many important men, in the course of my lifetime, and they, like President Roosevelt, did not always follow my advice. I don't believe that I need have heard the talk of the early part of the evening because I am sure that it was about States and nations, armies and politics, power and propaganda, and all the other issues which at this turning-point in the war beset the President and the Prime Minister.

What would you like us to discuss, old fellow? asked Roosevelt. Stamp-collections and water-colors?

You could do worse, Mr. President. Which reminds me of what happened in 1912 when some Republican politician burst into the Republican National Committee with the alleged scandal involving Woodrow Wilson with Mrs. Peck. They were all for using it against Wilson in the national campaign, when up spoke the Committee's General Counsel, James Francis Burke of Pittsburgh. "Sure," said Burke, "it's the humanest thing I ever heard about the man." So they decided that it would be better politics not to humanize Wilson by a woman-story.

In England, Churchill said, we keep sex out of politics unless there's a divorce and then, as you know, even a King must stand aside. I'd far rather paint than talk about painting, as you know, but there does happen to be a war on and the President and I are planning to win it.

More power to both of you, Baruch replied, but I also hope that you will win the peace, not be content with having overpowered your enemies. Last time I saw how swift was the change from hatred of Prussian militarism to talk about "the good Germans." I know every station along that line.

What's your idea, Bernie? the President asked. Where did we get off on the wrong foot? We're trying to find the way to beat Hitler in such a way as to win the peace.

I can best illustrate my meaning by telling you a parable, which can possibly be forgiven to one of my ancestry. I see a long, high wall. It is topped by electrified barbed-wire and it is many feet thick. In the center of the wall is a large gate, wide open. Foot-prints show that many people have passed the wall through this gate but none are using it now. On either side of the great gate are a number of smaller gates, each of which is under control of a group of well-armed officials. The entire human race is pressing toward the wall and each of the groups in control of the smaller gates is intensely busy devising new rules and regulations to control admission. At one gate they are killing Jews. At another gate they are taking the rich to one side and shooting them. At still another gate, they occasionally pick out a colored man who has jostled a white person in the crowd and hang him. At every gate, the guards go through the pockets of the people and take some and often all of their money away from them.

The management of the different gates has become a science in itself, concerning which professors are forever writing books and theses. Control of the gates is so profit-able that there are always rival groups trying to displace the guards and take over for themselves. For some, it is a life-long career to be trained to handle the crowds as they press towards the wall and trickle through the gates. For others, it is assumed that all that is required is Aryan ancestry or a gun or a voice or a vote. In every gate there are numerous officials who are forever busy inventing new ways of taking money and property from those who wish to pass the wall, or the formulation of new tests to determine those who are considered worthy to pass.

The queues before each little gate become longer and longer and the grumbling of the crowd is continuous. In the crowd itself there are differences of opinion as to how to pass the wall. There are radicals who wish to seize control of the gates. There are liberals who hope to persuade the guards to look the other way and forget the regulations. There are anarchists who wish to climb over the wall with ladders. There are conservatives who believe that, bad though it is, it is still better to use the gates than have no wall at all. And there are reactionaries whose chief complaint is that there are any gates in the wall at all. And there are dreamers who say that in the future there will be no gates and no guards and no wall.

Yet all the time, Baruch concluded, there is a wide and open gate in the center of the wall, through which everybody could pass. A gate without guards, without regulations, without executions, leading straight ahead to the main road along which the crowd wishes to pass. Nobody is using that gate. I myself believe that this is because the crowd no longer sees it or, seeing it unused, avoids it as being some kind of trap. Since nobody is using it, the crowd concludes that there must be some overwhelmingly powerful reason and makes a stern example of anyone who strays in its direction.

I can understand, Mr. Baruch, said Putzi, what you

mean by the little gates. They are the different governments of the world—England, Germany, Russia, America *und so weiter*. But what is the big gate which nobody uses?

Yes, Bernie, explain your parable, the President said.

2

Hanfstaengl is quite right about the smaller gates but I am surprised that none of you recognizes the big gate.

Human brotherhood? I guessed.

Freedom from fear? asked Roosevelt.

The world must have governments, Churchill said.

Naturally the world must have governments, Baruch agreed, but does that mean that the people of the world must be ruled?

You mean?

I mean that people came before governments and that their needs supply the only reason for governments. I do not agree with those of Jefferson's thought that government is a necessary evil. I believe that good government is a human necessity just as good hotels and good railroads are a necessity, but I believe that governments have forgotten their origin and have ignored the only important part of human life—the development of personality.

I don't think I agree with you, Bernie, Roosevelt said. Here, at any rate, we limit the scope and powers of government so as to give full sway to the development of human personality.

On the contrary, Mr. President, Baruch insisted, this country is limiting human personality more and more every year. I am now nearly seventy-three and I have seen bad times and good times, both here and abroad, and I have made my own way from poverty to financial success. I can assure you that there is infinitely less real freedom in this country today than when I was a boy in South Carolina. We have the income-tax—a necessary measure, no doubt—and the inheritance tax, which is also considered necessary. These interfere with a man's right to keep what he earns and to leave it to his children. We have compulsory military service—which is also necessary—and we applied it in time of peace for the first time in our history. When I was young, America allowed me to make a fortune, if I could, and keep it, if I chose. Today, I would not be allowed to do so. I could neither buy nor sell with freedom, nor could I keep my profits.

But that's only true about money, said Hopkins. I'm damned if I consider money the measure of human freedom.

It's the most important measure because it is the most obvious one. But there are many others. Can a European doctor, whether or not he is a Jew, be admitted freely to practice the art of healing in this country, without the permission of the medical association? Can a born teacher get a chance to instruct young Americans, as did Abelard and the Schoolmen in old Europe? Unless he can produce a certified Ph.D. from some recognized university he cannot qualify even as a junior instructor in the United States. About a hundred years ago Brigham Young—or was it Joseph Smith?—was free to have a revelation from the Angel Moroni permitting polygamy among the Mormons. Today it is a criminal offense under Federal law to drive your girl across a State line on a romantic excursion. Only ten years ago, there were States in this country where you could be lawfully condemned to life imprisonment if

171

you were found with as much as a pint of liquor in your possession. And as for pure science, which is the very citadel of human personality, what scientist is today free to continue his research without regard to industrial property or the political effects of his discoveries?

That has always been true, Baruch, said Churchill. Think of Galileo and Copernicus. It's less true now than it was a few centuries ago.

Is it, Mr. Churchill? Suppose that a British scientist made a discovery that rendered navies obsolete. Would he be allowed to develop his device or broadcast his findings?

The Admiralty would certainly make him a very handsome offer, Churchill answered.

Exactly. An offer which he would not be allowed to refuse. Again it is the power and policy of government that rules the scientific brain. We have lost that adventurous spirit that said: "Give me a place to stand and I shall move the world." Instead, scientists must say: "Give me a patent and perhaps I can sell this to General Motors."

Don't forget, Bernie, that we're at war now and that it is total war, the President remarked. In self-defense, we could not allow our scientists to publish and exchange information freely. After victory, with a durable peace, science will be far freer than ever before.

Will it? asked Baruch. I hope so. Somehow I doubt it. We Jews sense these things in our bones. We have had to leave too many places in too much of a hurry since Titus drove us out of Jerusalem to afford the luxury of self-deception. The world which the statesmen are building is at best going to be a sort of U.S.O. recreation center for the troops in their hours off-duty. At worst, it will be a mass concentration-camp with no room for individual personality except as it may amuse the guards to humor the inmates.

3

chill objected, individualism is all very fine but we still must have some kind of bobby to direct traffic and some set of rules for drivers, if we are to avoid injury.

Of course, we must, Mr. Churchill. But the motorist doesn't like to feel that the traffic cop is his master. In the last few years, the police have come to rule more and more of life.

Ach! those chauffeurs around Hitler! Putzi exclaimed. They told the Fuehrer: "Give us the carburetors and Germany shall rule the world."

Take the matter of travel, Baruch continued. If there is any right in nature it is the right of people to move from place to place and earn their living so long as they obey the rules of the community. This is particularly true of the Jews, who are always being told to move on. They don't ask charity or special privilege. They do ask the right to try to earn a living as people. Yet year after year, the difficulties pile up. Today, it almost requires an Act of Congress or a treaty for anybody, let alone a Jew, to cross a frontier in order to live, work and earn a living in another land.

Do you remember, Winston, Roosevelt asked, how before the last war you could travel anywhere in the world without a passport?

Except for Russia and Turkey, Hanfstaengl said.

Today, Baruch added, and for the last twenty-five years you could travel nowhere without a passport, for which you must pay money, and then you must have a visa, for which you must pay more money, and in addition you pay a tax on the cost of your ticket. I won't even mention immigrant quotas or residence permits.

My wife is British, I said, but we were married at a time when she remained a British subject under our laws, although losing British citizenship under British laws. In 1927, when we went to France she had to travel on an affidavit from the Secretary of State of the United States, the Secretary of State of New York and the Clerk of the County Court. It cost her $50, not counting visas. Today, after twenty years in this country, she must have a border-crossing permit or an alien reentry permit, in addition to her Canadian passport, every time she leaves this country.

Why doesn't she become naturalized, Jack? asked Roosevelt.

Because her idea of individuality is to remain British. So she is penalized at every turn for failing to conform to the pressure of police-regulations.

That is what I'm trying to tell the President, Carter, said Baruch. These governments, with their regulations, take no account of individuals and try to suppress personality.

In wartime, Roosevelt said, we must keep a check on goings and comings, in order to control Axis agents.

I've always been convinced, sir, I answered, that any Axis agent would be damn well sure to have his papers in perfect order. It's the innocent who have the inconvenience.

I have not done much travelling since September of 1939, save as the guest of Allied governments, Hanfstaengl said. I have no complaint on the subject of passports. I went from England to Canada to America, without passport or visas, as a P.O.W.

174

4

Well, coming back to the real topic, Baruch continued, the Jews supply the real test of human brotherhood. We are often accused of clannishness but that is the precise point. We are a race, with distinct characteristics and a definite code of ethics. We are hard-working, ambitious and we usually stand by each other. All we ask of the world is a fair field and no favor. We do not believe that brotherhood means a vast indeterminate melting-down of people into sheeplike conformity. We believe that brotherhood is an active principle by which individuals and groups of widely different abilities and qualities can work together under a common set of rules. So the Jews provide the final challenge to all the nations which talk about toleration but insist on assimilation.

Now Bernie, Roosevelt objected. It's only human nature for people to want others to conform to their standards. The Jews are a race apart, a religion apart, a diet apart, a special group inside every other nation. Such separations have always caused suspicion and trouble.

I grant you that, Mr. President, said Baruch, but the idea of human brotherhood has always assumed that the opposite could be true and that different men could work and live together. We Jews have always been good citizens of the countries which admit us to citizenship. We pay our share of the taxes, and more. We don't rock the boat. We are self-reliant, self-respecting and, on the whole, reasonably honest and well-behaved.

I have worked for both Jews and Gentiles, I said, and

the only people who really swindled me were white, Nordic Protestants of old American ancestry.

That's one reason why there are so few Jews in New England, Roosevelt said. They can't stand up against the sharp business methods of the native Yankees. No, Bernie, I see your point and I agree with it, but both the Prime Minister and I must deal with the world as it is and with people as they are. War is always worst for the non-conformists.

Times are always hard for the Jews, Baruch replied, since we are non-conformists and stiff-necked individualists. And the world and its rulers usually value people chiefly for their willingness to say "Yes."

Like Hitler, said Putzi. He always wanted a ninety-nine percent *"Ja"* in all his elections.

The whole world is set against individualism, said Roosevelt. It's caused too much trouble in the past to be let alone by society.

5

The world is confused, Baruch answered. What it is set against is greed, stupidity and force masquerading as individualism.

I say, Baruch, the Prime Minister interrupted. I don't agree with you on that. In every way the world is much more closely tied together than when you and I were boys. In those days, there was room for many individuals to rise or fall by their own efforts. Today, everything is linked to everything else: in industry, banking, trade and government. Freedom of the individual in these important spheres of human activity leads straight to chaos.

176

Exactly, Winston, Roosevelt agreed. When I came in after Hoover in 1933, I had to fight to make business realize its simplest responsibilities. Rugged individualism had to be put aside in the interest of social security.

Granted, said Baruch. You sought to do so by legislation instead of allowing business to learn by experience. If matters had been left alone, within the year the businessmen would have discovered that their responsibilities were a matter of fact and not an issue of political opinion.

All that would have happened, said Hopkins, would have been the complete victory of monopoly, cartels and trusts. Morgan, Rockefeller, DuPont and Mellon would have owned the country.

What good would that have done them? Baruch asked. They would all have discovered that their power and ownership was nothing unless the country was prosperous. Thanks to the New Deal, government interference saved them from this knowledge. Next time they will again follow the policies which lead to collapse. You wouldn't let them learn the facts of economic life.

So you think that we ought to have let the country go to the dogs in 1933 just to prove that rugged individualism was out of place in the Twentieth Century? asked Hopkins. The unemployed and their families wouldn't have agreed with you.

I'm not arguing past politics, Harry. I am trying to show that this country no longer believes in individualism and is busy finding reasons why it should be set aside. My contention is that individual personality is the only thing worth while in life. Otherwise, we are nothing but termites or white ants. I deny that U.S. Steel or General Motors are individualistic. On the contrary. They are private economic governments. I also see that the real individualists, men like Henry Ford and Tom Girdler in industry, are ignored and derided because the government rushes in to protect the clumsy, muscle-bound big business concerns from their competition.

What about Henry Kaiser? the President asked. There's a rugged individual who got his start under Federal regulation.

And I ask, Mr. President, what will happen to Henry Kaiser when the war ends and he is no longer asked to build unlimited ships at guaranteed profits? He may be really good but we won't know until we see whether he can fight off the post-war wolves as ably as Henry Ford did in the 1920's.

The trouble with you, Bernie, said the President, is that you talk as though individualism was confined to a handful of big powerful, successful men. There are millions of individuals in this country, many of them Main Street business men and small town manufacturers, who have not got a chance to show their real ability and character because the field is held by your big business executives, with Wall Street banking-connections. Harry and I tried to preserve individual freedom and personality for the little people, even in the breadlines.

And you were eternally right, Baruch said. The same result might have been achieved at less expense if we had followed Hoover's advice and let nature take its course. The American people, having gone hungry and lost its sense of certainty, was coming to life in 1932. You and the New Deal sent them back to sleep.

In 1932, I said, my office made up a list of at least seventy-five new political and economic movements in this country. And that didn't include Howard Scott's Technocracy, which came close to sweeping the nation at that time. Two years later, after W.P.A. and deficit spending, there wasn't anything much left of all this upheaval. The country had really gone back to sleep.

I hear that Howard Scott's still active, Hopkins said.

Of course he is, I said, but his followers aren't. Ten years ago, when he had a following, he was only one of many people who had got the country doing a little direct thinking and acting on their own problems. Since then, the people have returned to the old idea of let George do it, George being Roosevelt.

We've moved on a lot since then, the President said. And Congress has its own ideas about who George is. Our problem is to win the war.

The problem, Mr. President, as I see it, said Baruch, is not to win the war, but how to win it wisely.

6

I'm not sure that you're right, Baruch, when it comes to science, Churchill said. Scientific research has become a tremendous industry in itself and must, like other large industries, be thoroughly organized and directed. Freedom of inquiry is essential but there is no point in a scientist wasting his time in duplicating something that another scientist has done or is already doing.

One of the world's greatest scientists is a man named Albert Einstein, said Baruch. Without his free inquiries in the realm of physics, under liberal German governments before Hitler, the world would be much poorer. When Germany drove him out under the Nazi race-policy, they removed a great barrier to the kind of research that you have in mind, Mr. Churchill.

We gained by it immeasurably, Roosevelt commented.

The truth is, Churchill insisted, that the scientists—like the generals—have become confused by the size of their job and need encouragement and direction which can now only come from the government. For instance, the Admiralty not only thought but said openly that I was mad in the spring of 1940 when I ordered them to give top priority to the development of landing-craft for the invasion of the Continent. After a perfectly frightful amount of grumbling, and much wasteful trial-and-error, the naval architects were able to perfect the craft needed for the North African campaign. Thanks to having started at the time of the fall of France, it is now possible for us seriously to consider landing an army on Axis Europe. Left to themselves, neither the technicians nor the admirals would have done this. As for Einstein, he has—

Careful, Winston, Roosevelt warned.

What? Ah, yes. Quite.

If it would relieve your mind, Mr. President, I said, at this point I will remark that a few years ago I bought shares in the Eldorado Gold Mining Corporation of Canada. A friend of mine who writes scientific articles for *Collier's* told me that Eldorado controlled the uranium deposits of the Dominion and that they were using U-235 to experiment with atomic energy. I remember, too, how suddenly all references to atomic energy dropped from our newspapers. Since then I have heard a few official rumors about some gigantic experiments being conducted at fantastic expense somewhere in Tennessee.

Good Lord, Jack! The President exclaimed. You don't mean to tell me that there's been a leak?

There's been no leak that I know of, sir, I replied. Anyone who has kept track of pre-war developments, particularly the cyclotron, knows that atomic energy is just around the scientific corner, and when there is a blackout of all references to atom-smashing it stands out like the dark nebula against the Milky Way. I am certainly no scientist but it doesn't need a scientist to reach conclusions when a series of dramatic atomic discoveries are followed by complete silence.

We can always be thankful, Franklin, said the Prime Minister, that the Nazis are much too clever to see the simple, obvious things. As a matter of fact, we know a jolly sight more of what their scientists are up to than they know about ours. All because they are so sure that simplicity is a trap set to deceive them.

Like the Russians, Putzi added. They cannot believe the obvious.

Coming back to the Prime Minister's point, Bernie, said Roosevelt, and without admitting or denying anything that Jack Carter has suggested, let's put it this way: The development of atomic energy as a weapon or as a source of industrial power is quite obviously an enormous and enormously expensive project. So far it has taken us about forty years, since the Curies discovered radium, to reach a point where we think that we're on the right track. Normally, if we relied on the individual scientists and private or industrial research funds, it would take at least another fifty years to get there. Perhaps, by concentrating men and funds on the problem now, we can speed the process. This is not a violation of scientific freedom. It is simply making use of what science has already discovered, with the added impetus of war. What's wrong with that?

Nothing is wrong with it, Mr. President, replied Baruch, if that is all that will happen. I foresee that something else may interfere, that your scientists may discover a force that could explode the earth or blow the solar system as far as Aldebaran.

Schrecklich! said Hanfstaengl.

If this is the nature of the discovery, you will pay for your interference with the free and natural process of scientific freedom by placing scientists and research in a political straitjacket. They will become like Soviet scientists, all linked to Five-Year planning in laboratories like assembly-lines.

Nonsense, old fellow! That's balmy.

I don't believe that, when the time comes, you or any other government leader would dare release such a frightful secret to all nations. Self-defense would prohibit anything of the kind. It would be too powerful, the possibility of world-disaster would be too great. So you would be forced to multiply your police-powers, security controls, military rules and regulations, in order to keep the secret from becoming public knowledge. Thus you will, with the best of intentions, bring to a full stop the creative process by which men of science, working in freedom of investigation and exchange of information, have been able to build civilization.

You know, Franklin, said Churchill, I believe he's right.

7

If that is so, Mr. Churchill, said Putzi, the future will be a choice between Sovietism of the West and Sovietism of the East. The new world will be a world of policemen and chauffeurs. What will become of art when bobbies and bus-drivers rule the earth?

Art is our only hope, Baruch observed, but I doubt that art can live if it is divorced from science, which is knowledge, and is reduced to the role of decoration.

Ja, Mr. Baruch. Art can live. It is the only thing that lives. When I was a P.O.W. on the Isle of Man I heard a Luftwaffe pilot say that he had been driven back from London by a fat knight named Falstaff who rolled out of a cloud and laughed him back over the Channel. It was a fancy, of course, Mr. Churchill, but it is a fancy that tells that England has powerful defenders. Chaucer and Shakespeare, Milton and Samuel Johnson, Keats and Shelley, Dickens and Thackery, Tennyson and Browning, Sir Christopher Wren, Sir Joshua Reynolds, Rommey, Mrs. Siddons—when England is in danger, it is not Drake's drum but it is these who summon free men from the ends of the world to fight for England and the English ways. The poets alone are worth an army to the British Government in time of war. H.G. Wells and G.B. Shaw are worth at least a flotilla leader to the Royal Navy and *Pickwick Papers* is better than a squadron of Spitfires any day of the Blitz.

I agree with you, Hanfstaengl, Baruch observed. The same is true of France. It is not the General Staff or even the Tricolor that defends the French. It is the cooks, and wines, the perfumes and the modistes; it is Monet, Manet, Gauguin, George Sand, Montaigne, Voltaire, Verlaine, Victor Hugo, Dumas, Anatole France—all of the brains and talents that have created so much wisdom and beauty for the world. In war after war, when France is in danger, even when France is beaten, it is these who drive back the invader and liberate the land. They are much greater generals than Bonaparte.

When the time comes, asked Putzi, will Goethe and

Schiller, Hans Holbein and Albrecht Duerer be allowed to plead for Germany? When Hitler is silent and Goebbels is dust, will the world agree that Bach and Beethoven, Mozart and Strauss are extenuating circumstances?

Of course they are, the President said. That was what we were saying earlier in the evening. The old German culture—not Kultur—is too important to the rest of the world to be sacrificed in revenge for even the crimes of Hitler.

In Italy, I said, there are many besides the Church to plead for mercy. There are Titian and Michelangelo, da Vinci and Cellini, Dante and Tasso. They have always helped the Italians to rise smiling from the dust of defeat and survive the grim conquerors who always come thundering into Italy, stay a while, learn to laugh and relax, and when they must withdraw, leave with affection and regret.

You see, gentlemen, Baruch said. That is my argument. These great artists were not men of a system or the products of a police-state. They were innovators, rebels, fierce independents, anarchists even, who remade the discipline and tradition of their arts in order to find new truth or beauty. The spirit that drove Van Gogh to Provence and sent Byron to Missolonghi is not the spirit which Detroit wants in the assembly-line or the Army encourages in the ranks. It doesn't fit the blue-prints for your tightly-knit new world.

No, Mr. President, Baruch continued, I do not believe that the artist will find freedom of expression in this new world which is in the making. England and America will probably be hospitable to genius, especially to foreign genius, but where will Germany after Hitler find the means to breed a new Bach or Mozart and how can another Dostoievski grow in Stalin's Russia?

8

There is also the moral principle, Mr. Baruch, said Hanfstaengl. Perhaps you did not know but it is fair to say that I am here, with the President's most courteous permission, to try to persuade Mr. Churchill that the British Empire will be safe if I am released on parole to help fight Hitler.

Morals have nothing to do with it, Churchill observed. It's merely a matter of common prudence and the rules of war.

There is this, Mr. Churchill. When the war ends, I, as a German prisoner of war, will be returned to the Reich, *nicht wahr?* The Nazis, they will not forgive that I have helped you and they will try to assassinate me. I have taken this risk for the Allies. It is not unreasonable that I should ask protection in return.

We'll take care of that problem when we come to it, Hanfstaengl, the Prime Minister replied.

A moral problem still remains, Mr. Churchill, I said. I know that I am troubled by the question of how a decent world can be built of betrayed hopes and broken promises. Our arrangements with Darlan and Giraud in North Africa may have been bad politics but it was worse politics to let Darlan be assassinated and to let DeGaulle repudiate our agreement with Giraud. A little time ago you spoke of the Chetniks in Jugoslavia. I understand that we are shifting our support from Mikhailovich to Tito. Have we any assurance that the Chetniks will not be liquidated by Tito as a result, after they have fought on our side for two hard years?

We'll do our best for them, Churchill said, provided that

Mikhailovich plays our game and not the German game.

But won't our shift force Mikhailovich to get support from the Germans if the Partisans attack the Chetniks?

Perhaps.

There is also the question of Palestine, said Baruch.

We have kept our promises scrupulously there, the Prime Minister said.

You have kept them to the letter but you have not kept them in the spirit of the Balfour Declaration, Baruch replied. I do not happen to believe that Palestine is the solution for the Jews and I am not a Zionist. I am also fully aware of your problems and I do not criticize you. Yet in this case great expectations, with British encouragement, were aroused among the world's Jews on the basis of the Balfour Declaration. These expectations were dashed by the White Paper limiting Jewish immigration into Palestine. As a result a sense of betrayal and bad faith has grown up among the Jewish extremists. The problem has been a source of considerable embarrassment to the British Government only because a moral issue has been raised which cannot be settled within Empire policy. That is why I say that any conflict between a State and an individual is always a moral issue. To the British Government, the White Paper is a statesmanlike solution for the conflicting interests of Jews and Arabs in Palestine. To a Roumanian Jew who is turned back by British police from the border of Palestine, it is a matter of life and death for him personally and for his family.

I can assure you, Baruch, that it is also a matter of intense personal concern to the Arabs, Churchill said. That is why we must keep police in Palestine. That is the sort of thing which gives birth to the police-states. We do as little policing as we can but we also do as much as we must.

I have no criticism to make of your conduct in Palestine or anywhere else, Mr. Churchill, and I am in no position to form an opinion on the subject of Hanfstaengl's release. But I insist that governments must keep faith with people—not masses of people, not classes of people, but people as individuals—or the human race will be condemned to a bitter and foolish struggle against their own institutions. In your concern over Sovietism, you might remember that it was the crucifixion of a single Jewish extremist that overthrew the Roman Empire.

I don't think that you and Mr. Churchill are in any real disagreement, Bernie, Roosevelt said. There is a great difference between the deliberate betrayal of an individual —which is a moral issue—and the self-deception of individuals who betray themselves.

Baruch chuckled. You have been a past-master at *that* political art, Mr. President. Washington is populated with people who blame you because you let them fool themselves.

Not all of Washington, only the Metropolitan Club and the best social circles. It happens all the time in politics. A man believes that he has got something he wants and then, because he wasn't smart enough, he blames somebody else for his failure. There's no issue of morals there, Bernie. It's simply what happens when people try to outwit each other.

When it happens the same way too often in the Stock Market, Mr. President, you get a Securities and Exchange Commission. When it happens too often in politics you spread distrust. And distrust is one of the greatest dangers a government or a system can ever face.

That's true enough, Churchill agreed, but what can you do about it when so few groups of people really like or get on with other groups of people? It's hatred that really creates distrust and hatred is human.

Hopkins strolled over and stretched himself in front of the fire. Bernie, he said, if I wasn't an unquarrelsome fellow, I'd say that your argument started out fine but is getting all wet. As it is, I'll say that you've gone just a little haywire.

What don't you agree with, Harry? asked Baruch.

It's this business of individualism. Put it in terms of art and science and everybody will agree with you. Carry it over into the rest of life and it doesn't add up. Take murder, for example. Except in war-time, murder is strictly against the law and is also forbidden by the Ten Commandments. From the murderer's point of view, this is a distinct limitation on his individual liberty.

Harry, we can hire police forces to detect murderers and execute them, without turning the government over to the Homicide Squad.

Well, then, since murder is out, Hopkins said, let's try something else. Individual initiative and private enterprise take other forms which must be discouraged: selling heroin or marijuana to school-kids or operating houses of prostitution. Society in self-defense orders the police to take a dim view of the personal liberty of a pimp or a dope-peddler.

If society wishes to curb any particular crime, vice or habit, Baruch replied, it has the right to try but it has not the right to kill the patient in treating the disease. Addiction to narcotics and prostitution are not considered desirable in this country. Yet great civilizations exist, as in China or India, without jailing every man who smokes or sells opium and without making it a penal offense for a woman to sell her body. I mention this to show that it is a fact that social existence is possible even in the face of vice and crime. That, too, is part of human nature, which is why they have never been wiped out.

I won't argue human nature with you, Bernie, Hopkins said, but I will say that you take a different view of things when the Nazis start killing Jews for fun or when the Ku Klux starts flogging anyone who can't prove that he is neither Catholic, kike nor coon.

All right, Harry. I'll tell you why. It's nothing new for Jews to be massacred. They don't like it, of course, but they have got used to it, in a way, thanks to the very intelligent reasoning on the part of the Gentiles about the Jewish problem. What we are doing is to point out the danger of this Jew-killing to the whole human race. If men can be killed out of reason in Germany, because they have hooked noses and Semitic blood, then men can be killed in other countries because they are blond, blue-eyed Nordics. If it is legitimate for Catholics to kill Communists, as being atheists, then it is also legitimate for Communistic atheists to kill priests and nuns because they are Catholic mystics. If it is pardonable for the Ku Klux Klan to flog or lynch a man because his skin is black, it is also quite in order for a Japanese to kill Americans or British because their skins are white.

All right, Bernie, said Roosevelt. We all agree with you on that.

But the point is, Boss, said Hopkins, that this proves the precise opposite of what he has been arguing. Now, Bernie, I'll say that you have compared the ideal government to a good hotel where all the guests receive fair and courteous treatment so long as they obey the house rules and pay their bills.

Did I? Well, it's not a bad idea.

All right. I'll accept it. Now, what is the management to do when the old lady in room 902 complains that there is a noisy party in 904, when sneak-thieves take control of the laundry and pickpockets appear in the lobby? Is the management going to allow some of the guests to be annoyed, robbed and possibly injured or killed by others of the guests? No, sir. They employ hotel detectives who are careful to put a lid on many activities which could be called individualism—drunken, noisy and inconsiderate behaviour included—and they are quite prepared to call out the riot squad if necessary to protect the comfort of their guests. Individualism and freedom are fine so long as *we* are the free individuals. When we get a load of other people's freedom is when we send for the patrol-car.

That isn't true when it comes to labor, Baruch said.

9

Labor? asked Roosevelt. What's wrong with labor now?

Labor is doing a magnificent job of turning out the ships and planes, the tanks and guns for victory, Hopkins said. Outside of a few tough guys like Lewis and Petrillo, labor is all right.

We've actually had more war-time strikes in England than you have had here, Churchill said.

Yet you, Mr. President, Baruch continued, have ducked the whole problem of labor from the start of the war. You have never told labor the true situation.

I've kept down strikes, Bernie, and the production-lines are rolling. We had everything we needed in Africa and we've plenty more piled up for the next move.

And I say, Mr. President, that you've paid too high a price for it. No. I'm not talking about wage-rates or profits. For all I know they may be too low rather than too high. A few minutes ago we were talking about your skill in permitting—to use no harsher word—other people to deceive themselves. I say that your whole national policy on prices and wages has encouraged labor to betray itself.

That I do deny, Bernie, the President replied.

Very well, you have asked for it and here it is. You have not stabilized prices. Food prices are rising and Congress is behind the rise. Rents, too, are rising and so are the costs of building. Business rents and costs are rising. Price-control holds down the price of some raw materials and manufactured goods, but the general cost of living has been going up since the start of 1941. Am I right?

That's not my fault, Bernie. Congress left loop-holes for farm-prices.

So they did. Then you turn around to labor and say, "We have stabilized prices and it is only fair that we should stabilize wages." That statement contains a whole ocean of violations of personal freedom. What right have you, even as war-time President of the United States, to decide what a man's profit shall be or at what wages he shall work? That is an extreme of political arrogance for which I do not hold you personally responsible, since it was forced on you by the whole trend of the times. It is that trend which I criticize.

We can't have costs and wages pyramided in war-time and we can't permit bootlegged labor. If we're going to beat the Axis we must keep the price and wage situation under control.

I agree, Baruch said, but it need not be done by flim-flamming labor. What you have done is to fix wages while prices are rising. Then labor comes to you and says, "We can't make a living at these wage-rates under the Little Steel Formula." You turn to labor with a broad wink and tell them to go ahead and work overtime with time and a half pay for every minute over forty hours a week. So labor goes home and rubs its hands joyfully at their cleverness in electing a President who can get them a high weekly wage in the form of freezing wage-rates.

Well, said Roosevelt, there's nothing wrong with that, is there?

Nothing, except God help you when the war ends and overtime stops and labor finds itself forced to pay wartime prices with peacetime earnings. Then you'll be sorry that you didn't tell labor the truth and give them to understand that corporations are the only individuals that get rich in wartime, that war always impoverishes the people.

Bernie, the President replied, I would agree with you one hundred per cent if I didn't know that neither of us really knows the extent of this country's economic power, Fanny Perkins has hundreds of economists and statisticians in the Labor Department and even they have no accurate idea of this country's capacity to produce or to consume. I haven't flim-flammed labor and if labor has flim-flammed itself I am not aware of it. At the end of the war there is bound to be a lot of criticism of me and of my policies—lots of it fully justified—but if by then we have won the war, I won't mind the criticism and the country can survive.

In other words, Baruch asked, you would say that, in terms of the war, the end justifies the means?

Only because we are trying to conquer for a just and lasting peace, Roosevelt replied. For that I'm ready to risk even my moral reputation, but I'm hanged if I think I've betrayed labor.

No, said Hanfstaengl, but even if labor has only betrayed itself, Mr. President, will there not be a great growth of confusion and distrust that will be of great value to Communism?

192

Putzi, Roosevelt replied, quite frankly I am more worried about the racial questions after the war than any amount of industrial unrest.

10

I thought that we had settled that point, said Churchill.

Not on the basis of Baruch's theory, the President answered. Bernie, suppose you tell us how the race problem strikes you.

It isn't the way it strikes me, Mr. President, but the way it strikes millions of other people, particularly in Asia. I really can't tell you what it means to them.

Tell us the way it strikes you, personally, Churchill said.

Again, said Baruch, I must take refuge in a parable. Or, if you prefer, call it a hypothetical case.

When I was in the State Department, I said, it was the rule that the Department never answered hypothetical questions.

Which explains why it is in such high repute, the President observed.

My hypothesis is that it is the Japanese that beat us to the discovery of atomic power. San Francisco and San Diego have been blasted off the map and it is my painful duty to advise the President that unconditional surrender to Japan is the only hope of American survival. We surrender and, after a little guerilla fighting, hostilities end with the United States under complete Japanese control.

Japan, in order to govern its conquest, is forced to use color. The Negroes and, with some exceptions, the Mexicans are summoned to rule the United States. They are in a minority but they have tremendous power behind them. I like to persuade myself that John Rankin and Senator Bilbo will be among the first to advocate whole-hearted collaboration with the yellow conquerors and their colored viceroys.

I will now, Baruch continued, imagine that perhaps fifty years have passed—long enough for the Japanese conquest to be confirmed and the futility of white insurrection to have been accepted. What I try to do is to put myself in the place of one of Japan's white American subjects.

I find that, without any reference to my ability or my loyalty to the Mikado, there are many occupations denied me. I find that where white women are. encouraged or compelled to consort with Japanese, Negroes and Mexicans, white men who make eyes at a geisha girl are liable to immediate execution. No matter what my occupation or skill may be, I am always paid less than a Mexican, Negro or Japanese for the same work. If business goes badly, I am the first discharged from employment. I have no real equality under the law. Now, Mr. President, what is my point of view?

I would say, Bernie, that you were ripe for revolt.

Yes. Now, Mr. President, carry it one step further. Let's suppose that Japan faces a terrific war and that Japan's survival as a great power depends on the attitude of her white subjects. Imagine that Tokyo promises all kinds of advantages and liberties if only we support her war-policies. As the war comes to a victorious close, will we white American subjects of the Japanese Emperor receive our promised liberty or will we except betrayal of our hopes and renewed subjugation?

Subjugation, said Churchill.

There, said Baruch, is the whole story of "Asia for the Asiatics." It is entirely a matter of fact. The Europeans

194

conquered Southeast Asia because they had superiority of weapons. All concessions to Asiatic nationalism have been based on European convenience and necessity, never on abstract human or racial justice. Can you imagine a Caruso who is forbidden to sing in the Scala at Milan because he is a Neapolitan, as Anderson is forbidden to sing in Constitution Hall because she is a Negress? Would Fritz Krisler be content if Negroes forbade him to play the violin except in a dance-hall, on the ground that he was white. That is the essence of the race-question. It is not a matter of groups or races or nations. It is a matter of individual people, of personalities. What do you think are the feelings of the West Coast Japanese-Americans whom the Army deported because they had slant eyes and yellow skins?

They have showed superb patriotism, Roosevelt remarked.

But white patriotism was contemptible when it encouraged the Army to remove decent American families from their homes on a mere issue of racial origin. That, weakness, was your crime, Baruch remarked.

11

That was General DeWitt's doing, I said. In 1941, a government survey was made which showed that the Japanese-Americans were fully as loyal as the Southerners or the Mid-Westerners. Why, sir, I asked the President, did you let the Army do it?

Jack, said Roosevelt, it was a matter of martial law. The Army asked for special status on the Pacific Coast. After Pearl Harbor, they were entitled to get what they said they needed. Once they had this status, they decided that the Japanese-Americans must move east of the Rockies. I had no choice but to back them up or discredit them.

I agree with Mr. Baruch, I said. It was a shameful transaction. They will gain by it but we have lost.

When the war is over, they'll go back, the President said. It's a small matter compared to the war itself.

Mr. Baruch's point is that no arbitrary invasion of personal rights can be considered a small matter.

That is right, Carter, said Baruch. I'm not talking perfectionism. I simply ask how a good world order can be built on the denial of personal liberty. Granted that the Nisei in California will benefit from their dispersion by the Army, by what right can anybody justify the Army's attitiude? How can we atone for the complete denial of human and civil rights to those of our citizens whose ancestors were Japanese instead of German, Italian or Anglo-Saxon?

Bernie, said Roosevelt, I'm without defense on that one.

Are you not commander-in-chief of the Army? asked Baruch.

Yes, in constitutional law, I am.

Did the Navy agree with the Army on this wholesale deportation?

No, but they had no jurisdiction.

In other words, Mr. President, you allowed the Army, for its own reasons, to commit a wholesale violation against the rights of our citizens of Japanese origin.

Yes, I did. It was wrong but the Army said it was necessary.

Did you think it necessary, sir? I asked.

I accepted the Army's judgment, Jack.

Now then, Baruch continued, what is the relation of the

American government, which boasts of its devotion to liberty, to other minority groups?

What about Jehovah's Witnesses? They are not atheists. They believe in God and accept the binding power of oaths but refuse to be sworn into the armed forces because they do not believe in war. Where do you stand with regard to them?

Many people do not believe in war or in God but still must fight for their country. I don't believe in war and I'm sure that many of my friends are convinced pacifists but we have no choice but to support the war. Fortunately it is so immense that it is possible for conscientious objectors to support it without fighting.

That, said Baruch, seems to me a moral evasion, rather than an answer. If the war is wrong, then anything that supports a war is wrong. That is the basis of the law regarding accessories. You cannot deny your suppression of personal pacificism by saying that, so long as individuals are not required to fight, the issue does not arise.

Bernie, you are theoretically right, yet your theory would throw the door wide open to millions of draft-dodgers. It's better to take a chance on violating a few honest convictions than to expose the country to defeat.

12

Much as I truly sympathize with your point of view, as as artist, Mr. Baruch, Putzi said, I cannot agree with it as an historian.

Do you deny that human personality is the source of everything that is worth having in civilization?

No, I do not deny it. I agree with you entirely. But I believe that the impulse to give expression to personality is much more strong than any measures which can be used to suppress it.

If you were a Jew or a Communist in Germany today, said Baruch, you would not find room for your body let alone your soul. They do not even let you die with an individual flavor. They just push you into a gas-chamber along with the others. How much personality can survive that system?

I can only answer you as an historian, Hanfstaengl replied. This notion that the individual and his personality can be considered important is very new. For thousands upon thousands of years, men have lived in tribes, surrounded by taboos which forbade the individual to be in the slightest degree different from his fellows. Even the Romans provide an example of a tribe that became an empire and remained tribal. To Cato, any departure from tribal tradition was a sin. We all know that Athens punished with death the greatest of her individualists. Even in Western Europe individuality has been confined to a very small group until perhaps the last two hundred years. The world-shaking importance of *Figaro* is that for the first time the French aristocrats admitted that a servant might be an individual. Even today, the English, who are the most individualistic of people, are also strict conformists in matters of dress, always excepting the Prime Minister.

You mean that legend about the Englishman always dressing for dinner even when alone in the African jungle? I asked.

Ja, there is that. There is also sport. I do not forget that Rudyard Kipling almost lost his popularity when he made a sneer at the game of cricket—"the flanneled fool at the wicket." I dare say that even the President of the United States would hesitate to say publicly that he did not enjoy that dullest of games: baseball.

It happens that I do like baseball, Putzi, Roosevelt remarked, but I see your point. You think that all of us are prisoners of our tribal customs and that these customs suppress individual personality.

Yes, Mr. President. I will tell you something droll. When first I came here and stayed at the Fort, I was treated like a military secret and was allowed to walk for exercise only in the early morning or late at night, when I could not be recognized. It was summer and I can assure you that my G.I. guards were deeply shocked when they learned that I preferred to walk in my bare feet on the grass. They considered me almost insane when I told them that I really like to feel the cool grass with my toes, that it was healthful.

What have your feet to do with the case, Putzi? I asked. You were talking about personality.

Ach, thank you, John. Yes, it is this, Mr. Baruch. For countless generations men have lived for the most part without expressing their personalities. They were born, they bred, they died. That was all. You would have said that individualism was not in the breed, especially as the punishment was always so terrible to those who did not conform, even to crucifixion. Yet, when the pressure of the tribe relaxed only a little bit, there was the most incredible flowering of personality. From that I deduce that many waters cannot wash away individuality. *Nein,* I have no fear for the future of individualism even if it must go into hibernation under the police-state.

It's a real political problem, Bernie, Roosevelt said, to decide how much individualism any state can allow.

What I object to, Baruch replied, is the assumption that

it is for the State to encourage, tolerate or disallow personality. It is none of the State's business.

In Japan, as far back as 1931, they were prosecuting people for what they called "dangerous thoughts," I said.

The Japanese are almost as logical as the Soviets, said Putzi. To the policeman, all thoughts are dangerous.

In any case, the President observed, we cannot allow the individual to decide how much he shall pay as taxes, whether he will fight for his country or how many wives he shall marry. If we start from there, Bernie, perhaps we'll find that even what you call the police-state leaves plenty of room for the individual.

13

Perhaps. But there is another matter that you should consider in this connection, Baruch replied.

Which is it?

That this is a Christian country and that Western civilization is Christian civilization.

Naturally it is. You aren't going to complain about history, are you?

I have no complaint at all, Mr. President, but you sometimes forget that Christianity produces its own forms of politics and society and that those who are not Christian may find those forms oppressive.

Name an instance, the President urged.

I can give you instances of what I mean, even if they are not very good illustrations. In Canada, there is a sect of Russian Christians called Doukhobors. On certain religious occasions they do not wear clothes. To them it is a matter of religious principle that does no harm to their neighbors.

To the other Canadians, this is shocking and the police are frequently summoned to compel the Doukhobors to cover their nakedness.

The Doukhobors are Christians, Barney, and Canada has a cold climate.

Yes, Mr. President, I told you that my illustrations are far from perfect. Then here we have the Quakers. They do not believe in war and, after years of persecution, America and England have learned to respect their religious convictions, possibly because the Quakers are not very numerous. I cannot believe that you or General Marshall would tolerate Quaker pacifism, if there were five million young Quakers of military age who refused military service.

They are fine people, Bernie, said Roosevelt, and I'm glad that the issue isn't forced on me. But they, too, are Christians. Have you another example?

There is always the case of the Mormons, Mr. President. They are fine people, too, as we both know, and they follow their own religion based on the revelations of the Angel Moroni to Joseph Smith somewhere in up-state New York.

Rex Tugwell used to speculate about the state of American agriculture, I observed, if the Mormons hadn't been driven out of the rich farm-lands of Illinois, Iowa and Missouri into the Utah desert. He said that the Mormons had developed the only stable agricultural system in the United States.

They were driven out of Illinois and Missouri, Baruch said, because they were hard-working and prosperous. That is an old story to the Jews and it is instructive to see it repeated in the case of the Mormons.

They broke the American taboo against working too hard? Putzi asked.

Yes, Hanfstaengl. But the other thing was polygamy.

This was a special revelation given to Brigham Young in person. He took it with him to Utah, which then lay outside the effective jurisdiction of the United States. It was successful and popular among the Mormons, men and women alike. So the Federal Government in the course of time passed and enforced a law against Mormon polygamy. From the Mormon point of view that was an act of Christian persecution.

The Mormons are sensitive about the subject now, I observed, especially the women.

Society has always had the right to regulate marriage, the President said. Even the Moslem countries are abandoning polygamy.

That is true, Baruch answered, but it is *they* who are abandoning it. They are not being ordered to do so by an outside power.

What would you do about beastly things like suttee? asked Churchill. Hindu women burning themselves alive on their husband's pyre? And how about the Thugs who believed that murder was a religious service to the Goddess Kali?

I don't believe in human sacrifice, Mr. Churchill, but it is not logical to use an extreme to justify interference with moderate forms of worship, Christian civilization is a fact and I suggest that it is a fact worth serious study, since it has recently produced such expressions as German Nazism and Russian Communism.

Both of those movements were outside of and directed against the Church, Roosevelt remarked.

Yet neither could have succeeded if they had not corresponded to some quality in Christian civilization that harbored such doctrines and was hospitable to the idea of persecuting those who did not or could not qualify as True Believers.

14

There I do disagree with you, the President told Baruch. Earlier this evening, while you and Harry were gallivanting around the Catoctins, we discussed that subject. The point was made that the great challenge to Christianity came from the two countries—Germany and Russia—that had never submitted to Roman Catholicism or Roman power. That means that Nazism and Sovietism are tribal paganisms which are independent of the Church and in rebellion against it.

Ja, Mr. President, Hanfstaengl said, but we also agreed that Fascism was a political system that was very congenial to Roman Catholicism. There are not very great differences between Fascism and Nazism and Sovietism. All of them persecute the unbelievers in the name of their lousy faith.

I think that Hanfstaengl is right, Baruch added. Certainly, in the past Catholicism was not distinguished for its spirit of toleration. England under Elizabeth had no illusions as to what happened to heretics in Toledo.

"The thumbscrew and the stake for the glory of the Lord," Churchill quoted.

The Inquisition, Baruch continued, was a Catholic institution which was paralleled in the Prostestant countries. Eccentric old women were burned or hanged as witches long after the Holy Office had spent its force. To the Church at all times the spirit of free inquiry in matters of faith has been heresy.

The separation of Church and State, I said, seemed to put an end to that kind of thing.

But now Church and State have come together again in a

203

different way, said Baruch. When the Church was the State, heresy was treason. Now that the State is the Church, treason is heresy. Even the President and the Prime Minister will agree that, after a certain point, the State *must* persecute the Church in the interest of winning the war.

Nonsense, Bernie. I would agree to nothing of the kind. Our record during the war, in the case of Jehovah's Witnesses, for example, is proof that the Constitution protects every kind of religion, even anti-war religion.

I still ask if you would keep hands off Jehovah's Witnesses if millions of men joined the sect in order to escape the draft?

That would raise the issue of their good faith, the President said. We couldn't allow them to use that excuse for escaping military service.

In other words, you would undertake to pass on the spiritual motives of the individual who joined a religion before accepting his right to be considered a member of it. That is the final expression of tyranny.

You're both right and wrong, Bernie, Roosevelt replied. There is a more human and much simpler solution of the difficulty.

15

I see no solution that is easy or simple, Baruch observed. The process of persuasion is long and hard and unless you can persuade the individual the only alternative is tyranny. I do not agree with those who argue that the State is Public Enemy No. 1, but I believe that the power of the State is everywhere eating away the freedom of the individual.

Don't you think, Mr. Baruch, I asked, that human progress has rights of its own as against the will of individuals? It seems to me that what happens in politics, at least, is that after men have tinkered with a problem for a while, they decide to sacrifice the patient and save the disease. That is the way we get rid of institutions that are out-of-date. At first, we honestly try to save them and then, when that becomes too difficult, we save what has attacked them.

That is roughly true, Carter. I am not now talking about institutions. They change constantly and ought to change. What is important is that people shall be free to decide whether and how to change them. The modern State prefers to try to change the people.

So long as we have representative government, Roosevelt said, it will be hard to act against the will of the majority of the people.

But what if the majority is wrong? Hanfstaengl inquired. It is true that the safety of the people is the supreme law but it is also true that often in history the people themselves were mistaken.

People can be persuaded, Putzi. Take this country. Before 1939, it believed that its safety lay in isolation. That was a mistake. Even after Pearl Harbor there were strong and intelligent leaders who still believed that we could have stayed out of this war.

It took bombs on London and on the Pacific Fleet to persuade them, sir, I said. Your arguments only got you the reputation of a war-monger. It was even necessary for you in 1940 to promise that our boys should not be sent to fight in foreign wars. Ed Kelly told me on election day that the Republicans would have won the election if they had campaigned all-out for peace and isolation.

Jack, said Roosevelt, the war we are fighting is *not* a foreign war; the Axis made it an American war on December 7, 1941.

The country didn't understand the distinction, sir. People here believed that you meant it as a pledge to stay out of war altogether. I agree that this is a strange problem. For example, at the 1940 Democratic Convention, the Committee to Save America by Aiding the Allies took a poll of the delegates. They were asked whether they believed that this country would be directly involved in the war. The overwhelming majority said "Yes." Yet an equally overwhelming majority refused to put the Convention on record in favor of the conclusions they had reached as individuals. It needed bombs to change that kind of institutional thinking.

Men learn almost entirely from events, said Baruch.

I haven't taken an unduly active part in this recent talk, Franklin, the Prime Minister remarked, but I come back to the British idea that the rights of free men are best defended in their own minds and hearts. We have no fear of the power of a mistaken majority in England because we know that the individual Englishman is alert to maintain the liberty of the subject.

The problem of persuasion still remains, Winston. During the 1930's, you were trying to make England realize the Nazi peril and England was deaf. The country preferred Chamberlain's umbrella to your shillelagh. It took Norway and Dunkirk to convince them and by then it was almost too late.

Can the democracies afford the time for persuasion in future? asked Churchill. Events have been enormously speeded by these devilish new devices of warfare.

Unless men *are* persuaded, Mr. Churchill, Baruch said, there is no choice but tyranny.

No, Bernie, there *is* another choice, Roosevelt replied. That is defeat and destruction. Our problem is to find the way in which free peoples can be persuaded to take timely measures necessary to their own saftey. This is the last war in which we can afford to wait for events to teach us.

And how do you propose to persuade the people to consent to their own salvation? asked Baruch. That is the oldest question of human society. To be specific, what measures do you propose for the Germans that will permanently disarm them? That is the key to the immediate problem of peace.

16

Bernie, I refuse to let you put me on the spot. You have raised the issue of individual freedom as the key to all our problems. How would you apply individual freedom to the conquered Germans?

I was really hoping that you would ask me that, Mr. President. Since I missed the early part of the discussion I thought that you had already covered the subject thoroughly.

Not from that angle, the President said. According to Putzi, the Nazi race-policy is the key to Germany. How are you going to reconcile the idea of the Master-Race with individual freedom?

I would solve that problem in the same way that the Jews have solved their problem.

I wasn't aware that the Jewish problem was solved, Churchill said.

The Jews, said Baruch, are themselves a former Master-Race which has become a race of individuals. They have not been a nation since the Dispersion, which is why they survived where Rome perished.

Do you mean, Mr. Baruch, that the German people are to become like the Jews? asked Hanfstaengl. That would be frightfully difficult.

I mean that Germany is as bad for the Germans as for the rest of the world. When Germany falls, the Allies will have the chance to make the greatest experiment in modern history, to set the German people free by abolishing the German state and nation.

That's not a bad idea, said Churchill. How can you do it?

Before Germany existed, Mr. Churchill, there were Germans. They were and are a highly gifted race. They and the Jews are the only two peoples that have produced great men without the help of a nation. The great Germans—Bach, Kant, Duerer, Goethe—were produced by the German race before the German nation came into existence. There was no Germany until Bismarck, less than a hundred years ago. Since then there has been a great Germany and very few great Germans. If the world must choose—and the Germans insist that we choose—it must be between Von Moltke and Mozart. Let's take Mozart.

But how would Germany be governed? The President asked.

Europe cannot survive with a strong Germany, replied Baruch. The government of German territory is a matter of indifference, so long as it is not a national German government. I suppose that the Russians and Poles will govern the east and that we and the French will govern the west.

Ach, so, it would be another Polish partition, said Hanfstaengl. That would make a new war necessary.

It might be like the conquest of Ireland, Putzi, I said. As soon as the English had conquered them, the Irish became a world-race. They ceased to be a world-race, when England recognized the Irish Free State. Between the Battle of the Boyne and De Valera, there were great Irishmen in every walk of life and in every country. What great Irishmen have been produced since De Valera took over?

That is what I have in mind for Germany, Baruch observed. If we are going to have a free world, let's see what happens when you set a particular race free from the State idea. We'll have to occupy and police Germany anyway, in our own defense. What I want to do is to make a virtue of necessity by abolishing Germany and freeing the Germans.

But Mr. Baruch, Putzi objected, I do not think that you understand that the Germans do not wish that kind of freedom. They need the State.

What the Germans wish is a matter of almost complete indifference to me, Hanfstaengl. You will probably believe that I, as a Jew, seek revenge against Germany but that is not the case. There is a great attraction between the Jews and Germans. We were set free from the Jewish State by Titus nearly two thousand years ago and we are still going strong. The Germans will still be on earth two thousand years from now if President Roosevelt and Mr. Churchill dare to free them from their crushing State.

If there is no Germany, who will restrain Russia? asked Churchill.

I do not think that Russia will need to be restrained, Mr. Churchill, provided that you follow the liberation of Germany by the liberation of science.

17

I thought we had given science a pretty thorough work-out, Bernie, Roosevelt remarked. What do you mean by the liberation of science?

If the problem is to restrain Russia or to curb imperialism, including Russian imperialism, you have only to turn the scientists free. We are already getting ready to develop atomic energy. What will that do to imperialism? It will mean that the problems of food supply fuel, raw materials and military security will cease to exist.

I doubt it, said Churchill. To the end of time men and governments will struggle for power.

No, these objects of empire will cease to exist in terms of the political State. The State is only a very powerful tool for getting access to food and markets and natural resources. Of what earthly use would the wheat-ranches of Canada be to the British Empire if all of England's food could be produced in a single factory in Kensington?

They've already developed a yeast-cell that turns molasses into meat, I said. What it means is that a single acre of Cuban land produces in a single year as much "beef" as fifty acres of Prairie in three years. The ratio is changed enormously but you still need the land.

The problem of fuel, particularly oil, Baruch continued, becomes almost meaningless if science can turn, say, a tea-cup full of salt into the equivalent of a thousand barrels of gasoline. When ships can cross the Atlantic on a thimble full of coal, the heart will go out of empire and the State will wither on the vine.

The idea of the State will last long after the need has

passed, said Churchill. People cling to their institutions. They are afraid to go home in the dark.

As for military security, what use will Constantinople be to Russia or Gibraltar to England, when the whole Mediterranean can be closed by rocket-projectiles from hundreds of miles away? What has happened to the old British idea of the buffer-State since the airplane?

That's gone, Churchill agreed. There are no buffer-States. The Nazis taught us that in Poland and the Low Countries. There are only zones. We must control the European zone, if we are to be secure against Russian power.

What I say, Mr. Churchill, Baruch said, is that it is science that is your frontier, and science is a matter of freedom. You cannot direct science as to what it shall discover next, because you don't know. Many of the greatest discoveries, like X-Rays, have been quite accidental. And you cannot determine how these discoveries will be used. The Chinese used gun-powder in fire crackers to frighten the demons for generations before the Europeans used gun-powder to kill each other in battle. The airplane is one of the greatest single scientific developments of all time, yet so far its chief use has been to kill and destroy.

That's all very true, Churchill replied. What are we to do if the Russians don't turn science free but use it to devolop weapons?

Soviet science can never catch up with Western science, so long as Western science is free and Soviet science a slave to State-planning. My idea would be to establish great scientific foundations with public funds, free of political controls, and to make provision for the free licensing of discoveries. In twenty years, Western science would have advanced so rapidly that Soviet science would look like alchemy and the Soviet state would be as obsolete, compared to the West, as Ethiopia was compared to Italy in 1935.

Wouldn't the Soviets try to stop this—perhaps by war—if they saw themselves being outstripped in science? I asked.

Not if our science was really free, Carter. Because then, under our system of personal profit and freedom of enterprise, the greatest rewards would go to the scientists who did most to make life more comfortable and pleasant and secure for the mass of people. That means that our competition would be in terms of consumer goods and services, the one kind of competition that really terrifies the rulers of the Soviet Union. We can make them melt, like a lump of sugar in a cup of coffee, if we forget about the State and turn to human comfort, security, personal prestige and satisfaction.

I can see how that might work in international relations, I said, but I still don't see how the national State can be altered. Up to now, every new invention has simply strengthened nationalism.

18

Carter, Baruch replied, I don't see that there is any problem. Without an international problem, nationalism is no longer necessary.

How do you work that out, sir? I asked. It seems to me that international relations are by definition based on nations. Unless you can get rid of the nations, as expressed in their national governments, you are still going to have the problem of the individual as against the police.

I don't see that that follows in the least. Take the question of States Rights in this country. We had a Civil War which decided that the Federal Government was supreme. As a result, the rights of the States withered and it was never necessary formally to acknowledge the change.

I think that the cheap automobile did more to break down States Rights than Appomattox, I said. Yet even there I find no escape. The States continue to tax me for the right to use my own car on the public highways and the Federal Government has a number of laws which apply to me if I cross a State line. So far as the automobile is concerned— and it is a product of free science—all that happened is to make two laws and two sets of taxes grow where only one grew before. The insolence of saying that I cannot take my property on the public roads unless I pay a special tax. They never dared do that with a buggy or an ox-cart.

On the other hand, you do not seriously object to the State registration and so forth, do you, Carter?

Not seriously. Even though the system has been imposed upon me, it is not unfair or unreasonable. The taxes go to build the roads over which I drive my car. That's fair enough.

In other words, Baruch said, a fair trade is no robbery and a reasonable arrangement is enough to satisfy you that the rights of the States are part of your own rights when it comes to operating an automobile.

I have some reservations when it comes to Virginia, with its high taxes and its bad roads, I said.

That sounds like the Byrd machine, said Roosevelt.

They call it States Rights, sir.

Virginia represents the ideal of States Rights at their lowest and most sordid level, the President observed. They don't care how many two-headed calves or six-toed babies are born in the Old Dominion so long as they can get their apples picked at sweat-shop wages.

All that I am trying to argue, Mr. President, I said, is

that the multiplicity of sovereignty increases the opportunity for undetected graft and hampers personal freedom. I am a citizen of the United States. I pay taxes in Virginia, in the District and to the Federal Government. If we join the United Nations, so far as I can see it merely means that I must pay another set of taxes. In all this building of a new world, I think that you and Mr. Churchill may lose track of the men who pay your bills. Sumner called him "the Forgotten Man."

, Jack, the Forgotten Man has changed since Sumner's time. He thought that the taxpayer was forgotten, today it is the wage-earner.

Sumner's point, sir, was that all of the great plans of statesmen for reform and so forth had to be paid for by some one. He said that the man who paid for them was the forgotten man. Who is going to pay for the United Nations?

All of us, Jack.

Are we going to be consulted as to what it will cost or how much each country or each citizen will pay? I asked.

In effect, yes, the President answered.

Does that mean, sir, that if any country wishes to avoid paying its share it can refuse? Does this mean that I can withhold my share of the income tax that covers the American contribution to the United Nations?

Of course not, said Roosevelt. The Congress as representing you, will speak for your personal interest in the matter.

That's fair, too, I said, assuming that I or my children have the right at any future date to refuse to pay the freight. Is it understood that this country can refuse to contribute to the United Nations?

It is, said Roosevelt.

Then what earthly good is it? I asked.

It is better than war, Jack, the President replied. In war, you have no choice at all but to pay whatever the military say is needed. Even that may not be enough for victory, but you have to pay it. You give Harry Stimson what Marshall says is needed, and no questions asked. The United Nations will represent a predictable risk much cheaper than the established risks of war and in practice the nations will prefer to pay their contributions than to risk the unlimited budgets of national defense.

If we are going to avoid war, even under the United Nations, Baruch said, we must be prepared to run still greater risks.

What's your idea, Bernie? the President asked. After all, this world of personal freedom is your baby. How would you avoid the hatreds and risks that build up between peoples and groups and make for war?

I can only suggest a policy which was recommended by a great Jewish leader, and which has since been ignored.

Which is?

It is the policy of turning the other cheek. Let me drop the metaphors, Mr. President. The real problem of national society is the basis for common agreement, the freedom, in which each can contribute to the value of the whole and still be protected in his personal rights and liberties.

That is true.

Very well. The only course which has not been followed is the policy of toleration. If lynching occurs, it is an evil, is it not?

It most certainly is, said Roosevelt.

What is the cure for that evil? Federal legislation?

I'm not sure, although an anti-lynching law might help.

Or is it the conscience of the Southern communities where lynchings generally occur?

I would prefer it to be the latter, the President said, since then there would be no need for a law.

So should I, Baruch agreed. In other words, we feel that the answer to an extreme of bigotry is not a similar extreme of coercion. If we are concerned for freedom, freedom flies out of the window when the policeman breaks through the door.

There's a limit to that point of view, Bernie. There is a line where firm authority must exist if freedom is to be maintained as between strong and weak individuals or groups.

We are discussing lynching, Baruch said, which is an unlawful expression of mob-violence against an individual. When it becomes a subject of law it is dignified into a legal issue. I contend that there is greater freedom in a system of lynching which has no relation to the law than in a system of law which attempts to codify and define the illegal execution of an accused person. In Mexico, for example, they have the special law by which the police are authorized to shoot a prisoner who is trying to escape. As a result, in Mexico they have no lynchings but they have many prisoners who are shot in the alleged attempt to escape.

I'm not sure that I quite get the drift of your argument, old fellow, the President said.

My argument, Mr. President, is in favor of greater freedom for the individual, even at the risk of an occasional lynching, rather than for a police system under which lynchings are technically impossible.

I still don't understand how you think that would be an improvement.

It would be an improvement, Baruch replied, chiefly in the sense that toleration is an improvement over bigotry.

216

Voltaire said it when he denied the truth of his opponent's argument but asserted the right of his opponent to promulgate error. The answer to bigotry must be toleration—if necessary, for bigotry.

The Nazis used that argument to their own advantage, Churchill said. They employed all of the arguments of liberalism.

The same is true of the Communists, also, said Hanfstaengl. They believe in freedom of speech *und so weiter*, when they are in the minority. When they possess power it is farewell to the bill of rights and freedom of speech.

Putzi, I said, the real argument is not the bill of rights or freedom of speech—which are civil liberties—but the freedom of the human spirit—particularly the artist—to create and operate. That is the test of freedom. So far, Mr. Baruch has the best of the discussion, from my point of view.

19

I don't think that there's any real argument between Bernie and me on this subject, Jack, Roosevelt said. From the very start of the New Deal Harry and I did everything we could to promote art and the theater.

If it hadn't been for the Boss, Hopkins said, we would have lost a great many first-rate artists and authors.

No doubt, said Baruch. Yet it would have been better to have lost them than to make their art dependent on a government program, Harry. Art is the loneliest and least disciplined of all the careers known to man. If you let the artists and dramatists follow their own talents, they will give us better than we deserve. The government can't help them. They can help the government, usually against the will of the politicians.

You mean, "I do not care who writes my country's laws, so long as I may write the songs"? I asked.

That's part of the idea, though it goes far beyond that. Give me the freedom to develop their personalities and their individual liberties without interference from the State and you may find that a new world has appeared overnight.

So, Bernie, said the President, your opinion is that it all boils down to the matter of liberating the individual.

Yes.

You would set men free from the State, starting with the Germans as guinea-pigs, and you would put an end to some of the restrictions on freedom of travel. You would also grant the broadest possible scientific and artistic freedom.

That is what I hope for. It is not what I expect.

For the Germans you mean, Mr. Baruch, said Hanfstaengl, that you would give us the status of honorary Jews, much as Hitler gave to the Japanese the droll rank of honorary Aryans. In this way you would lead the human race out of Egyptian bondage to Church and State, to Capitalism and Communism, *nicht wahr?*

I hadn't thought of it in quite such Biblical terms, said Baruch, but that is roughly the idea.

Something is still missing from your picture, Bernie, said Roosevelt. After all, what we are trying to do is to establish the vital difference between the Allies and the Nazis, so as to bring the war to an early victory. You, Bernie, propose to attack regimentation with unregimentation, tyranny with freedom. But many people do not welcome freedom, some fear it. In any case, it is a question whether Germany is less free than Russia.

You can't escape it, Franklin, Churchill said. Any way you approach the problem, you must end by smashing the Germans. We'll have to worry about the Russians and freedom afterwards.

I think that you are mistaken there, Mr. Churchill, Baruch said. I agree that the solution is to smash Germany but I insist that the way to smash Germany is to free the Germans, whether they wish it or not. You don't propose to exterminate the German people as they have tried to exterminate the Jews?

Rather not, though it is jolly difficult to see how you can smash Germany without smashing Germans. You can't make an omelet without breaking eggs, you know.

Bernie's idea, Winston, is to persuade the Germans to give up Germany before it smashes them.

That is correct, Mr. President, Baruch said.

The only way to persuade a bully is to bash him, Churchill said.

No, Winston, said Roosevelt. I believe that there is another way.

I wish we'd hear from Cunningham, Franklin. Then at least we'd know whether Musso is open to persuasion—on wings.

V
Earth

1

We'll be hearing soon enough, Winston, the President said. In the meantime, let's see if we can't come to some sort of conclusion on this discussion.

Why not take a vote? asked the Prime Minister.

I don't think we're ready for a vote on this, Roosevelt replied. We may be in a little while, but not just yet. Bernie, your wall can be passed without a mob-scene or a massacre. There is a bridge between the individual and the State. Whenever it is used, you find your crowd moving forward in reasonably good order and with good humor. That is the result of persuasion, as expressed in the idea of consent. Jefferson laid it down when he said that governments derive their just powers from the consent of the governed.

Like many other things American political leaders have said, it sounds reasonable but what precisely does it mean? asked Churchill.

From the start, this country has experimented with government by consent, said Roosevelt. It's far from perfect but it is the only thing that holds us together. Back in 1620, before they landed on Plymouth Rock, the Pilgrim Fathers drew up the Mayflower Agreement by which they agreed in advance on their rights and duties in the new world.

As I remember, Franklin, that agreement didn't work perfectly. Even psalm-singing Puritans couldn't outlaw human nature. Down at Jamestown, in 1607, there was another colony and that was based on two ideas: military force and John Smith's rule that the man who did not work should not eat. Virginia did quite nicely under that rule and produced in time your leaders like Washington and Jefferson. New England never produced men to touch them, for all that they believed in government by consent.

That is quite true, Roosevelt agreed, but the idea of consent was necessary to the larger union of the colonies. Neither the Confederation nor the Constitution would have been possible without it.

It could not prevent your Civil War, Churchill observed.

It was inevitable that the psalm-singing North and the fiddle-playing South should come into conflict. The test of the principle was not the war itself but the reconciliation that followed the war. This is one of the few instances in which a crushing military conquest did not result in permanent estrangement between victors and vanquished. That was because the ideas of Jefferson and Lincoln were sound enough to overcome the passions of war.

I won't argue American history with you, Franklin. Yet I could observe that other political systems have worked equally well and for longer periods of time.

You may not wish to argue American politics with the Boss, said Hopkins, but I do. I'm here to say that American politics are lousy and that the far-famed or far-flung American Constitution stinks.

Harry, said Roosevelt, how often have I told you not to say "stink" in the presence of company.

That is nothing to the words I'd like to use, said Hopkins. Here we have this country which is based on the consent of the governed and the Bill of Rights. What do we get? We get practically the entire South where they have

224

reduced the effective right to vote to about ten per cent of the white adult population. We get Western states like Montana and Colorado that are owned body-and-soul by one or two Wall Street corporations. We get Eastern city bosses like Pendergast in Kansas City, Ed Crump in Memphis, Ed Kelly in Chicago, Frank Hague in Jersey City— not to mention Tammany in New York and the Boston Irish —where voting is handled on the efficiency-plus basis. I'm damned if I know of a single state or city where the vote is honest or where the election laws are rigged to protect the voter and not the machine.

I remember, Harry, I said, that you told me that after the '36 election how Frank Hague had told you that you were the greatest political boss in American history.

Yes, damn him! He meant it as a compliment, just because I had tried to get people to vote in Pennsylvania and a couple of other states.

There are worse things than a good city machine, Harry, said the President.

Oh yeah! I know. A bad country machine, like Harry Byrd's in Virginia or the up-state Republicans in New York, is worse. And so what do we get? We get a Congress which is owned by Big Business. We get a government which is a call house for every lobby that commands the dough to make a noise. We get newspapers which are ninety per cent wrong on every test of public sentiment and we get courts that resolve every issue in favor of industrial property and against human rights.

We made a dent in their power, said Roosevelt.

We did not, Hopkins replied. All we did was to slap a few ears back and kid the people that we had changed things. What happened was that the really smart guys made a few nice sounds and the courts handed down a few tough-sounding decisions and everybody said, "Ah! that's taken care of!" Nothing's been taken care of and the next generation will have the same job that we had, only next time it will be worse.

What about T.V.A.? Roosevelt asked. That, at any rate, was different.

T.V.A. was a good campaign slogan to lick Willkie with in 1940, but I'm damned if it really made any difference. We lowered rates in the Southeast and distributed electricity to the hill-billies but who got the real benefit out of T.V.A. and the other big power projects? It was not the common man, as Henry Wallace calls him. It was the uncommon corporation, like Alcoa, Monsanto and Cyanimid. Is it the little guy who is getting the break from Bonneville, Boulder and Grand Coulee? It is not.

We can't do everything at once, Harry, Roosevelt said. We gave the country as much change as it could stand.

Again, Boss, said Hopkins, I say that we did nothing of the kind. In 1933, the country was ready for any change at all, the bigger the better. What we gave them was a stream-lined breadline that delivered the bread to your door, the ploughing under of cotton and pigs to hold up prices, planting of lots of little trees—"Only God can make a tree", and Roosevelt—and a lot of tough talk and soft action where the big business rackets were concerned.

We had to get ready for this war, Harry, and you know it.

Okay, so we got ready for this war and we seem to be winning it, but I'm damned if I think we ought to boast about our pure Jeffersonian democracy when we pay less respect to the rights and sentiments of the voter than does

Iceland, France or Denmark or any of a dozen other countries I could name. We kid ourselves that we are good Jeffersonians but we are really run by what Hamilton called the rich, the wise and the good.

Well, admitting that we don't live up to our ideals, said Roosevelt, we still have the ideals themselves. Take this idea of consent. Jefferson picked up political philosophy where the British thinkers had dropped it and introduced French clarity and logic. Jefferson and Franklin were not only important thinkers, they were also great individualists. Franklin was one of the leading scientists of his time and Jefferson was original to the point of eccentricity. He invented the swivvel-chair, the dumb-waiter and the mould-board plow; he founded the University of Virginia, established religious toleration and designed Monticello. Among other things, he was a brilliant architect.

When he built Monticello, I said, he forgot to put in the stairs. By the time this oversight was discovered, there was room for only a narrow, twisting staircase between the first and second floors. When he gave a dance, the ladies with their big skirts had to climb a ladder and enter through a window, in order to reach the ballroom.

Really! Churchill chuckled. That's illuminating. Most reformers *do* forget the staircase, you know.

Accidents happen, sir, I said. In the early days of the New Deal, the big new Pittsburgh Post Office was completed before they discovered that they had forgotten to put in any mail-boxes and the Army Engineers had almost finished building Bonneville Dam before it was realized that they had neglected to build a lock for ships to pass the dam, although the purpose of the project included improvement of navigation on the Columbia River.

2

That kind of thing is apt to happen in a free country, said Roosevelt.

I can see that Jefferson had technical as well as political heirs, said Churchill. No stairs, eh?

But the ladies still got to the dance-floor, the mail-boxes were built, the ship-lock was added to Bonneville. Nobody was shot or sent to prison because of the blunder. Jefferson's real legacy was a workable form of the social contract.

Ach, ja. The social contract, Putzi said. America is then the child of Rousseau and the French philosophers. Did you know, Mr. President, that the colonies offered the Crown of America to a German prince and also to a member of the British Royal Family during the Revolution? Frederick of Prussia refused his consent.

Who was the British prince? Churchill asked.

The Duke of Cumberland, Mr. Churchill. He was not in favor with King George III but he hesitated to become legally a´traitor, as he must have been if he had accepted the offer of Congress.

Pity! Churchill said. It might have saved us bother.

It wouldn't have worked, Winston, said the President. American had to make her own political system. Long before the revolution, Locke was hired—to draw up a constitution for South Carolina. The greatest British political philosopher of his time produced a very logical document that became a dead letter the day it was written.

The revolution began long before it broke out, I said. One of the first changes noted was in Virginia where hot weather and bad roads forced the Church of England to change the rule that its members must be buried in the churchyard. This was not a matter of theory but one of fact.

Exactly, said Roosevelt. I admire Jefferson because he found in the French thought of the Eighteenth Century some general principles that helped the American colonies to become a new nation without any serious break with European civilization.

That is so, Mr. President, said Hanfstaengl. It was not like the Soviets which insisted that everything must be new after the Communist revolution—Soviet art, Soviet science, proletarian literature, Stalinist music and Commintern medicine.

The French did much the same as the Russians after 1789, said Churchill. Robespierre was not so different from Lenin. Religion was abolished and they even had a new calendar. They certainly had plenty of murder, beastliness and secret police. I'm not sure that I would take pride in claiming intellectual descent from the French revolutionary thinkers.

But that is the point, Winston, said Roosevelt. The same ideas that led in France to the Terror and the guillotine, when handled by Jefferson, became part of the Anglo-Saxon tradition of liberty. What Rousseau called the social contract became something much more sensible. It became government by common agreement, government by consent of the governed, as Jefferson called it.

And in 1776, had America reached the age of consent? Putzi asked.

I'd say we'd been consenting ever since, said Hopkins.

Joking aside, Harry, the truth is that this idea of consent was the means by which the political separation of America from England was reduced to just that. There was no break with religion, with culture or civilization. There was no wholesale abolition of the laws or property. It was not even Utopia. That is what puzzled Frenchmen like DeToqueville and Englishmen like Macaulay and Bryce when they came to study the results. They were looking for results when what confronted them was a process.

3

It sounds most splendid, said Churchill, I wonder whether our historians would agree with you. The United Empire Loyalists who were driven out of the Colonies into Canada during the Revolution have another tale to tell. They describe a revolutionary terror and confiscation of Loyalist property that was a curtain-raiser for the bloody events that followed in France.

The Tories told the truth, Roosevelt admitted. The facts were ugly enough at the time. The important fact, however, was that, under the principles of Jefferson, the excesses of revolution were abandoned and the Americans remained a part of the general world-order, even to the extent of paying our debts to the London merchants after those debts had helped bring on the war.

Is America governed by the ideas of Jefferson, Mr. President? Putzi asked. So far as Europeans can see it, your government is controlled by Big Business.

That was true until 1933, Roosevelt agreed. In spite of what Harry Hopkins says, since then we've come closer to a real democracy. It's still far from perfect, and we have a long way to go before we can call ourselves Jeffersonians.

If you ask me, Baruch observed, we're worse off than we were in 1933.

God forbid, said Churchill.

No, Bernie, Roosevelt replied, we've learned how to handle these tough problems. The Civil War taught us that about slavery. When the Constitution was signed, there was a general belief that slavery would soon come to an end, as being unprofitable and barbaric.

Then came Eli Whitney's cotton-gin and slavery became as profitable as the liquor or the opium trade. The circumstances which had existed at the time of the Constitutional Convention had changed and the issue between freedom and slavery began. The country didn't know how to settle it without fighting.

England had no great difficulty, said Churchill. We abolished the slave trade and liberated the slaves without losing any lives.

The British slaves were not in England, said Roosevelt. With us, powerful commercial and financial interests were on the side of slavery and they commanded votes and majorities. The Constitution protected the South's "peculiar institution" and, after the Louisiana Purchase, a whole empire was opened to the cotton-planters. When the Mexican War confirmed the slave empire, the irrepressible conflict appeared. Men like Garrison in Boston declared that the Constitution was a "covenant with Hell" because it gave sanction to human slavery. And when Southern postmasters refused to deliver Abolition pamphlets in the mails, the entire fabric of constitutional consent was shattered.

I still find it difficult to understand, Churchill said, why a four years' war was needed to decide the issue and why fine men like Lee and Jackson would have fought simply to defend slavery. Why did your Civil War occur?

The late Justice Holmes was asked that question by Tom Concoran, I said. Corcoran was Holmes' private secretary and was curious to know why the young men of Massachusetts had enlisted so eagerly in the Civil War. Was it to save the Union? Did they burn to free the slaves? "Tom," said Holmes, "in those days all the jobs in New England were taken and New England was entirely inhabited by New Englanders. We were bored to death, so we went to war."

I can understand that, Carter, Churchill observed, but even boredom is no reason for a four years' war.

Lincoln tried to make the Union, and not slavery, the issue, said Roosevelt. His hand was forced by the reformers and what might have been settled even after the fighting began became a struggle for survival on both sides. It ended in the greatest single act of confiscation in our history, when we freed the slaves without compensation.

No wonder the South is solid, said Churchill. Loss of property is a powerful political motive.

4

The same issue remains, I said. Today, on one side is industrial property and on the other what is left of Jeffersonian democracy. If democracy is to survive we've got to find a peaceful way to change property rights.

How is that? asked Churchill. How can there be any stability in the world if there is no clear, firm understanding about property and contracts?

I can answer that for Jack, said Roosevelt. Let's take the present agreement between Great Britain and Egypt. Do you depend on Egypt to defend the Suez Canal?

Of course not, Franklin. The Gyppos couldn't hold the Ditch for ten days without us.

That's not what I mean, the President continued. Your

standing in Egypt is a matter of force, and not a matter of treaty.

On the contrary, we have a treaty with Egypt.

Believe me, I'm not twisting the lion's tail, Winston, Roosevelt continued, but it is a fact that you have been in Egypt since the early 1880's without the invitation of the Egyptian Government. And as far back as the Battle of Omdurman, where you distinguished yourself, it was clear that Cromer and the Foreign office were running the country.

Quite! What does that lead to?

It leads only to the conclusion that there is no real agreement between Egypt and the Empire. When you refer to the treaty, you refer to arrangements which you have dictated and which you are ready to modify or maintain, as suits your convenience.

The same is true of your position in Panama, Franklin.

I don't deny it. There, as at Suez, we both say that the end justifies the means.

Would you allow the Colombian Government to jeopardize the right of transit at Panama? Churchill asked.

No.

No more could we allow the short sea-route to Asia to fall under the blackmail of a Levantine potentate, said Churchill. The agreements which we urged the Egyptians to sign were not unreasonable.

What has reason got to do with it? the President inquired. You command the North Sea and the Channel, Gibraltar and Suez. Your naval power is also a matter of life or death to other countries. If Egypt or Colombia had had the power to hold or develop the canal-zones within their sovereignty, there would have been no question of their submitting to authority. It was their weakness and our strength that gave us the right to take charge.

Our own rule in the Pacific is based on the extremely drastic treatment accorded to the Hawaiian Kingdom by American diplomacy, I said. Queen Liluokulani was effectively dispossessed of her power by American naval force and we control the Central Pacific, because we compelled rather than persuaded the Hawaiians to submit to our power.

I agree, Roosevelt said. The only point in our favor is that we were frank enough to annex Hawaii.

That means that America is an imperialistic power, said Hanfstaengl. How does that differ from Hitler's taking of Austria or the Sudetenland?

Putzi, I replied, islands are the tail that goes with the hide. The power that rules the seas takes the islands of the sea. Otherwise they would starve. That is a matter of economics, not of morals or politics.

5

We have been talking about the idea of agreement by consent, as the foundation of government, said Putzi. Can Germany invoke such a right?

Why not? inquired Roosevelt.

I am asking this because of the Hitler propaganda against the Treaty of Versailles. When Woodrow Wilson announced his Fourteen Points, it was as a contract to which the Germans, if they agreed, could be a party for a just peace. When the German Government agreed to the Armistice of 1918 it was in terms of the Fourteen Points. Hitler and the Nazis have always said that the Dictate of Versailles was a violation of the Fourteen Points and so was to be considered as a fraud. Germany has signed the Armistice under false pretenses, the Nazis said.

Germany signed the Armistice because the German Army had been hopelessly defeated, said Churchill.

I agree, Mr. Churchill, replied Hanfstaengl, but the terms of agreement were on the basis of the Fourteen Points, *nicht wahr*?

Just a minute, Putzi, I interrupted. Which of the Fourteen Points were violated by the Treaty of Versailles?

There was naturally the question of Germany war-guilt, John. That was most important.

But, Putzi, I said, war-guilt was not one of the Fourteen Points.

I do not like to disagree, John, but war-guilt was the basis for reparations.

Germany aggression and the damage done by Germany to the Allies were the basis for reparations, said Churchill.

No, Mr. Churchill, the legal basis for reparations was the untrue Versailles thesis of exclusive Germany war-guilt.

Putzi, I said, that is where you and the Nazis are barking up the wrong tree. If there was any fraud in reparations it was all on the German side. Germany never paid reparations. What happened was that America loaned Germany the money with which to pay the Allies and they in turn paid some of it to us on account of war-debts. Before Hitler came in, Germany was paid more by the world than Germany paid to the world. That was the colossal fraud of reparations.

But, John, there was also the pledge of disarmament in the Fourteen Points. This was a fraud. Germany disarmed but the Allies did not disarm. How do you justify that?

Germany lost the war and was disarmed by the Armistice itself, I said. I agree that the Allies failed to disarm, despite years of negotiations at Geneva, but that was long after the Germany General Staff had migrated to Russia and after the Treaty of Rapallo placed Germany and Russia in alliance against the West. That was another fraud of which Germany and not the Allies was the beneficiary.

Good for you, Carter, said Churchill. I'm tired of hearing the Germans squeal that they have been betrayed. The truth is that we let them off jolly lightly after the last war because we hoped that Germany would see the value of keeping faith and working with other nations. Instead, they wasted not a moment in devising the most ingenious and systematic methods of evasion and intrigue to break their pledged word. And then, under Hitler, they made a completely successful effort to persuade the Germans that their troubles were not due to having lost a war of aggression but to the failure of the Allies to keep faith with Wilson's Fourteen Points.

Why didn't we go ahead and occupy Berlin in 1918? I asked.

That was because the French had the wind-up, said Churchill. Old Foch was afraid that that would leave France under British and American military occupation. The real reason why we lost the peace in 1919 was that the French were too timid and suspicious to trust us. Served them right that Hitler rolled over them in 1940.

That's what Wilson said, I observed.

6

How is that, John? asked Putzi. Woodrow Wilson wanted Hitler to conquer France?

Don't you remember? It was in the House papers. During the Peace Conference, Wilson said to House that he hoped that next time the Germans would clean up on France and that he'd like to tell Jusserand so to his face.

Jack, said Roosevelt, that was because the French were trying to make the peace of the world secondary to French security. They kept digging up the Treaty of Vienna and the Treaty of Westphalia, not to mention the Treaty of Utrecht. Wilson was a good historian but he knew that there are times when the past is much better forgotten.

I'm not quite sure that I follow you, Franklin, Churchill said. Government by agreement means that agreements are sacred unless the parties agree to change them. There is no escape from that.

What is to be done, Mr. Churchill, asked Baruch, with an agreement which is entirely obsolete but which is adhered to by one party against the general interest?

There are always ways of bringing pressure to bear so as to make an obstructive party change his position, the Prime Minister observed.

That sounds like power-politics in a dinner-jacket, said Roosevelt.

Without forced agreements, Franklin, often there will be no agreement at all.

We found a way around that, Winston, when we came to draw up our Constitution in 1787. There is a way to get rid of unworkable contracts by the simple process of ignoring them. Did you know that our present Constitution is itself unconstitutional? It was adopted in complete violation of the Articles of Confederation. A convention was called and measures were discussed. After many debates and compromises, the new charter was offered to the states for ratification, with the provision that it would come into force when nine of the thirteen states had ratified it. The old Confederation provided that amendments must be

237

adopted unanimously. Well, the new one was ratified and the others decided to join the majority. That's an illustration of how practical men can get around a theoretical difficulty.

I agree, Franklin, that there is a good bit too much of government by dissent in this world. Yet it is difficult to see how there can be any kind of public law of nations unless it is founded on the scrupulous respect for agreements.

It's hard to draw any line in theory, Roosevelt admitted. Sometimes it is necessary to have a practical demonstration before the minority is convinced.

That was true of Prohibition, I said. Within two years after adoption of the Eighteenth Amendment, it was clear that the dry law wouldn't work. But it took more than twelve years to convince the Prohibitionist minority which was in a legal position to block repeal.

Well, here's another case, Jack, Roosevelt said. Every government in the world knows that the Hapsburg Monarchy has been practically discredited in Central Europe. Yet there are a lot of sentimentalists as well as deeply religious people who think that a Hapsburg restoration of Otto in Austria would be an ideal solution.

Felix Frankfurter? I asked.

Felix among others. It's an attractive idea. If it was possible it would solve many problems. But it just simply is not practical. However, before the supporters of the idea would admit that the Hapsburgs have gone with the wind, it was necessary for the Army to take time out from fighting the war and try to recruit a Royal Austrian brigade under the authority of young Otto. Only when Otto and his brothers discovered that the Austrians in this country would much rather be part of a big army than a small one, did the idea languish.

Am I to conclude, Mr. President, Hanfstaengl asked, that *this* war has rendered obsolete the rights of the small nations for which the Allies fought the *last* war?

Their rights are not obsolete but small nations, as such, are becoming out of date. They are too small to defend themselves and so they are losing their absolute sovereignty.

7

Do you believe, asked Putzi, that God is really on the side of the biggest battalions?

Perhaps it is the biggest battalions that are on the side of God, I replied. The airplane has wiped out the Buffer State. The Wehrmacht and the Red Army are wiping out the small nations. These new secret weapons may wipe out the big nations, too.

That is why I call this a war for survival, said Roosevelt. It can't honestly be called a war for small nations or even a war for democracy.

There is still the question of the individual, said Baruch. Whether you have a world government or no government, you must first get the consent of the individual or you will have chaos. As nations are losing their sovereignty, they compensate themselves at the expense of the liberties of their people. We have fast planes that will take us anywhere in a few hours and it is harder to get permission to cross the Atlantic than in the days of the ten-day boats.

Just so, Churchill said. That is why I say that the peace ought to go back to established rights and interests, including of course the freedom of the individual, or what we call the liberty of the subject.

What are you going to do about vested rights that are against the freedom of the individual? asked Hopkins.

What have you in mind, Harry?

Well, back in 1933, when we started to pull this country out of the depression, we found that there were any number of vested rights, all based on perfectly legal private contracts, that stood in the way of the simple matter of seeing that our people should not starve. As a matter of fact, they still stand in the way, except for war profits. There wasn't time to persuade the beneficiaries of these vested interests —even if they could have been persuaded—so we had to go ahead without them.

As I remember, Harry, I said, your formula was: "Tax and tax, spend and spend, elect and elect."

Harry never said that, Jack, Roosevelt observed. The Supreme Court fight was the thing that really turned the trick.

You couldn't change the law so you changed the judge? asked Churchill.

Something like that, the President admitted, except that the first judge had already changed the law. However, Winston, there's a much better example of what Harry means—the I. G. Farbenindustrie.

How so?

Both before and after Hitler took power, the German Government used I. G. Farben to establish a world-wide control of the chemical industry in the interest of Germany. It was all done quite legally, operating through the normal channels of business law and the rights of industrial property, including patents. We were all sucked in, one way or another—Imperial Chemicals, Standard of New Jersey.

And it wasn't exactly a cartel so it did not run foul of our own anti-trust laws. We had the devil of a time here, before Pearl Harbor and even after the Germans had welshed on their agreements, to break their hold on American industry. You would have thought that we were proposing to send all businessmen to the salt mines the way some of them carried on at the time.

I'd like to hear what Baruch has to say to that, said Churchill.

Mr. Churchill, Baruch said, there the trouble lies not with the individual or the contract but with the American system as a whole. In England, when the time came, you had no trouble with your businessmen. I. G. Farben and the other German cartels were no obstacle to the defense of Britain. Here, there is no clear understanding of the rights and duties of individuals or business corporations. They fear that the State has lost restraint and wisdom, so they resist government policy from an instinct of self-preservation. Personally, I do not think that any American businessman should have sold his corporate soul for a mess of German patents, but there was no public policy here to which he could refer for guidance and support. He was forced to follow his immediate self-interest.

There is another limitation on the sacredness of contract, said Hanfstaengl, that cannot be reconciled with Mr. Baruch's theory of freedom for the individual.

What's your idea, Putzi? the President asked.

Let us suppose, said Hanfstaengl, that John Carter and I should sign a contract between us that we should assassinate the Prime Minister.

For God's sake, why? asked Roosevelt.

For any reason at all or because we do not like him.

Speak for yourself, Putzi, I said.

I happen to admire him, too, John. This is an hypothesis. I ask you, Mr. President, is our agreement to murder Mr. Churchill a sacred contract?

It is a criminal conspiracy, Putzi, and you know it. No court in the world would uphold such an agreement.

Very well, Mr. President, Hanfstaengl continued. Let us suppose that both John Carter and I have a persecution complex on the subject of Mr. Churchill. Let us suppose that we sign an agreement that if either of us considers himself to be attacked or menaced by Mr. Churchill, both of us shall try to kill him. Is that a sacred contract?

Not in the least. The Court would hold that redress lay with its processes and not with you.

Ganz gut, Mr. President! Now then, how are we to deal with the alliances and counter-alliances between the nations? Germany agrees with Italy and Japan to sign the anti-Commintern Pact against Russia. Is that a criminal conspiracy?

Of course it is, said Churchill.

I agree, Mr. Prime Minister. So in 1939, Great Britain signs a pact to defend Poland against aggression. Is that a criminal conspiracy?

Naturally not, Churchill replied. The pact became effective only if Poland were attacked.

But you knew that Poland would be invaded, *nicht wahr*?

The invasion was not of England's making. The defense was a defense not only of Poland but of all civilization.

I agree, Putzi said. Now here is what Americans call the sixty-four dollar question. Germany invaded Poland in September, 1939, and England declared war against Germany. A little later, Soviet Russia also invaded Poland. Why did not England declare war against Russia?

Quite obviously because Russia's invasion of Poland was aimed at Germany, the aggressor, said Churchill.

Very well. A little later, Russia without provocation invaded Finland. Finland was a good little country. It had paid its war-debts. The people of Helsingfors carried umbrellas, like good citizens, and Finland was in high repute. Why did not England declare war on Russia when the Soviets attacked good little Finland?

You know the answer, Hanfstaengl, Churchill replied. Finland was a base from which Germany could attack Russia. Germany was the world aggressor. Russia was the only possible check on German power in the east of Europe. We had signed no pact to defend Finland. Much as we regretted it, we could not allow our sympathy for Finland to divert us from our own safety or our purpose to destroy Hitler.

Very good, Hanfstaengl said. I do not disagree with your reasons. Yet what you have said, Mr. Churchill, makes it appear that vested rights, including treaties, must yield in the face of necessity and that obligations are not to be fulfilled except in the light of interest. Is that true?

Not at all, Churchill said. It is the boast of British diplomacy that, despite these most exacting limitations, we have never broken our word.

That reminds me, sir, I said, of a story I heard the other day. A couple of English Army officers in a railway carriage were grumbling about the Foreign Office, what terrible mistakes it had made, and so on. After a while, a languid, young ornament of Downing Street lowered his newspaper and stared superciliously at them. "Shut up," he said. "Don't you realize that if it were not for the Foreign Office you wouldn't have your bloody war?"

Just the same, Jack, said Roosevelt, Putzi has made a

good point. You cannot respect a contract in which two individuals conspire together against a third. Yet this is exactly the kind of agreement in international affairs that we are being asked to support.

8

All these agreements must be reconsidered in the light of reason and existing circumstances, of course, said Churchill.

But that is exactly what we cannot do, Winston, if you begin by assuming that all agreements are sacred.

There is no real difficulty, the Prime Minister replied. Casting back a bit, we did make an open pledge to defend Poland against aggression. We made no such pledge so far as Finland was concerned.

What about the Covenant of the League? I asked. Didn't you pledge yourself to defend all State Members of the League against external aggression?

Quite true, Carter. Yet the League procedure itself prescribed the course to be followed in case of aggression. When Russia invaded Finland, the League expelled the Soviet Union but did not vote to apply sanctions against her.

Since England and France dominated what was left of the League at that time, I said, didn't that mean that you yourself decided whether to defend Finland against the Russian attack?

We had our hands full at the time, said Churchill.

Of course you did, I agreed. All I am saying is that the defense of smaller nations has, up to now, been a matter of choice by the Great Powers, and not a matter of agreement. And I'll add to that the American refusal to join destroyed the League from the start. If the future of the world is to be based on the idea of the consent of the governed something more reliable must be offered. Otherwise the small nations will automatically fall under the control of the strong powers.

They always have and never more so than now, said Churchill. No, Carter, I think that the President is right when he says that this war marks the end of the rights of small nations, as such—much as your Civil War marked the end of States Rights in this country.

The most illuminating speech ever delivered in the Senate in recent years on the subject of States Rights was that uttered by Cotton Ed Smith of South Carolina, I said. "No man," said Senator Smith, "could believe more firmly than do I in the sacred principle of the rights of the States, but—" How would you apply the idea of the consent of the governed to post-war world organization, Mr. President? I asked. Can we allow, as in 1939, Roumania or Poland to have full power to commit the great powers to a war? Suppose that after this war Persia or Turkey, neither of which are democratic nations, should decide to defy Russian pressure. Will we give them full backing, in the name of sovereignty, or will we follow another course?

I'd like Winston to answer that, said Roosevelt.

I would assume, of course, Churchill said, that neither Persia nor Turkey would make any major decision without consulting the interested powers, which would certainly include Great Britain. It they neglected our advice, we would have no responsibility. If they followed our recommendations, we would naturally support them.

How does this differ from the sort of alliance we were discussing? asked Hanfstaengl. Instead of it being a written agreement, it is an understanding that advice must be followed.

Hanfstaengl, said the Prime Minister, you're getting lost in the Black Forest again. The interests of the great powers determine their course of action. The smaller nations, if they are prudent, consider these interests in shaping their own course of action.

Yet what you say, Mr. Churchill, Hanfstaengl said, means that in Turkey, for example, the consent of the governed means "the consent of Great Britain," just as in Panama or Cuba it means "the consent of the United States" or in Eastern Europe "consent of the Kremlin." I do not see how this is consistent with a world order which is based on the sanctity of treaties or on the principle of freedom.

Franklin, Churchill said, this is *your* problem. So far as the Empire is concerned we have been doing quite nicely without this deluge of philosophical doubts.

9

In spite of the fact that we've a good many blots on our copy-book, the President replied, we have found a fairly practical solution to some of these problems. Back in 1787 we had to resolve the problem of the great states as against the small states, New York against Rhode Island. The politicians tried to settle it by means of a senate in which each state—large or small—was guaranteed equal representation. This was an ingenious as a compromise but it wasn't enough. The real answer was provided by Thomas Jefferson. His Bill of Rights—the first ten amendments to the Constitution—represented his point of view. It was decisive.

How so?

The Bill of Rights made the Constitution more than a

plan of government. It was an agency to guarantee the personal individual liberties of the common man, said Roosevelt. That made all the difference between a political blueprint and a free society, eh, Bernie?

I agree, said Baruch, that without the Bill of Rights, the Constitution would never have been adopted.

But it was more than an election deal, Roosevelt insisted. Popular demand for liberty lighted a fire under the politicians and forced them to accept a Constitution which many of them opposed.

But we're still a long way from keeping the Bill of Rights any better than we keep our other election promises, I said. We don't even let the District of Columbia vote, in spite of "taxation without representation." And everybody knows that the Southern Negroes don't have the votes which were guaranteed by the Fourteenth Amendment. In fact, one of the reasons advanced for not giving us the vote in the District, is that there are too many Negroes who would be enfranchised.

Yes, said Hopkins, we're a long way from government of, for or by the people and getting farther every minute. The best that can be said for our system is that there is a rough kind of popular sovereignty that gives public opinion a veto power over the government. It can't get things done but it can sometimes stop things from being done. It's about the only democratic thing in America.

Whichever way it is, said Churchill, I don't see how it applies to the present problem. It seems to me that our greatest bond of unity is the need for beating Hitler.

When Hitler is beaten, we'll need something else, said Roosevelt. I tried to outline a sort of World Bill of Rights in my Four Freedoms speech and we both signed the Atlantic Charter along the same lines in August of '41. Since we need a world order, we'd better copy Jefferson and offer people greater freedom in return for joining the United Nations.

You have mentioned the Four Freedoms, Mr. President, said Putzi. Freedom of speech and freedom of religion I can understand. That takes care of Nazism, Fascism and Communism. But what do you mean by freedom from want and freedom from fear?

That's chiefly addressed to Asia, said Roosevelt. Asia has been starving for centuries and has been preyed upon for centuries. To Asia, the political freedoms—of speech and religion—mean very little. But the freedoms from want and fear mean everything.

Ja, I can see that, Mr. President, but how does that differ from a war to end war, a war to make the world safe for democracy? Is it not like the promise to have a chicken in every pot? The Full Dinner Pail? Is not this the obtaining of agreement under false pretenses? Isn't it what John Carter would call the bunk?

Putzi, said Roosevelt, the Ten Commandments have not yet been realized anywhere near one hundred per cent, not even in the life of a single man. That does not mean that the Ten Commandments are bunk. The Four Freedoms are not bunk, even if they should never be fully realized. They represent the goal towards which all organized society is striving. They can be realized in part without too much strain on an imperfect world filled with imperfect men.

Really, Franklin, Churchill laughed. I agree with you quite fully but I had never thought that you would succumb to the special vice of all American Presidents—dabbling with the Decalogue.

When Wilson produced his Fourteen Points at Versailles, said Hanfstaengl, Clemenceau observed that *le bon Dieu* had needed only ten.

Well, Franklin has boiled down the political Decalogue to four.

Christ, Baruch said, reduced it to two: love God and love your neighbor.

Unfortunately, Bernie, the world likes to have these things spelled out for it. We can all agree on general theory. Russia might claim that she is a democracy, as we claim we are, but neither of us would like each other's definition of democracy.

10

Very well, Mr. President, said Baruch, how would you spell out the idea of government by consent in the case of the major nations involved?

Do you include France? I asked.

No, Carter, said Baruch, I don't include France. France is still vital but is no longer a great power. I refer to America, England, Germany and Russia. They are the major powers engaged in Europe and the mastery of Europe still means mastery of the world.

To speak of government by consent in terms of Germany is absurd, Roosevelt said. The Leader-Principle and the Master-Race idea are absolutely opposed to the ideas of Jefferson. I think we can take it for granted that the Third Reich does not consider popular consent an important element in government.

What about the Soviet? asked Hanfstaengl. Do they consent?

Before dealing with Russia, Putzi, let's take the other extreme. This country, as you know, is founded on the idea that the consent of the governed is essential. That is our theory, at any rate, though we don't really live up to it. In distributing the powers of sovereignty, under the Constitution, it is provided that all powers, unless otherwise specified, are reserved tó the States and to the people, respectively. It is on these reserved powers that the President, as agent of all the people, draws for authority in time of war.

Good manners are essential to that kind of government, sir, I said. Joe Guffey claims that at least six Democratic Senators and I forget how many Congressmen lost their seats last November because Leon Henderson ran the O.P.A. as a crack-down operation and not on the basis of public cooperation. When you draw a check on these reserved powers it is just as well to explain things to the cashier.

Leon is a fine fellow, Jack, and there simply wasn't time to persuade everybody as to the necessity for rationing and price-control

I still believe, sir, I said, that you need a good bedside manner when you operate on the rights of the American people, if you're going to avoid serious complications.

I wouldn't dispute that, said Roosevelt. Moving on from our theory of government, I would say that the British Empire is based, in practice, on much the same idea. An empire cannot operate under any single, formal political philosophy, but consent can take many different forms. The government of Great Britain and the Dominions is much more democratic than our own. In India and the Crown Colonies the government is less democratic than in the Philippines. In the British spheres of influence, consent takes the form of treaties, concessions and vested rights. Is that correct, Winston?

Yes, Franklin, if you *must* reduce the Empire to a formula. No country is strong enough, by itself, to operate as a world empire except on the basis of agreement.

And what of Russia? Putzi asked.

There, said Roosevelt, I should say that the process of consent is somewhere between the Nazi and the British systems. The Soviets do not, in theory, follow the Leader-Principle. Decisions are taken by the Politburo and the Supreme Soviet, representing the party and the bureaucracy. In practice, I suppose that whatever Stalin or his mysterious committee decide is done, but they must go through the forms of consultation with the Party and with the political administration.

Do you believe, sir, I asked, that the Soviet Government is becoming less or more absolute?

More absolute, Jack, like every other government at war. When peace comes it will be interesting to see whether Moscow clings to its dictatorial war-powers or evolves into a more democratic form.

It will be interesting to see if we do, too, I said.

At most, Mr. President, said Putzi, the Communist Party is not ten per cent of the Russian people.

Perhaps, but in their theory, Moscow must govern with the consent of at least that ten per cent. That is important.

11

From a purely propagandist point of view, Mr. President, I asked, how do we justify ourselves against the criticism of the Communists or, for that matter, the Nazis?

In what way, Jack?

Well, let's take the matter of the Negroes in this country. The Nazis contend that our Jim Crow and other racial discriminations, show that we are in real agreement with their race doctrines. The Communists say that they are the true friends of the Negro and that our so-called democracy pays only lip-service to the idea of equal rights. Most Europeans regard us as hypocrites who pretend to be democratic but are really a Big Business empire and a ruthless one.

Well, Jack, what answer would *you* give?

On the subject of the Negroes, I'd tell the truth, sir. I would say that it is true that in certain States and in many localities we do not give effect to the ideal of full social, political and economic equality for the Negroes. I would say that, notwithstanding these inequalities and discriminations, the American Negroes have made and are making enormous and unprecedented cultural advances. I would say that progress doesn't operate like an assembly line but in waves.

That wouldn't hold the Communists, said Roosevelt. The Russians would tell their people that the mass of Americans live in a state of abject economic servitude.

And so we do, said Hopkins. But as we're too dumb to recognize our servitude, it doesn't seem to make much difference.

That's another blot on our copy-book, I said. It is all very well to speak of government by consent but unless it extends to economic opportunity, what does it mean? Maury Maverick once pointed out that you can't eat the Bill of Rights, and you yourself, Mr. President, quoted that British judge who ruled that "necessitous men are not free men." The ballot, representative government and guarantees of civil liberty don't mean much if you can't get a job or a meal. What good is democracy if it leads to strikes and breadlines, evictions and bankruptcies?

I think I agree with Harry, the President said. A bad economic system that works because people believe that it is good is better than a good system that people have lost faith in. My own experience is that you must always doubt logical conclusions.

Spoken like an Englishman, Franklin, Churchill said.

Aren't you getting close to what Hoover and the Republicans meant when they talked about "confidence"? asked Hopkins.

Not exactly, said the President. This is a very rich country and we are a very energetic people. We haven't started to solve our big political and social problems chiefly because we've never tried to. We've been too busy making money, as in the 1920's, or too busy recovering from a depression, as in the 1930's, or too busy fighting a war, as now. Some day we'll wake up with a bang and start to put our own house in order. All that I have been able to do in the last ten years is to keep alive the ideas and methods of Jeffersonian democracy so that when the time comes they will be at hand to be used. I'm convinced that they are our only real defense against a bloody revolution or a terrible tyranny.

America has had things too easy, said Baruch. Individual Americans have led hard lives—millions of them—but there was always so much wealth that it was always too much trouble to work out a better system for distributing it.

I still think, Bernie, said Hopkins, that it won't be nearly as tough to fix things here as most people think. Any nation that can fight two wars at once and still raise its living standards can settle its business system anytime it wants to.

It's whether we want to that worries me, I said. That is where our prejudices may become dangerous.

I do not think that I understand you, John, said Putzi. How can prejudice interfere with these economic problems?

Ask the President. He has been forced to set up a Fair Employment Commission to see that, even in war-time, men shall be allowed to work without reference to race, color or creed.

Jack is quite right, Putzi, Roosevelt remarked. This has nothing to do with what is known as toleration. It's a simple, practical matter of mobilizing our manpower. There are parts of this country where Negroes are barred from war-jobs, simply because labor unions wish to keep certain kinds of employment as a reserve for whites. In other communities, Catholics or Jews or Mexicans or Filipinos or Japanese-Americans are kept out. In some cases it is employers, in some it is the unions, and in some it is simply a matter of local custom.

But that is a great defect in the idea of government by consent, Mr. President. It is also a great opportunity for the Nazis and the Communists, Hanfstaengl said.

I agree, Putzi, but it is the nature of consent that it cannot be forced. Leaving logic to one side, it is better to deal with prejudice on the level of private employment than to have it in the form of law, police regulations or political philosophy. We can hope to widen the area of consent in time.

12

That is all very true in the States, Churchill said. What does it mean in Asia? I agree with you that Asia supplies the test of all political power and philosophy. How can you convince the Asiatics that you love them as customers when you reject them as citizens?

We must work that out, said Roosevelt.

How can you work it out in time, faced with Soviet propaganda and influence?

We must work it out, the President repeated. When my cousin Theodore arranged to send Dewey's squadron to Manila in '98, he knew what he was doing. The American people did not. Before they realized it, they had conquered the Philippine Islands. Poor old McKinley didn't know what to do with them. He prayed to God for guidance and then decided that it was our Christian duty to keep them.

Like Brigham Young and polygamy, Baruch suggested.

Bernie, you're a cynic. No, McKinley was quite sincere. Then Bryan decided to oppose him for reelection in 1900 and campaigned on the issue of anti-imperialism. We put down Aguinaldo and the Filipino insurrection and kept the islands but Bryan, though defeated, won the debate. Over the years the American people and government came to realize that you cannot reconcile a colonial empire with Jefferson's ideals. We decided to keep the ideal and give up the empire.

Wasn't that also because we feared the imports of Philippine sugar and vegetable oils? I asked.

Yes, Jack, it was. That is further evidence of the anti-imperialistic character of our institutions. We would rather surrender foreign sources of wealth than expose our citizens to competition from that wealth.

All that I can say, Franklin, Churchill remarked, is that you have made matters extremely awkard for the Dutch and ourselves. Since you passed the independence law for the Philippines every Hindu and Javanese is demanding the same.

Why don't you give it to them?

Are you serious?

Certainly, Winston. You should give it to them as we did. We did not grant Philippine independence until after more than forty years of public education and about thirty years of local and insular self-government. Then, when we decided that the islands were almost ready, we announced that they would become independent after a further period of ten years. If you and Queen Wilhelmina wish to keep your Asiatic empires for the next thirty years, all that you need do is to announce a program for getting rid of colonial government at the end of that period. Then, when you keep your word, your former subjects will be your best customers and firmest friends.

Hm!

But what about South America? Putzi asked. That is an American sphere of influence in which the greatest propaganda can be brought to bear against you. They are nominally independent, so, you cannot give them independence. They already buy and sell with you almost exclusively—except in the Argentine—so you cannot expect them to become better customers. And they are a Catholic, somewhat colored, and Latin civilization. They know very well of the prejudices of this country. They would prefer to do business in London, Paris, Berlin or Madrid. Is there an element of consent here?

Yes, Putzi, there is, said Roosevelt. I know as well as anyone the barriers to full understanding and cooperation in the Americas. Yet it is a fact that, under the Good Neighbor policy, we have mutualized the Monroe Doctrine, abandoned our policy of intervention and given practical effect to hemisphere solidarity.

13

It would seem to me, Mr. President, Putzi said, that this Monroe Doctrine and these British spheres of influence are the great danger to future peace.

Rubbish! said Roosevelt. It seems to me to be the most solid and simple political relationship that exists. It does not involve any extension of our sovereignty and yet makes possible a very close and friendly cooperation without pain or imperialism.

Is it in fact painless? asked Putzi. It would appear to me that on the contrary it might be very painful to be a citizen of a country which was also a sphere of influence. There would be no clear responsibility anywhere and so consent would not be possible.

I still consider the Monroe Doctrine type of policy better than a program of conquest and colonial administration.

There I cannot agree, Hanfstaengl replied. The British Empire is most admirable when it is most imperialistic. The Empire wants South Africa—boom! boom! boom!—and the Empire takes South Africa. If the South Africans become discontented with British rule they know whom to blame and where to protest.

As you know, Churchill said, we gave Dominion status to the Union of South Africa not long after the conquest of the Transvaal and the Orange Free State.

Did not that mean that South Africa, as a Dominion, became a super-sphere of British influence, with divided powers and responsibilities?

I don't quite follow you there, Putzi, the President remarked. Surely self-government is better than conquest.

Let me put it another way, Mr. President. Is the island of Cuba really free? Not quite. If things go wrong in Cuba, who is to blame? Who knows? It might be the Cuban Government or it might be the sugar companies or it might be the New York banks or it might be the State Department. How can you have government by consent when there is no clear responsibility by the government to the people?

I see what you mean, Putzi, but I still think that the people of Cuba are better off than they were as a Spanish colony.

There I do most heartily agree with you, Mr. President, said Hanfstaengl. Now I see this danger for the post-war world which you are making. Up to now there have been only British and American spheres of influence. With some small exceptions, the two Anglo-Saxon powers do not seriously collide. America does not covet the British sphere in the Near East. England does not wish to meddle with the Monroe Doctrine. The two countries have agreed to work together in China since the time of the Boxer Rebellion.

That is true, Churchill said.

Now let us suppose, Putzi continued, that when the war ends and Germany and Japan cease to be great powers, the Soviet Union should also create a sphere of influence.

They probably will, said Roosevelt. Why not?

They will most certainly attempt to do so, Churchill agreed.

But that may not be convenient, Mr. Churchill. If the Soviets are what you call reasonable and content themselves with Eastern Europe, you will not object.

The Vatican will always be interested in Catholic Poland, I said.

Ja wohl! But let me finish, please, John. What if the

Soviets want a sphere of influence over all of Persia or Austria or Jugoslavia or Norway?

We shall oppose them, naturally, said Churchill.

But how will you oppose them if they are in a position to use the independent sovereignties of these countries against you? Suppose, Mr. Churchill, that the Persian Government or the Austrian Government or even the French Government agrees to work with Russia?

They will probably decide against it.

But can you stop them? And can we, in our general support of the sacredness of sovereignty, deny to these sovereign nations the right to agree to become part of a Soviet zone. That is a very great danger.

We shall meet it if it comes, Churchill said. I agree that it may make some difficulty.

14

It took England over twenty years after the Napoleonic Wars to usher Russia out of the Eastern Mediterranean, I observed.

Putzi, said Roosevelt, your idea about spheres of influence is a good one, but only on the assumption that the war ends on the basis of power politics. The truth is that the war is being fought and will be won by a coalition and a coalition is held together by the fullest application of the principle of mutual consent.

Quite so, Churchill agreed. Common necessity forces us to sink our differences and work together.

Won't the differences return when the danger disappears? I asked.

Not if we handle the policies of coalition wisely, Jack,

the President answered. We can commit each other to programs and policies which will carry over into the peace.

May I ask what these policies of coalition are, sir? I inquired.

Well, there is no hard-and-fast rule for making the eagle, the lion and the bear work as a team, but there are some general principles, between allies, which are workable. First of all, there is the idea of mutual aid, rather than indiscriminate requisitioning. Take Lend-Lease. Harry here sits on the lid and we pass out what is available according to the judgment of the Combined Chiefs of Staff.

Is Russia represented on the Combined Chiefs? Putzi asked.

Not directly, Putzi, because Russia is a deficit country in terms of munitions. Now this system of allocation works better than if each government had the credits or authority to acquire whatever their own staffs considered necessary. This mutual aid extends into food, oil, raw materials, finance and shipping. Such a system will prove invaluable in the post-war period and can be used to by-pass all power-politics.

Then Lend-Lease will continue after the war? I asked.

In fact if not in form, Jack. Then there is the principle of mutual forebearance towards operations in the various theaters of war. We do not propose to tell the Red Army or the Soviet Government how they shall conduct their operations in Finland or Roumania. They do not dream of telling Winston and me what policy we should follow in Greece or Italy. On that basis, we are establishing a live-and-let-live relationship in every theater of the war.

Just the same, Franklin, Churchill said, it will be wise to make some firm, clear agreement with them on future arrangements before we get into Axis territory.

Which is why we must see Stalin, Roosevelt agreed. Free agreements between the major belligerents can forestall general grabbing of territory and special advantages when the fighting stops.

You had better get those agreements, Mr. President, Baruch observed, well before the war is won.

Rather Churchill agreed. "When the devil was sick."

There's more than one devil in this picture, Winston, the President replied. We're all apt to forget our good resolutions when the headache passes.

Do you believe that the Soviets will keep agreements made under the duress of war? Hanfstaengl asked.

Yes, Putzi, I do. We shall not ask of Russia anything that is unreasonable. And, after all, as we said earlier in the evening, the three great Allies all depend on the idea of human brotherhood and are all deeply opposed to Nazi race policies. If we keep that clearly in mind, we can find common ground for agreements that will start to make the peace long before the war is over.

The war is the thing that really holds us together, Churchill remarked. We must win it and the Kremlin knows it as well as Downing Street and the White House. Hitler is a powerful argument in favor of mutual accommodation and agreement.

15

But could not the principle of consent also be applied to Germany, Hanfstaengl inquired, especially if Germany is, as I hope, to be joined to the West?

It could, Churchill admitted, but what would be left of the Third Reich?

Um Gotteswillen! There is much in Germany to which the world can well agree.

Of course there is, Roosevelt remarked, but the problem is to persuade the Germans to agree with the rest of the world. Bach, Mozart and Beethoven have become field-marshals in the German Army. Kant, Hegel and Schopenhauer are not philosophers: they are German drill-masters.

Without discipline there is no Germany possible, said Putzi.

With Prussian discipline there can be no Europe, replied Baruch.

Then how can Germany be born again? asked Hanfstaengl. Can the eighty million Germans crawl back into Prussia, Bavaria, Wuertemberg and Saxony? Is it that which the world wants? The repeal of Bluecher and of Frederick?

The repeal of Prussia is clearly indicated, Roosevelt said, because Prussia is the grandfather of Hitlerism and we now see to what Prussian militarism leads.

So, Mr. President, you want the Germans to be nice, quaint, beer-drinking, song-singing inmates of Central Europe, ready to fight the French or the Russians, if needed, but otherwise quite, quite harmless? Good dogs!

What you suggest sounds both novel and alluring, Churchill observed.

We must rid the Germans of this urge for empire that has flung them against Europe and the world, said the President. The Germans are admittedly a great people but by outlawing the idea of government by consent they have become a great nuisance and a greater danger. Do you deny that, Putzi?

Aber nein, Mr. President. I do not deny but I do say that there are other nations in Europe that have pressed on

Germany. If German power, which means Prussia, is destroyed, there will be no Germany at all.

And not a bad idea either, said Baruch.

What we want, said Hopkins, is to establish conditions by which the Germans can produce new Bachs, new Goethes, new Duerers, instead of Himmlers, Hitlers and Goerings. After all, empire is a very narrow measure of greatness. The world judges civilization by a handful of individuals who had no part in empire: Socrates and Christ, Euclid and Galileo, Shakespeare and Pasteur, Einstein and Montaigne. Does German genius require an army before Germans can contribute to the world?

Nein, Mr. Hopkins, Hanfstaengl pleaded, you are right of course but still you do not consider the very real pressure of Bolshevism from the East. That is the Soviet night which ends all stars. Where the Marxists tread only red flowers are allowed to bloom.

That is special rhetorical pleading, Putzi, I said. It was Germany that attacked Russia, in time of peace, not Russia that attacked Germany. What greater proof of moral weakness can be imagined that Hitler at his strongest must make an undeclared war against his Soviet partner?

What, then, does the idea of consent mean for Germany? Putzi asked. That Cossacks and Commissars should patrol the streets of Berlin and Dresden?

Quite probably, said Roosevelt. If Germany is to achieve government by consent it means the end of the Nazi Party, of the Leader-Principle, of the Master-Race. It means admitting Poles, Dutch, Danes and Czechs to the franchise and to marriage. It means the abolition of the Army and the secret police. It means a Germany which is harmless to Europe.

How long would such a Germany last? Revenge alone

by the slave workers and the people of the occupied nations would forbid leaving Germany defenseless, Putzi said.

How long did France last after the wars of liberation had driven the French from Spain, Italy and Germany? How long did France last after the British and Prussians marched into Paris after Waterloo?

You believe then, Mr. President, that Germany and the Germans can survive even if they are weak?

Yes, Putzi, said Roosevelt. If Germany cannot survive in weakness then there is no power strong enough to save Germany. I am gambling that the Germans, in spite of Hitler, are so important and so vital that even the conquerors must spare them in the moment of victory.

That is true of the British and Americans, of course, Mr. President. Will it be true of the Russians?

16

Don't forget, Putzi, I said, that the two strongest conservative forces in the world will be on the side of the Germans once that Hitlerism is destroyed.

You mean, John?

I mean the British Empire and the Catholic Church.

But it is Mr. Churchill who has proposed to solve Hitlerism by killing the Germans and it is the Vatican which must oppose Nazi paganism.

That is true now, Putzi, I said. But let us suppose that the fighting has been over for a year, that Germany is prostrate under the Allies, and that the Russians are pressing in from the East, as you expect. Would you turn to Washington for support?

With the greatest respect for President Roosevelt and

you, John, I do not think that Germany could expect useful support from Washington. There will always be too many newspapers and too many last-ditch Jews—with all respect to Mr. Baruch—who would oppose any action on behalf of Germany.

So you would turn to London? I asked.

Ja, to London and to Rome, Hanfstaengl agreed. *Ach,* yes, John, I see what you mean. England will need the strong buffer state against Russia. If Germany did not exist, it would be necessary to invent her, *Gott sei dank!* And Rome must always hold back Asiatic atheism and Marxist Communism. Without a Germany, this would not be possible.

Before you start rebuilding the Third Reich on this basis, Putzi, you had better ask yourself what price London and Rome would ask. After the last war, Germany was trusted and betrayed our trust. This time, there must be pledges.

To England, Hanfstaengl said, we would gladly pledge an unconditional offensive and defensive alliance. We could restore monarchy and otherwise establish guarantees of orderly government. German industry would affiliate itself with British and American industry. There would be no difficulty there.

How about Rome? I asked. How could you persuade the Vatican of your sincerity?

Rome would be easy because Rome is wise, said Putzi. We would simply negotiate a new Concordat in good faith and live up to it. We would espouse the Catholic cause in Eastern Europe, especially in Poland. We might even take a Catholic monarch, in the Wittelsbachs. No, there need be no quarrel between Germany and Rome.

How would England and the Vatican know that you

were to be trusted? asked Baruch. After the last war, the Germans were supple and reasonable right up to the moment when they burned the Reichstag.

But England and the Vatican would understand that their interests were the same as ours, in keeping Bolshevism back from Europe.

In other words, Hanfstaengl, Churchill said, you would expect the Foreign Office and the Vatican to swallow Hitler's anti-Communist talk and make that an excuse for a soft peace?

England could do worse than make a soft peace with Germany, Mr. Churchill, Putzi replied. A hard peace that brought Russia to the Rhine or to Gibraltar would not be a soft peace for England.

There again you have the typical Nazi threat, said the Prime Minister. Support me or the Communists will get you.

No, Winston, I don't think that Putzi means it that way, said the President. It is a warning rather than a threat.

Thank you, Mr. President. I assure you that I am in no position to threaten the British Empire.

What he has in mind, Winston, is a rational understanding between the three powers of Western Europe—Germany, England and the Vatican—that European civilization must be preserved.

That is right, said Putzi.

The question can be settled only by agreement and consent among these three powers and two of them—England and the Vatican—are agreed that agreement is impossible unless Germany gets rid of Hitlerism.

If the German Generals were to blow up our dear Fuehrer with a bomb and offer a rational peace, would England listen to them? Putzi asked.

Of course we would, Churchill said. It's all bloody nonsense our having to fight the Germans. If they should show the sense to stop it, come to terms and play the game, Germany might yet be saved.

And Europe? Hanfstaengl asked. Can Europe too be saved?

Do you agree with Spengler, that the West is doomed? I asked.

No, John, I do not believe in the necessity for western collapse. I sometimes wonder whether the West can find the wisdom to survive.

Is survival a matter of wisdom or is it instinct? Baruch inquired. I have often wondered, contemplating the survival of the Jews, how much of it was due to the wisdom of Judaism and how much to the qualities of the race.

It is true, Mr. Baruch, Hanfstaengl replied, that men often achieve great things that are not deliberate or planned. Let us say, when Columbus discovered America he thought that he had found a way to the wealth of India. That is an example. Let us take the Crusaders, who believed that they were rescuing the Holy Sepulchre from the Saracens. In fact, they did not rescue the Sepulchre but they did restore contact between Europe and Asia for the first time since the fall of Rome.

There are plenty of modern examples, Roosevelt said.

In this country, remarked Hopkins, poor old Hoover thought that he was fighting for individual initiative. In fact, he was preparing us for socialism.

For that matter, Harry, I said, President Roosevelt is regarded as a great radical. In fact, he has been a great conservative.

With us in England, said Churchill, it was Chamberlain and his brolly and Baldwin and his pipe and their hope of peace that prepared this war, while I was regarded as a fire-brand because I urged the only policies which could have prevented Hitler from declaring war.

Hitler himself, Putzi remarked, desired only to make Germany strong, peaceful and prosperous. He regarded himself as a great builder. He wanted German girls to find husbands and raise families. He wanted German men to find work, dignity and security. So desiring, he led the German people into this frightful destruction and death.

I have heard that Lenin, I said, was deeply disappointed when Russia went Communist. According to Marx, Russia was the last country that should have had a social revolution. Germany was the place where Marx expected the Communist Revolution. When it came in Russia, Lenin was much embarrassed. Some of Soviet irritation with the Nazis is due to the fact that Germany had made a liar out of Marx.

It also seems to be true, Jack, said the President, that the Japanese really expected to be welcomed with open arms in China and the Philippines. They thought that they were liberating Asia. All they did was to enslave and impoverish Asia, including Japan.

In English politics, said Churchill, it has been the cynics like Disraeli who have been the most romantic in their policies, while the idealists like Lloyd George were the most realistic.

In other words, said Roosevelt, people rarely know—especially people in public life—what they are doing and how they will be regarded by history.

I know how we shall be regarded, Churchill said.

How? asked Hopkins.

I am far too wise to give my own opinion, Harry, but I suspect that the historians—especially if Hanfstaengl and the Germans have a voice in the matter—will describe

Franklin and myself as two unscrupulous Jewish statesmen who deliberately lured Japan and Germany into declaring war on us in order that we might, for selfish reasons, do away with all barriers to our power.

I think, Mr. Churchill, said Hanfstaengl, that history will say of President Roosevelt that he checked an economic depression and prevented a political revolution in the United States, that he prepared the American people for a great war and led them to victory in that war. Of you, history will say that you had the courage and patience to wait—alone— until Russia and America joined the Empire in a war which had threatened England with destruction.

So far as I am concerned, said Roosevelt, I hope that history won't record that, at the turning point in the greatest war in history, neither the Prime Minister of Great Britain nor the President of the United States were quite sure of what they were fighting for or how they would use their victory.

17

I'm sure, Boss, said Hopkins, that we ought to be able to strike a balance between what you and what the Prime Minister expect from history.

Harry, I've seen enough contemporary history in the form of the newspapers not to give a hoot for what history may think until all the returns are in.

On the contrary, said Churchill, in England we have been suckled on history until Oudenarde and Blenheim seem as recent as Dunkirk or Crete. In England we have to think of history because we live with and by it.

Coming back to what the Boss just said, Hopkins remarked, it is important to see where America stands in relation to the Empire from now on in.

Harry, Roosevelt replied, I would be hanged, drawn and quartered in public print if this ever leaked out but I don't think that there is any problem at all which America must decide in relation to the Empire.

Just a moment, Franklin, Churchill said. I agree that there is no purpose in making detailed agreements and commitments as between our two countries, yet I think that we in England are entitled to ask for something quite definite from the States in the post-war world.

Winston, you are entitled to ask for it but can anybody give it to you? I cannot commit America and neither, for that matter, can Congress. It all depends on public opinion.

Surely, said the Prime Minister, a firm understanding with America is not asking for the moon. How can Britain possibly settle the affairs of Germany, adjust relations with France and the Low Countries or adopt a line of policy towards Russia, unless we first know clearly where America will stand?

I can tell you right now, without the necessity for an agreement, where America will stand, said Roosevelt. We will disapprove of your colonial policies, envy you your raw materials, suspect your diplomacy and criticise your motives —and we will fight to protect you if you are again threatened with disaster in Europe.

That's not nearly good enough, Franklin. We can do better than that.

Where? asked Roosevelt.

We could get a firm agreement with Russia.

Which would break down the moment Moscow moved on the oil-fields of the Middle East or dipped into the Mediterranean.

It isn't too late to make a deal with Hitler, Churchill said. He might consider such a thing at this stage in the war.

You can't make a deal with Hitler, Winston, now. You might make us and the Dominions accept it but you couldn't persuade Europe that it was wise or necessary. England needs Europe, both as a market and as a source of supply, even more than England needs Canada or Australia. You would simply throw the Underground into the arms of Hitler and make sure of a United Europe under German control.

We could make things jolly difficult for you if we asked Hitler for a negotiated peace, said Churchill.

It wouldn't stop us fighting, because we are fighting Japan as well as Germany, and Hitler has no control over Japan. A separate peace with the Reich wouldn't restore Rangoon or Singapore. This Pacific War is a war that must be fought out, Winston. It can't be called off on account of rain, like a cricket-match or a ball-game.

Then you say that we have no choice but to continue fighting? Churchill asked.

No, Winston. I simply say that this war has grown beyond your power and my power to control or even to direct its course.

And for the future? What do you see?

I see that America, in some ways, is annexed to the British Empire, said Roosevelt.

Good. Our comradeship on the field of battle should lead to closer partnership between the two countries.

And I see that, in other ways, America annexes the British Empire. In still other ways, the two countries remain independent and even rivals. I know no formula which describes what is happening. It is without precedent in history and it will certainly puzzle the historians, let alone the Soviet Foreign Office. The two countries are interpenetrating each other without change of sovereignty and without formal recognition of the event. That is too important to be confined to a written agreement, in my opinion. In fact, I think the less it is discussed the better it will be.

18

Does that mean, Mr. President, asked Hanfstaengl, that America is committed to oppose the Soviet Union?

Not necessarily, Putzi. I see America and Russia as the two poles of the post-war world. They are opposite in almost every sense of the word. It is true that the South and the North Poles are opposed to each other, but neither does anything about it and, between them, they determine the way the earth turns.

Yet it is very difficult for me to see how America can support the British Empire and still not oppose Russia.

It will be difficult, Roosevelt said, but it may be a mistake to assume irrevocable natural hatred between nations. It is true that England and Russia are opposed on many issues but it is also true that, thanks to Hitler, it has been easy for England and Russia to sink their differences and work together in this war.

But what of our relations with Russia, sir? I asked. What about men like Martin Dies and red-baiting newspapers like the *Chicago Tribune?* How can we deal coolly with the Russians so long as our public opinion is at the mercy of emotional propaganda?

Jack, said the President, our relations with Russia are really the easiest in the world. We have no geographical contact at all, except possibly across the Behring Straits to Kamchatka. The two peoples know almost nothing about

272

each other. Any real alliance between us is out of the question because of the enormous difference in language, religion and political ideas. We are bound to bump into each other in Europe and the Far East but not in any way that is crucial for either country. Once Germany and Japan are out of the way, we are sure to develop a lot of friction with the Russians, but friction is all that it need be, not war.

Mr. President, said Hanfstaengl, I do not think that you really understand the danger of Communism. If Russia was just simply a nice national state, with geographical limits and recognized political needs, what you say would be quite correct. But Russia is also a social revolution in action and this revolution is not confined by geographical boundaries or by political considerations.

What about it? I asked. That has been true since 1917.

It means, John, that you can make an agreement with the Soviet Government and they will keep it most scrupulously. Yet at the same time, the Commintern and the Communist Parties outside of Russia will conduct their own policies and execute their own decisions. Against this there is no diplomatic or military defense.

There is a defense, Putzi, Roosevelt said. It is to make American democracy and American opportunity work so completely to the satisfaction of our people that the Communist can't even find a soap-box.

It wasn't until the apple-sellers and the breadlines under Hoover that Communism was taken seriously in this country, I said. If we have a post-war depression, it will happen again, only more so.

Do you know, Boss, said Hopkins, I think I have the solution for Communism over here. Insist on treating them as members of a religion and not as a political party. Let them have their Marxist Churches with readings from

Das Kapital. If a Communist is arrested, tip off the Civil Liberties Union to defend him under freedom of religion. They couldn't stand up against being classified with the Holy Rollers or Jehovah's Witnesses.

Harry, the President replied, you have some practical ideas but this is not one of your best. The Communists would claim religious persecution if you treated them as a religious sect.

It's what they really are. I'd like to see Yale and Harvard giving honorary degrees—D.D.M., Doctor of Divine Marxism—to Earl Browder and Maxim Litvinov. I'd like to see old maids leave their fortunes to repair the organ in the First Communist Church. That would cripple them.

It would serve them right, Harry, I said, after treating their own churches as though they were speakeasies or houses of mental prostitution, but there doesn't seem to be much consent in it. I'd rather see us and Russia square off and make an agreement, about the small number of things on which we can agree and then see if we can't widen the area of consent. Then we'd be getting somewhere.

A telephone-bell rang. A moment later Colonel Starling appeared.

That was the Combined Chiefs at Washington, he said. They asked the Prime Minister to stand by for a call from Malta.

Tell them I'm ready, said Churchill.

19

I told you we'd be getting word, Winston, the President said. While waiting for the call, we might as well wind up this talk. I'm not sure that we've proved much except that the consent of the governed is the vital difference between the Allies and the Axis.

Where does that take us after the war, sir? I asked. If our invasion of Europe succeeds, we must make peace on some basis, and how can we apply consent to a world that has forgotten freedom and can only think of food and revenge?

Jack, we must create a world order of some kind, any kind. We must bring Russia into that order, no matter what the price we pay. Russia must learn and we must learn that peace is really indivisible and that world-organization is the only alternative to chaos.

How would you persuade the Russians that this is so, Mr. President? asked Hanfstaengl. They might prefer famine and chaos as recruiting sergeants for the world revolution.

I doubt that Russia wants chaos in Europe, at any price, said Roosevelt. They can't be immune from famine or disorder along their frontiers. They need European goods for reconstruction.

Ja, I can see that, said Putzi. Then how will you prevent the Communists from exploiting for their own advantages the troubles which must exist in Europe when Germany falls?

Putzi, if Europe cannot resist Communism, it doesn't deserve to be saved from Communism. Just as in the case of Germany, I am willing to gamble that Europe is vital enough and strong enough to preserve itself against all the Commissars.

The call is coming through, sir, said Colonel Starling. Will you take it here or in the other room?

I'll take it outside, said Churchill.

Before you go, Winston, I think you might tell us whether Putzi goes on parole or remains a prisoner.

And I think, Franklin, that Carter might say whether I get the cigars or you win the cigarettes.

How about it, Jack? asked the President.

The telephone bell jingled.

The call's here, sir, said Starling.

The Prime Minister jumped up and left the room, closing the door behind him.

Do you seriously believe, Mr. President, asked Hanfstaengl, that America and England can succeed in binding the Soviets to a world league? How can there be peace between Europe and Asia?

I don't know how there can be, but there must be, said Roosevelt.

There was a pause, while we heard the murmur of the Prime Minister's voice in the next room. He seemed to be excited.

Then the door burst open and Churchill stood in the doorway, beaming.

That was from Cunningham, Franklin, he said.

What did he say?

The fleet opened up on Pantelleria at dawn, he replied. The results were good. Little return fire and no air opposition. The balloon's gone up, Franklin, and we're on our way into Europe.

We are on our way, Roosevelt agreed, and, as we say here, we don't know where we're going.

Well, what about it, Carter? Churchill asked. Do I get those cigars?

20

I suppose, sir, I said, that in a talk like this everyone privately considers himself the only impartial person present. So I'll take advantage of this opportunity to tell you what I really think. Yes, Mr. Churchill, you win the cigars.

The best Havanas, Franklin, please.

I'll give them to you anyway but first I'd like Jack to tell me why he thinks you have the better argument.

Back in 1933, Mr. President, I explained, you and Harry Hopkins and a lot of less important people, including myself, set to work doing what Rex Tugwell called "remaking America" after the depression. It now seems clear that what we were really doing was to measure America for uniform, to get the country ready to fight this war. I don't object to that particularly, but it happened to be the last thing we thought we were doing and it's a good thing to remember how far apart were our plans and the real results. No wonder that the Isolationists raged! After a few years of the New Deal, it was pretty clear that Americans didn't particularly want to be remade by us or by anybody else. They stopped the process of reform in 1938 and would have voted us out in 1940 except for the war.

That's true, Jack, but how does that apply to tonight's talk?

Tonight's talk was pretty much of the same pattern as the New Deal. We are saving the world from Hitler and are going to remake the world after Hitler is defeated. The world wants to get rid of Hitler, just as America wanted to get rid of Hoover, but I'm pretty sure that the world is tired of being saved, as we call it, by America, when we are really saving ourselves. And I'm absolutely convinced that the world doesn't want to be remade by America or by England or by Russia or by any combination of the three big powers. If the world wants anything it is to be helped to save itself.

The world, I continued, will be tired, hungry, poor and morally exhausted at the end of this war. The people won't want to be saved after they have been delivered from the Axis. They will want food, kindness and a breathing spell, and they won't want to be pushed around any more. In any case, sir, I doubt that we Americans know enough about the world to save it or to remake it acceptably, when we haven't even solved the simple problems of security and employment and political liberty in this land of abundant wealth. Mr. Churchill is the only man here tonight who has really travelled all over the world and knows it. He has no fixed formula for saving or remaking the world. Hs is concerned with saving the British Empire. Mr. Baruch's ideal of personal freedom and individual liberty will be safer with him than with an America that has convinced itself that it has saved the world and is entitled to lay down the principles for its future moral guidance.

Then, Jack, said the President, you think that we should do nothing about all these future problems?

We shall have to deal with them, of course, sir. But can we solve them? Or will they solve us? They have existed for many centuries and will continue to exist. If we defeat the Axis and protect our interest in peace and victory, that is enough. For twenty years after the war, we should make it our business to learn as much as possible about the rest of the world, and trade as much as possible with the rest of the world, and travel as much as possible in the rest of the world. In that way we might get the knowledge and experience to make our advice worth listening to. Then, perhaps, our advice would be followed. Today the world doesn't need advice, only help.

Winston, asked Roosevelt, do you agree with Jack? That we should take care of the war and let the future take care of itself?

I do, Churchill said.

Let's take that under advisement for the moment, Roosevelt suggested. And now what about Putzi? Does he get his parole?

Churchill shook his head. No, Franklin, he's better off and safer in custody than he would be if he were at large. With him, as with other issues, let's wait and see what happens. When the war is over, he may fit into the pattern of things. He certainly does not do so at the moment.

I'm sorry, Putzi, the President said. At least you can't complain that you did not have a chance to state your case.

I wish to thank you, Mr. President, and Mr. Churchill, said Hanfstaengl, for your very great consideration in allowing me to do so. The way the world is going, perhaps it is better to be shut away from it.

21

Now, Winston, said Roosevelt, let's clear up the other matter. Both you and Jack Carter are half-right and half-wrong. We can't afford to win the war with no program for victory except victory itself. I have a better plan.

What is it, Franklin? More points? More Freedoms?

I propose, the President said, that we face the fact that this war ends the sovereignty of small nations and whittles away the sovereignty of big nations. Let's make a virtue of necessity and work for a world-organization along those lines.

That's all very well so far as Western countries are concerned, Churchill replied. What about Asia? It may be difficult to persuade Russia and China that the nationalistic game is played out just when they are coming into position to capitalize on their national power.

That's where Bernie, here, gave me the right idea, the President continued. As Jack Carter says, the world is tired of being pushed around and saved. Every time the world is saved, taxes go higher and government breathes more hotly down the necks of the people. Let's make our platform for winning the peace the promotion of the rights of the average man against the State, the policeman, the tax-collector and the politician.

Russia wouldn't go for that, said Churchill.

It's the only answer to Russia. The Soviet Union looks mighty attractive because people are tired of insecurity as well as of being pushed around. Let's stop pushing people around. Let's get production and employment rolling. Let's lower trade barriers, get rid of passports and visas and exchange controls. Let's stop backing these damned monopolies and give people a chance to be themselves. Let's fight regimentation with freedom.

That's not a bad idea, said Churchill. Moscow is ready for anything but that. They thrive on being persecuted and always want to claim a foul. They are ready with the propaganda and the organization to capitalize on resistance to Communism. If we don't resist at all, simply let our people have freedom and food and as much security as is rational, the Kremlin won't know what to make of it.

How much would it cost you to drop Empire Preference

and all that and continue in peace the pooled economics of war? Roosevelt asked.

I suppose we could scrap it for about a thousand million sterling, Churchill said. Could you give it to us?

It will be a bit of a struggle but I imagine we can work it through Congress, the President replied. Four billion dollars only a small part of what we spend for a month of war.

Good. That means, of course, that we'll have to settle all this muck about airways and oil-wells and ships and such. They're really more bother than they're worth. What about your tariff?

We've brought it down, but for the first few years after the war our tariff won't matter. We'll be exporting goods rather than importing. In five years, if you play ball with us, we can work out a system of trade, travel and exchange that will wash out the whole tariff problem.

Then when we see Stalin this summer we can go ahead and make any political deal that satisfies him, and still we'll be selling him a pup.

We'll sell him a pup only if he is in the market for dogs, said Roosevelt. Any time he wants to go swimming with the rest of the boys there'll be no extra charge.

What about Germany? asked Putzi.

Since the nations of the world are going to lose their sovereignty, said Roosevelt, we might as well begin with Germany and Japan. China has never had any sovereignty in modern times except as England and America insisted on it. The Chinese probably need a lot more government than they've had. We could do with a little less.

And the peace of the world will be safe as houses, said Churchill. Nobody's going to have the strength to fight a war for the next twenty years. That means that power will depend on industry and agriculture, rather than on weapons. There, I think, Franklin, we will still be on top of the heap.

So this will be a war to end the rights of nations, said the President, and to substitute individual freedom for the State and production for military power. That suits me.

Will it suit Stalin? asked Baruch.

He had better agree, said Roosevelt. Othewise Russia will be left at the stake, talking about political principles while we are busy saying it with ships and shoes and sealing-wax, with cabbages if not with kings.

Always excepting His Majesty George the Sixth, added Churchill.

How are you going to make the States consent to the loss of power? Baruch asked. As they lose sovereignty they will, as here, take away the rights of their people. Where is the compensation?

What's the matter with science and technology? asked Roosevelt. That is the new frontier, the source of new wealth and power. If we let the State turn to the development of this frontier, they will have all the power they need and all the revenues, too.

That will take a good bit of working out, Baruch said, but it can be done.

Harry, Roosevelt said, will you draw up a memo for Winston and myself to initial in the morning.

Shall I call it the Catoctin Declaration? asked Hopkins.

Why call it anything? asked Churchill.

Okay, I think I have the main points clear. First, Germany and Japan are to be denationalized as a start on denationalizing the world; two, the Big Nations will use their power to diminish the sovereignty of the smaller nations; three, England and America will use their technological power to diminish the sovereignty of the big nations, themselves included, in favor of the United Nations Organization; four, the United Nations will be popularized by basing itself on a program of world liberation; five, liberation will consist of freeing individuals from the police-restrictions and tyranny of the State; six, England and America are to lead in this program of liberation by freeing their own peoples in order to git thar fustest with the mostest goods; seven, the nations of the world will find new power and revenue in scientific and technical developments along lines which are still to be worked out; and eight, Soviet and other totalitarian powers are to be resisted by the creation of a world order based on freedom and abundance. Is that all?

Yes, said Churchill, that's all. It's going to take quite a bit of doing, too. We must make great changes in England.

Nothing to what we must do here, said Roosevelt, but we can't expect to lead the world to peace and freedom unless first we put our own house in order.

www.ingramcontent.com/pod-product-compliance
Lightning Source LLC
Chambersburg PA
CBHW020233260626
47156CB00002B/665